WALK THE WEB LIGHTLY

WALK THE WEB LIGHTLY

A NOVEL

MARY PASCUAL

SPARKPRESS

Published by SparkPress, a BookSparks imprint,
A division of SparkPoint Studio, LLC
Phoenix, Arizona, USA, 85007
www.gosparkpress.com

Published 2024
Printed in the United States of America

Print ISBN: 978-1-68463-232-9
E-ISBN: 978-1-68463-233-6
Library of Congress Control Number: 2023917585

Interior design and typeset by Katherine Lloyd, The DESK

To the best friends a girl could have

PART I

Walk the web lightly

Do not shake it, do not push

Just glide along the edge

Soft the web falls and slow

CHAPTER ONE

H e came for her the day her grandmother died.

Naya had seen him around the edges, of course. When she first told them about the man, her mother had looked worried. Her grandmother had narrowed her eyes and huffed through her nose. Then she shooed Naya toward the weaving room and set her to carding wool.

Late that night, Naya saw Grandmother reweaving the wards after she thought everyone was asleep.

"Be careful, my love, my sweet girl," her mother said, fretting. "Don't stand out. You can't be caught if you aren't seen." Mama pulled the brightly colored hair clip from Naya's brown curls and replaced it with a plain bobby pin. Naya wore her hair long and loose, the tight ringlets floating around her head like a cloud.

"But I want to be a doctor, Mama," she argued. "I can't be a doctor if I'm hiding."

"A doctor!" scoffed Grandmother. "Whoever heard of one of ours being a doctor! We create. We don't patch!"

But that wasn't true. They patched all the time. Naya should know, as most of the mending fell to her. Mama designed and sewed beautiful custom clothes. Grandmother could spin and weave anything, from wall hangings to the finest silk wrap. Most of their designed clothes were high-end and priced to match, but they both provided tailoring for their clients, adjusting special orders to the customer's taste. Naya mended and darned and picked stitches and hemmed until the tips of her fingers were dry and peeling.

"It will hone your skills!" Grandmother said.

Mama and Grandmother ran a boutique below their apartment, by appointment only. They liked it that way: discreet, controlled, secure. More importantly, Grandmother said, it left them time for their art.

But to Naya, it felt like a dress that had grown too tight.

After Naya told them about the man, Mama kept fretting, until Naya's insides felt threadbare and frayed, her skin held together by nothing but worries and what-ifs. She was supposed to finish up a hem order, but she slipped out of the house just so she could breathe.

Honestly, the man hardly registered for her. Something big was coming, something that would change all the lines. First, she saw just the possibility of it a long way off, a tiny but lingering potential, flickering in and out of the lines. Mama, wringing her hands, had told her not to worry.

But she wasn't worried. She was fascinated.

Naya snuck around the corner of the house and hurried down a side alley to the empty lot where the neighborhood kids hung out, thrilled to be out on her own. Mama was protective, more than the other parents. Their city neighborhood was a mix of old houses, newer apartments, and converted businesses, squished between the city's proper downtown and the outer suburbs. When Mama let her out of the house at all, she used to walk Naya back and forth to the lot, lugging a lawn chair with her. Then Mama would sit and read while Naya played. Or she'd hover just out of sight as Naya got older. Naya didn't mind when she was little, but it started getting embarrassing. The other kids had been walking around the neighborhood by themselves for ages! But she was fourteen now, and even Grandmother had argued Mama couldn't follow Naya around forever.

She was supposed to tell them before she left, though.

Tiggy Harris was already at the lot, trading cards with the other boys. He gave her a sideways smile, his green T-shirt setting off his hazel eyes and deep bronze complexion. She sat down on a tire under the big oak tree and scuffed patterns in the dirt. Grandmother would scold her later for getting her white shoes dirty *and* for not finishing the pants.

She thought about the something big again. A delicious shiver quivered down her spine. She wasn't supposed to walk the lines where anyone could see her; it was their family's biggest secret. But if she was careful, no one would notice. Naya leaned back so it looked like she was gazing up through the oak branches, and she let her eyes go blurry. The images came first, as they always did, crowding into her mind, random flashes of what might happen in the future, pictures of what happened in the past. Then she concentrated and zoomed out like a camera lens, and the lines came into focus: shining strings of linked events, layers and layers of them. The farther out she zoomed, each one appeared as the timeline for an individual person. Naya let her hand drift up like she was brushing back her hair and settled it lightly on a string near her face. Following the string, with her hand as an anchor on the images, Naya saw a woman she half recognized from the neighborhood, carrying groceries upstairs to her apartment. Behind the woman was a single shining line of her past. In front of her, the line split into new lines—cooking dinner, watching TV, leaving the apartment with a sandwich, walking into a restaurant—each new image based on a decision the woman would make in the future. On and on the future lines went, splitting this way and that. The most likely possibilities glowed strong and bright. Naya followed the brightest line, skating along it as far as she could. A jolt jarred her, and suddenly she saw the woman clutching her sweater, her face wet with tears.

Naya froze. There was dissonance down the line. She had felt it before, but she couldn't see what it was yet.

Isabelle Alba came bulling up. All the kids called her "Short Shorts" for the tiny shorts she wore and because she had laughed, delighted, the first time she heard the nickname. She was a full head taller than Naya's slight frame. Everything she said sounded like a shout. "You daydreaming again, Naya?"

Naya dropped her hand from the line as she sat up. "Yep." She grinned.

Short Shorts swiped at a tire to knock off dirt, then changed her mind and leaned on the tree trunk instead. She was wearing her going-out clothes—still in small shorts but also a trendy top and sandals, so Naya knew she'd leave soon to hang out with older teens. Short Shorts used to scuffle in the dirt with the best of them. Now her head was angled toward the street, watching for her ride in comfortable silence.

Not that any of them played the way they used to. The younger kids still ran around the patch of dirt in the center, edging out the grass with their energy and laughter. The lot was supposed to be a recycling yard once, before the enterprising soul who had started it gave up. There was still a big pile of tires in one corner that were perfect for playing king of the hill or lava monster. Near the open street side of the lot, a giant cement tube rested, good for rainy-day forts and littered with cigarette butts from high schoolers' night visits. But those days of running until your breath gave out seemed further and further away.

An argument over sports teams erupted, and Tiggy drifted away from the other boys. Naya tilted her head to stare at the leaf-speckled sky through the tree, pretending not to see him.

"Ha! I see what you're doing," Short Shorts teased, too loud.

"Shhh!" Naya hushed her out of the side of her mouth.

"Hey." Tiggy nodded at both of them, but his gaze settled on Naya.

"Oh. Hey," she said back. Her heart beat faster, just a little. One time, she'd overheard Grandmother saying, "There's no point in mooning over someone who isn't going to moon back."

She was still waiting to see if Tiggy was the mooning type.

He shuffled his feet for a moment before pulling out his phone. "You see this video yet? It's ridiculous!"

Naya grinned. She had seen the video, but she moved closer to watch.

The twins walked up, holding hands as usual, their long, dark hair bouncing against their backs. Marisol Fernandez and Sarai Patel weren't sisters. They weren't related at all, but they looked so much alike that they could be. They did everything together, along with redheaded Arnie Wilkins, who orbited around them like a satellite.

Marisol peeked over Tiggy's shoulder. "We saw that video already."

"Yeah, but did you watch it until the end? When he gets sick?"

Sarai shrugged. "It's just okay."

"Name a video that's better!" Tiggy demanded.

"I don't know." Sarai paused, pursing her lips. "I guess we're bored of them. What's the grossest video you've ever seen?"

All the kids looked at Naya.

"Okay." Naya smoothed down the front of her skirt, then leaned forward and whispered, "Have you ever heard of *Taenia solium*?"

"No," came the hushed reply.

"It's a type of tapeworm," she continued. "If you accidentally eat food with tapeworm eggs in it, the tapeworms will hatch and attach to the wall of your intestine. Then they eat all the food you eat, until they get really big. Like huge. Bigger than any earthworm you ever saw. Here's the part that's really gross."

The faces in front of her puckered, but everyone leaned in.

"I watched an operation where the doctor pulled a six . . . foot . . . tapeworm . . . out of this guy's intestine . . . through his *mouth*! You can see it on YouTube."

Gagging sounds, gleeful and exaggerated, erupted around her.

Naya beamed.

"That's so disgusting!"

"How do you find these things?!"

"Did you watch the whole thing?"

"Yep," said Naya.

"I'm going to be sick."

"I wouldn't have made it through the whole video," said Arnie quietly. His freckled face flushed. "You're pretty brave, Naya."

"Can you imagine," Marisol said, "being at the doctor's office for a regular appointment, and some random person walks in with a tapeworm?"

"Ew! Do you think the end was already hanging out of his mouth?" said Sarai.

"Nothing that exciting ever happens around here," Tiggy declared.

The mundanity of that settled around them like a weight.

Naya thought about the lines, and a thrill curled through her again. "Sometimes," she said slowly, "you've got to make things happen."

"Well, no one start eating any tapeworm eggs!" Short Shorts barked out. "That's not on the menu!" Her laugh was infectious, and they broke into new jokes and giggles.

Naya sighed. She still had to finish that hem. "I gotta get back. Homework," she lied.

"Yeah, me too," said Tiggy. "But, uh, if I have trouble, can I look at your math problems tomorrow?"

"Sure."

He smiled, bright and sunny, and Naya glowed a little on the inside.

<hr>

Naya eased the sewing room door open and slunk toward the sewing machine. If she finished the hem before dinner, maybe no one would mention . . .

"Naya!" The voice cracked like a whip. "Don't tell me you're sneaking in here like you snuck out! I hope you finished that hem order, young lady."

Her good mood dissipated. Naya could tell Grandmother already knew she hadn't finished the hem. Naya turned. Grandmother stood off to the side, sorting through customer orders at a table, as if she had been waiting for Naya. Grandmother's green, draped-silk caftan caught the light as she straightened, setting off her tawny skin, short, iron-gray finger waves, and the frown she aimed at Naya.

"I'm almost done. It'll only take a minute." Naya hoped her face was blank, but she could feel her jaw setting. Why was she working anyway? It was *their* shop, not hers!

Her grandmother glowered at Naya's smudged shoes. "Were you sitting in the dirt? Your clothes are too nice to be treated that way. They are practically couture!"

"No! I wasn't sitting in the dirt!" Naya muttered under her breath, "Handmade isn't couture anyways."

"That is exactly what 'couture' means! Do you know how many kids would love to have your clothes?"

Naya suppressed an eye roll. They'd been pushing and pulling at each other lately, but she didn't want to do it tonight. She stomped, with as much dignity as she could, to the sewing machine.

"If you keep shirking your responsibilities—" Grandmother started.

"You don't have to lecture me all the time!" It burst out of Naya, despite her best efforts. "I'm not a kid. I'm finishing the hem!"

Grandmother might have let it drop then, but Naya couldn't keep her mouth shut. "And couture is only for the French," she muttered.

"Oh, are you all grown up then? You know everything?"

"Well, I sure know how to *hem*!" She knew it was bratty, but Grandmother was so stubborn sometimes. Always thought she was right, or her way was the best way.

"Naya!" Suddenly Mama was standing in the door. She gave them both a long look as she said, "Hush now. Stop your fussing with Grandmother."

Grandmother held her head regally, but her face was squinty, the way it got when she went from irritated to mad. She swept out of the room. Naya could never manage an exit half so grand.

Mama walked across the room like she was coiled tight, clutching the edges of her richly embroidered cardigan. Unlike Grandmother's bold looks, Mama chose easy-to-wear, simpler lines in her clothes, but with exquisite details, like intricate stitching or unique buttons. Her brown hair, long like Naya's, was often tied back in a ponytail or bun to keep it out of her work.

"She worries about you when you disappear. *I* worry." Mama held Naya's shoulders to look her in the eye. "You know better. You can go out, but you need to let me know where you're going and when you'll be back." She looked anxious and hurt and stern all at the same time.

Guilt plucked at Naya, and she cast about for a reason to push it away. "She's more worried about the mending than me! She's *always* more worried about the clients!"

"That's not true."

"You could just check the lines to see where I am."

Grandmother made a dismissive sound from the next room. Naya scowled.

The anxiety on Mama's face grew. "You know it doesn't work like that. We can't see our own paths. Or family that's close to us. It's not good for people to see where they're going."

"So you can't see my path at all? Or Grandmother?" Naya said it like a challenge, even though she already knew what Mama would say.

"I can see bits and pieces sometimes, but only when it's really important. Like remember that time you fell off the jungle gym at school and cracked your head? Your grandmother and I both felt the lines shift. That's how I got to school so fast. I already knew."

Naya was meanly pleased they couldn't see her. There was a teensy worry too, because once or twice she had a glimpse of Mama and Grandmother. More than what she was supposed to see, according to them. But she'd keep that to herself.

Most of the time though, Mama was right. Naya had stared down the length of her body until she was cross-eyed, willing her own line to materialize. When she tried to call family lines, to pull them to her, all she got were blank spots and a headache.

"But that's not the point," Mama continued. "You're taking risks that you shouldn't."

Naya flushed. Did Mama know she'd been walking the lines at the lot? She changed the subject. "Something big is coming. Have you seen that?"

Mama stiffened, tension settling into her shoulders. "Don't worry about tomorrow, Naya."

But Naya knew Mama worried all the time. "But you can *feel* it," said Naya. "Something happens to a whole bunch of people at once. Maybe us too. I can almost see it."

"There are those who wander too far along the lines," said Mama. "There are those who get lost trying to see everything. A person can go crazy doing that."

Naya rolled her eyes. "Don't worry! I'm not going to go crazy."

If anything, Mama looked more worried. "Those kind of risks, wandering too far—it's not worth it. You know the lines can change at the last minute. People aren't meant to see everything, even us. Never let anyone know, my love. It's safer that way." Mama smoothed a hand over Naya's curls. She could feel the thrum of tension in her mother's touch, and guilt stabbed through her.

CHAPTER TWO

M ama said, "There are people who'll try to use you if they know. We used to get burned as witches! Or worse, forced to walk the lines for other people. Sometimes our kind goes missing. You shouldn't ever talk about it where people can hear. A great-great-aunt on your father's side disappeared for years . . ." Those tales always lowered her voice to a hush, like she could barely stand to share them. Her eyes grew tight and anxious.

But Grandmother had different stories. "We used to be revered as great prophets and seers. Worshipped!"

"Mama said we used to get burned as witches."

"Well, you can't be stupid about it! You don't walk the lines willy-nilly, to see what to have for dinner or for a lark. You can't blab or brag about it. What we do is a gift! A precious gift, worthy of kings. Not a party trick, and certainly not for the rabble of this day and age. Our secret belongs to us and no one else. We've always been a rare people, but there are fewer of us now. Who knows how many have been lost over the years?" Grandmother's eyes looked far away and distant.

Naya felt her own eyes widen. "How did we get lost?"

Grandmother's gaze sharpened. "That's in the past and not for you to worry about! The important thing is that you remember your heritage! Your training! Our gifts are near sacred, and you have a duty to preserve them. Why, one of your ancestors was high priestess during the reign of pharaohs. She lived in a temple . . ." And Grandmother would launch into a story.

No matter what stories Naya heard, it always came down to one thing: don't get caught.

◆━

In her room alone, Naya put up her hands and danced them in the air, like plucking invisible strings. She could see random images without much concentration, but it was much, much easier to follow a particular line if she used her hands. All their kind learned to do this—zooming out to see the lines, then running a finger along the line they wanted to follow. It helped them organize what they saw, and see more. Naya learned all sorts of things through walking the lines.

She watched the line of a woman who was a veterinarian.

She followed a young man leaving a boring office job to DJ at night.

She watched firefighters race to emergency calls.

A musician put in hours of practice on his guitar. Naya traced his lines backward to his weekend gig. After each show, the man would put on the movie *Babe* and start crying.

She watched two college students making videos in their dorm room. Then she followed the lines to their classes. The material was hard. She needed more study before she got there, but it was almost like she was going to college herself.

She watched a man in an R&D lab as he peered through a microscope and discussed bacterium with his lab partners. Naya wondered . . . do bacteria or viruses have timelines? Would those lines be microscopic too? She had never noticed teeny-tiny lines, but it would be amazing to see them. She'd have to ask Mama and Grandmother about that.

She always forgot, though.

It wasn't only people who had timelines but animals too. Anything that could make a decision had a line. Naya's earliest favorite lines to watch were animals. She could follow a cat's line as it roamed the neighborhood chasing prey, or follow the wolves' lines at the zoo. Once she spent an hour watching a rabbit move its babies to a new den. Animal lives were simpler than peoples', but they could be unexpectedly dramatic—a hawk appearing and diving for prey, or the eruption of ants into activity. Nature was fascinating.

She heard Mama and Grandmother arguing sometimes when they thought she was asleep. It was an old argument, but Naya listened every time she heard them.

"You're filling her head too big!" Mama would scold. "These aren't the ancient times. There are no more priestesses!"

"Well, you're scaring her! Too much, I think," Grandmother would reply. "And we *are* more. You know that. She needs to know her heritage and wear it with pride."

"I just don't want her to glamorize the past. Or think she can bring it back. Kids today . . . you never know what they'll talk about or put online. They're all influenced by celebrities or social media mavens."

"If we don't instill pride in her now, she might let her culture slip away because of those very online TokTubers. Or whatever you call them." Grandmother sniffed. "Besides, Naya has more sense than that."

"You know as well as I do there are reasons to be scared," Mama said, stern and tense.

Naya would wait then, holding her breath. Wait for Grandmother to disagree and prove Naya right . . . that Mama was just worrying when she didn't have to.

But Grandmother never did. She never disagreed. No matter how long Naya waited in the dark.

CHAPTER THREE

Airports always stirred his imagination. So many people, so many objectives, everyone hurrying this way and that. It was ripe with possibilities. He could sit for hours just watching, assuming there was good food available. But there was no time for that now. The man smiled and slung his leather overnight bag on the security carousel. He knew there were a number of irregularly shaped items in his bag. It would be unfortunate if he were stopped. He could see the security guard hesitate, peering at the screen. The man smiled genially at the guard who was waving him down with a metal detector. After a pause, his bag was passed through the checkpoint.

On his way to the gate, he strolled by a young lady arguing with her beau. The man indulged a moment to observe the couple. The boyfriend looked contrite yet slyly confident; she looked miserable. She was clearly torn. The man thought she should forgive her boyfriend. Everyone deserved a second chance at love. As he passed, she acquiesced and embraced her boyfriend.

Satisfied, the man quickened his pace to the plane. When he boarded, the attendant didn't bother to ask him for a ticket.

CHAPTER FOUR

M r. Ned, her science teacher, wanted to talk to her. Naya shifted in her seat while everyone else slouched out of class. She didn't think she was in trouble, unless he was mad that she almost always started her homework while she was still in class. Got it done most days too, while everyone else was still asking questions about the lesson. Sure, sometimes she let some of the other kids look at her notes, but she didn't see how Mr. Ned could know about that.

She wished, for the thousandth time, that she could see her own line.

"Naya?" Mr. Ned waved her to his desk.

She dragged her feet a little, walking up the aisle.

When he looked up from the paper he was grading, he laughed at her expression. "You're not in trouble! If anything, you're doing exceptionally well in class. You're a natural, and you seem to enjoy it."

Naya, surprised, warmed at the praise. "I like science a lot!"

"I wanted to talk to you about a summer program coming up. Have you ever thought about pursuing science as a career?"

A funny feeling went through Naya's head. She could swear the air around her chimed and the world slowed down. How did he know? Had her heart been showing this whole time?

Her mouth opened and closed like a fish. Finally she managed, "I want to be a doctor."

"Then this would be perfect. The university is holding a camp introducing science careers to teens, and one of the focuses is on medical. I think you even get to participate at the teaching hospital on campus! You're on the young side, but I have a friend on the board, and I can write you a recommendation if you're interested."

Naya couldn't breathe at all for a moment. "Yes! Yes, I am interested! Oh my gosh! Yes!"

He smiled and handed her a flyer. "Talk it over with your parents."

"Thank you!" She hurried out of the room to her next class, careful not to crumple the precious flyer.

The program looked amazing! The flyer listed "interact with professional mentors" and "college internships" among the bullet points. But it was a daily program for four whole weeks! Naya bit her lip. She usually worked at the boutique during her summer break. They had a couple of sale days with last-season clothes and bikini wraps, but the big push in summer was getting ready for their fall Open Studio weekend. It was one of the few times they were open to the public. Naya usually helped with inventory, the sales, and as much non-customer-related work as possible so that Mama and Grandmother could concentrate on their higher-end designs. Open Studio was a big deal, an art show in its own right, but also crucial for launching early Christmas shopping and landing new clients for the holiday party season. Sure, she got paid to help, more than her usual allowance, so it was like she was an employee. She frowned. She supposed she could *quit* a job, if she was really an employee. But deep down, she knew Mama and Grandmother needed her.

But she needed this camp! She wanted to go so badly it hurt.

She scanned the list of science careers on the paper again, the promise of laboratory time. It was like she was holding her dream in her hands, instead of just a flyer.

And . . . if she got into this program, if she did well, maybe it would prove to Mama and Grandmother that they didn't have to be so protective all the time, so careful. Not everyone was out to learn their secrets! Naya was older now, and she could take care of herself. After that, she could go anywhere, do anything—including studying medicine.

The application deadline was in May. That gave her a few months to convince Mama. Grandmother would be another story.

＋

When Mama and Grandmother started piling up sandbags in front of the door, the other shop owners pulled theirs out as well. No one ever said anything, but the neighbors had learned to watch the women of the Intertwine Boutique. Despite what the news said, as sporadic rain sank into the parched ground, the street prepared, building barriers and running to the store for last-minute supplies. While Grandmother readied candles, Mama and Naya hauled the most expensive fabrics and pieces upstairs.

By evening, the weather had turned for the worse, wind howling around the edges of the house, trying to find a way in. Naya snuggled into a knit blanket on the couch, checking her homework, while Mama and Grandmother worked on client projects.

Sharp banging shook the door, the sound ratcheting up the stairs like a ghost. Grandmother and Mama looked at each other with wide eyes.

"That can't be Ms. Norris for her appointment! In this rain?" exclaimed Grandmother.

"You know, I didn't even think to call her," Mama murmured back. "It's a matter of *sense*." She nodded at Naya.

Naya hurried down the stairs and threw open the door. The wind gusted in a wet, flapping figure, who collapsed on the floor like a drowned crow. Naya pushed the door shut against the pelting rain and peered at the huddled mess of black clothes. This certainly wasn't Ms. Norris.

"Thank you," mumbled the person. She pushed a floppy hat off her eyes. "My aunt sent me to pick up her dress."

"Hi, Niecy," said Naya. "I'm sorry, but her dress isn't ready. She needs another fitting."

"It's Calixta," she said automatically. "And of course she needs another fitting. The woman won't stop eating."

"You better come up now." Mama's voice floated down the stairs.

Naya looked at Calixta and shrugged. Calixta sighed heavily, holding out her hands so Naya could pull her up off the floor. She dripped all over the place as they clomped upstairs.

"Guess what, Niecy? You're spending the night," Grandmother announced.

"Really?" Calixta's face brightened. "Oh, that's wonderful! I could use the break. Aunt Norris is driving me batty. I'm not sure a college fund is worth all the aggravation." She took off her hat and hurried to the kitchen sink to catch the drips off her clothing.

"Is that why you do it?" Naya asked. She'd seen Ms. Norris bossing her niece around town. Calixta was part companion, part assistant, and fully miserable.

"Naya!" Mama chided. "That's rude! Now go get blankets to make up the sofa bed."

"No, it's okay," said Calixta. "My mom thinks that if I'm around all the time, 'being useful,' Aunt Norris will put me in her will." She rolled her eyes. "Personally, I'd rather just get a job waitressing."

"What do you want to study in college, dear?" Mama asked.

"Psychology," said Calixta. "Maybe behavioral development. I'd like to do some type of counseling work, but I'm not sure what my focus will be yet."

Naya couldn't quite picture Gothy Calixta with a pen and pad in hand next to a patient on a couch. She hurried to get clean sheets as Grandmother handed Calixta a towel and asked her where she wanted to attend college. It turned out she had quite a list and was happy to chat about them without her aunt around.

When Naya came back, Calixta bent down and hauled out the sofa bed for her. She was stronger than she looked. She tucked in the sheets, quick and efficient, while Naya unfolded blankets.

"College sounds amazing!" Naya said. "I can't wait."

Calixta laughed. "You have to get through high school first."

"I know. I just get bored sometimes. There are biology classes at college way more interesting than anything we're learning now."

"Oh!" Calixta looked surprised. "You're into science, huh? With the shop and the way you dress, I thought you'd be into fashion."

Naya shook her head. "I want to study premed," she confided quietly. "But they"—she nodded toward Mama and Grand-mother in the kitchen—"expect me to be an artist. To follow in their footsteps."

Calixta mulled that over. "Well, there's no harm in taking classes in both to try them out. You'll know what feels right. Just follow your heart," Calixta said kindly. "And if you're taking painting or sculpture or whatever, that will keep them off your back while *you* decide," she whispered.

Naya changed her mind. Niecy would make an excellent counselor.

◆—

Naya asked more than once. "Why are we artists? Shouldn't we be able to do anything?"

Mama said, "It's just something our kind has always excelled in. We're naturally talented. We gravitate toward art like fish to water. Many of our ancient ancestors were great weavers. Walking the lines and seeing the threads, understanding the picture in the tangle, it's no wonder they were artisans."

Grandmother said, "We were destined to be magnificent artists! Our gift allows us to see above the mundane into the divine! To touch miracle and translate it for the world. How could we not share that?"

"Art lets us leave our mark on the world," Mama said. "To create something new in the fabric of being, it's an honor and a blessing."

"Pieces of our heritage, our history, our souls," Grandmother said, "become part of our art, whether others know it or not. A glorious secret hidden in plain sight!"

Mama said, "I can't imagine living without art. It would be like not being able to breathe."

Grandmother said, "It's our duty to continue our traditions, to make our lineage proud. It's *your* duty too! We are gifted beyond mere men. Those of our kind who squander their gifts, turn away from them, it's . . . shameful. Like denying the grace of God." A ghost of sadness crossed her face, chased away by ferocity.

"If I couldn't create," Grandmother said with a flourish, "you might as well cut off my hands!"

CHAPTER FIVE

After the storm, the sunshine looked like candy, lemon yellow and crystalline. School was cancelled because the sewers had backed up. Naya helped clear the sandbags and haul the expensive fabrics back down to the shop. When she stood on the front stoop, taking deep breaths of the clean air, Mama laughed quietly.

"Go see your friends. But only go to the lot! No wandering, and be back for lunch. I need your help this afternoon."

Naya didn't need to be told twice. She practically danced around the corner of the house. The path was muddy, but early tulips sprouted all along the back fence toward the lot. She was glad to be out. She was glad she'd worn jeans today while cleaning too. She settled on her usual tire, sprawling her legs in front of her, enjoying that she didn't have to smooth out her skirt for once. She kept the embroidered hem of her blouse out of the dirt, though. It was one of her favorites.

Tiggy was all wound up about something. He was practicing flying kicks at the cement tube with the other boys, but he flew at the cement extra hard. There were twenty-six bones in the human foot, and one was bound to break at the rate he was going.

Naya frowned where she sat under the tree. "Are you okay?"

she asked when Tiggy finally left the boys and plopped down beside her.

He swiped sweaty hair off his forehead. "My parents are driving me crazy. They're just too strict, you know? There are rules for everything! Some of them don't even make sense!"

"What happened?"

"Nothing."

She squinted at him. He looked mad, but there was something else mixed in, a sourness, like his stomach hurt. "No, really."

He blew out his breath slowly. "Okay. My mom took me to the mall the other day. I needed new sneaks, you know?"

Naya glanced down at his shoes, already scuffed from his assault on the cement tube, mud staining the canvas edges.

"She was mad that she had to buy me a new pair, made me promise to do a million chores to make up for it. But I can't control how I grow, right?" He kicked at the dirt. "There were all these rich kids from Vista Heights there, acting like they owned the place. You should have seen them! Snotty and posing and buying whatever they want. Trying to act street. Trying to pretend they're from here, and this is a rough hood."

Naya scoffed. "This isn't a bad neighborhood!" Although, in comparison to the rich suburb of Vista Heights, it definitely wasn't fancy. It was a city neighborhood, with more businesses mixed in among the houses and apartments, and way fewer lawns than a suburb. But that didn't mean it was bad.

"I know! They acted all tough, and they don't even know! They think they know, but they don't. They're just a bunch of tourists."

An image of teenagers wearing white knee socks with sandals and big cameras around their necks popped into her head. She laughed. "Yeah, maybe they came in on a tour bus with the other grandpas."

"Tour bus. Ha! With cameras and those stupid hats?" Tiggy laughed out loud. "You always make me feel better."

But he still looked upset. She didn't have to walk the lines to know there was more to the story. She reached out, hesitant, and rubbed the spot between Tiggy's shoulder blades. He tensed. Then he dropped his head and sighed.

"They kept laughing behind my mom's back," he said quietly, "when she was telling me all the chores I had to do."

Naya stiffened, her eyes wide. She'd be so angry if someone was making fun of Mama! Or Grandmother. Even if they were mad at each other.

"Snickering and making comments," he continued. "And I couldn't do anything! Even yelling at them would be another broken rule. Even if they deserved it."

Naya's stomach tightened just thinking about it. She'd never be allowed to be so rude as to yell at someone. Not to mention out in public, where it would draw attention.

"My mom just kept going on and on, you know?" Tiggy continued. "All the rules, all the responsibilities I was supposed to be living up to. And they kept making fun of her. Following us around."

"They followed you?! What's wrong with them?"

"I know! I just wanted to punch them, but . . ." He rubbed at the brown skin on his arm. "My mom is always talking about being better. But . . . I don't think I want to be better. I want to be bigger. I want to be . . . more." He flailed his hands. "I know that sounds weird."

Naya was okay with rules, usually. Being polite, laws—they helped people get along, to make a society. And the world in general was all about rules. The rules of circulation flow, the way organs worked together, how each body was organized exactly the same. How geometry appeared in nature, in fractal patterns and beautiful spirals, unexpected and precise and ordered. The laws of physics, even though theorists got the time part all wrong. Even the rules at school made sense to her.

Then she thought about the other rules, the ones that didn't have good reasons but they had to follow anyway. Her skin wasn't as dark as Tiggy's, but it was still brown, making it even more important not to break any rules.

She looked up through the sun-dappled tree, the sky huge above them. She thought about having to hide all the time. She thought about working in the shop the rest of her life, having to give up her dreams *just in case*. Just in case of what? Nobody burned witches anymore. All that stuff Mama talked about was from years and years ago. What could she be if the rules weren't there? The rules *might* make sense. Or they might not. She knew better than most how quickly things changed over time.

No, she didn't like rules when they bound her. She didn't like that at all. "I know just how you feel," she told Tiggy.

❖

The small city was rather sleepy, as far as cities go. The man was used to more hustle and bustle—preferred it, even. This city was what many would call a model of security, but he called it middle-of-the-road. Full of midrange opportunity for middle-class prospects, neither too prosperous nor too poor, not a lot of excitement but not a lot of crime either. The type of place where families would want to put down roots.

Boring. But perhaps it was just what he needed.

He could always find ways to entertain himself.

CHAPTER SIX

S he could barely remember the first time she was taught about the timelines. She'd always been able to see things, as far back as she could remember, but they were random images, uncontrolled. She had a crystal-clear memory of being in the kitchen, holding her pacifier and chasing after flashes of pictures and light, laughing. She remembered how tall the counters seemed, like cliffs with cookies at the top she couldn't reach. When she began talking in full sentences, Mama had guided her through walking the lines. By the time she started kindergarten, she could block the images if she needed to. By kindergarten, she knew not to tell anyone. It took longer to learn the control of zooming in and out, how to trace a line of events.

Walking a line was like dipping her fingers in a stream but not. The lines *buzzed*. They were energy, but also something like light. The energy moved like a current, but it wasn't a direction Naya could describe if someone asked her. They were soothing, and pleasant, and invigorating all at once. When she walked the lines, she felt refreshed, the same way wading into water felt nice.

Sometimes, without even looking, she let her fingers drift, and she'd find one just by the feel of it, next to her desk in class or walking down the street. She always pretended she was listening to a tune in her head, waving her fingers in time. But really she was enjoying the energy.

Even though the lines were made up of possibilities and potentials, something you'd think would pop in and out of existence . . . the lines were always, always there.

—◆—

"But shouldn't being able to see the lines help us do other things as well?" Naya asked.

"Such as?"

"Like . . . understanding the intricacies of law, or testing the theories of physics or . . . computer programming. I wonder if code is like walking the lines?"

Grandmother said, "Ugh! Who would want to be stuck in an office of cubicles all day? All that gray grinding you down. And I've seen code. It's not pretty. We make beauty."

Mama said, "Some things are too painful to walk the lines . . . Imagine being a lawyer and seeing all those crimes being committed."

Grandmother said, "And those scientists? Ha! They think they know more than they do."

"What about . . ." Naya caught herself before she said, "a doctor." "What if you were a firefighter?" she said, pushing. "You could see where to fight the fires. Maybe save lives."

"No, Naya," Mama said. "That would draw too much attention."

"But . . . shouldn't we be able to help?"

"We watch, and we capture beauty. We don't interfere with fate," said Grandmother.

"We don't stand out," said Mama.

Naya sighed and let it drop.

Naya often thought about the something big while she was hemming or doing chores or walking home, any moment when she could let her mind drift. Then, inevitably, she would let her vision blur and, if she was alone, let her hands float up and walk the lines. Nothing happened much in their city. Lots of small somethings happened, of course, but the something big felt different. It was a bone-deep tremor on the lines. Like the world changed, but she didn't know how. Like maybe the world was opening up. She poked at the spots where it disturbed the lines, like poking a sore tooth. It was her favorite pastime besides watching medical videos.

But since talking with Mr. Ned, all Naya could think about was the science camp. It was driving her to distraction, trying to figure out how to convince Mama and Grandmother to let her go. She debated on the best approach . . . using a straightforward, reasoned argument with Mama, or trying to find an angle. She saw people use angles all the time on TV and in the lines. It always worked out for people on TV, and about fifty-fifty for people in the lines, she guessed. Sometimes she didn't bother to go back and see what happened. But still, an angle might be a good way to convince them, especially Grandmother. She already knew Grandmother wouldn't like her studying science. Honestly, Grandmother would be mad about anything that wasn't art or something their ancestors had done.

Naya shook her head like she was shaking away a gnat. She didn't see why she had to be an artist just because everyone else did art!

The problem was, Naya wasn't sure she could work an angle without messing it up, or what kind of angle would work in the first place. Mama worried too much already to use guilt; it would just shut her down. And really, Naya felt bad just thinking about adding any more guilt on Mama. She could use her college transcripts as a reason, but college was still a ways off. That gave her an idea, though: if she said she wanted to study a related subject—say history—Naya could argue it was to research their heritage. But how could she work in science? She might end up promising to go to an art institute when she actually wanted to go to a general university. Mama was usually straightforward, but Grandmother was wily. If she could get Mama to agree first, in private, then it would be easier to convince Grandmother. It would still be tough, though. Naya had been working extra hard to get ahead of all her sewing duties. She'd complained less (mostly) and was extra sweet (she hoped).

Maybe there was something she could offer, something to trade? But everything Naya could think to offer would push her more toward art and away from science. And really, she didn't want to compromise that much. She just wanted them to say yes! Would that be so hard?

Naya set her jaw. She'd figure out a way to convince them. She had to.

—•—

The rhinoplasty surgery was going well. Sometimes the surgeon started and found something he wasn't expecting. Naya squinted at her phone, the video too small to see the level of detail she wanted. She had pulled up a diagram for comparison, but every time she switched web pages, the video stalled.

"Are you watching videos again?" Grandmother interrupted. "I don't know how you stand those things. They give me the heebie-jeebies! Here, come help me with the weaving."

Naya sighed theatrically as she put her phone away, but she couldn't help a little grin. She followed Grandmother into the weaving room. Looms dominated the space, but one large window lit the room. When the breeze came through, dust motes danced across the shelves of thread spools that lined the walls, like a rainbow come to life.

Grandmother was working on a silk shawl, the threads so fine, if you blinked you could miss them. The shawl held a half-finished landscape, full of color and florals, both abstract and literal. That was grandmother's special gift—capturing a design inside a design inside a design, until what you thought was random resolved into a beautiful, precise image. Grandmother always put in a tiny spider somewhere in her weavings, her secret signature. Naya's eyes roamed the shawl searching for it.

"I need to start on the sky, sunset to night. What color do you think, Naya?"

Naya's hand hovered over the spools. She pulled a watery turquoise and a pale golden blush like light on water.

Grandmother beamed her approval. "And how would you use these?"

"Three rows turquoise, then float the blush." Naya held her breath.

Grandmother nodded. "Good. Let's see how good. Pick more, please."

Naya felt a surge of pride. She loved when they worked like this, her pulling threads off the shelves, Grandmother weaving. Sometimes Grandmother didn't use the colors Naya pulled, but more often than not she did. It was always a wonder watching Grandmother work, and it was like Naya was creating the piece too. A feeling of calm settled over her as she fell into the rhythm, drifting over to see what Grandmother was working on, then to the wall to pull threads she thought might match. Her intuition picked the colors more than her mind consciously did.

"Naya, come here."

She walked to Grandmother's side and looked where she

pointed on the shawl. On the branch of an abstract tree was a small black spider, cleverly woven to almost blend in with the burls on the trunk.

"You do one."

"Really?" Her jaw dropped. Naya had woven a row or two before, but only when it was a plain color, a simple pattern.

"Yes. Your practice pieces have gotten better and better. You're ready."

Naya's hands felt suddenly damp. She wiped them on her skirt, then picked up the shuttle holding black thread. She hesitated, then pulled a mustard yellow from the shelves and bent over the shawl. When she pulled away, there was a tiny black-and-yellow spider next to Grandmother's larger one.

"Ooh, look at that detail!" Grandmother crowed. "You're good at this, Naya. You'll be a fine weaver someday. Maybe it'll be your specialty."

The praise washed over Naya like a drug. Of all the arts they practiced, she did love weaving.

But she loved science more. In fact, the spider she wove was called *Araneus diadematus.*

CHAPTER SEVEN

Visits to three psychic mediums, a tarot reader, and someone who called himself a "quantum seer" yielded nothing. Unfazed, the man stopped for a trim at a hair salon. He kept his hair at a precise length, and it was always funny what could be turned up in local businesses. Two seats away, an overbearing woman talked loudly while having her gray roots dyed. He was alternately bored and amused by her pompous ramblings. People, he found, were worthy of study but predictable. He was on the verge of tuning her out when something she said made his ears prick up. Something trivial, nothing definite, but an . . . undertone that sounded promising. He complimented her choice of hair color and youthful appearance. She talked more and more and more until the man had pinpointed a particular neighborhood worthy of investigation. *Good thing*, he thought as he smoothed down a stray hair. He was in the wrong part of the city.

◆━◆

Their house was old. An old building, remade any number of times, from house to storefront to apartments to business again, until Grandmother and Mama had found it and reshaped it once more. A funny hodgepodge of a building, with walls that had been moved and windows added. There was half a kitchen downstairs, a chimney without a fireplace, and a warren of workrooms and closets. Part of the front shop still had a chandelier from when it was a grand dining room. The upstairs was more modest, with three bedrooms and one big combined room for the kitchen, dining, and living room, but the colors made it anything but sedate. Sometimes Grandmother or Mama would just start painting . . . walls, doorways, frames. Even Naya had doodled all over her room, from stick figures when she was small, to unicorns and kittens, to sketches of plant anatomy as she got older. They had yanked out the second washer and dryer to make more space for artwork. The units could have been separate. They could even have sublet some of the downstairs space to another business, but their lives spilled up and down the stairs until it was all one rambunctious house, and business, and art project. Even the garden in the back spilled in from the outside; plants placed here or there, morning glory curling around the window frames. Sometimes Naya could hear the echoes of other people in the rooms as she walked the halls. Sometimes she could feel the house's memories, warm and fond—theirs now, but also part of everyone else who had lived there.

She trailed her hand along the wall, listening to the house as she looked for Grandmother.

Mama was in the downstairs kitchen, painting. She'd taken over the breakfast nook as her own little studio. She said the light was best there, and it must have been true, because her face glowed while she worked. Where Grandmother's special talent was in weaving, painting was Mama's. Sometimes she painted leather handbags and sold them to clients. Naya asked her once why she didn't put her regular paintings in an art show, but Mama said she painted those just for herself.

Naya crept into the room and hovered over Mama's shoulder.

She was painting a scene full of marigolds, so many and so bright that Naya waited for them to spill, live, from the canvas.

Grandmother was out in the garden, planting seeds. This was her chance.

"Mama?" She glanced furtively at the back door.

"Yes, honey?"

"How busy do you think we'll be this summer? Usual busy or slower busy?"

Mama gave her a sidelong look. "Probably about usual. Why do you ask?"

"Well . . . we don't have any special events planned, do we?"

"Out with it, my love." Mama dipped her brush in yellow and gilded the edge of an orange marigold. The stroke was delicate and fine, and Naya marveled at it as she found her words.

"I know I usually work in the shop when school's out, but there's this program, a summer camp. It's only for a few weeks, not the whole summer, so I'd still be around to help. But this camp, it's a really important one. Prestigious!"

Mama stilled her hands and watched Naya stumble through her speech. "What are you saying, Naya?"

"I really want to go. It'll look good on college applications too. You know, like Niecy."

"You're too young to worry about college. Is it for art?"

"Um, what?"

"Are you doing art for the summer camp?"

Naya swallowed. "No, it's for students interested in medicine." Quickly she said, "My science teacher thinks I can get in because I'm so good at science! Better than a lot of the other kids. Top of my class! He says he'll even write a letter recommending me."

Mama fell quiet, a little furrow forming on her brow. Her eyes studied Naya's face.

"Honey," she started, "I know you like science . . . but people like us . . . I don't think medicine is the way to go. There are burdens with seeing as much as we do."

"But don't you see, Mama? That's why I could be good at it! I could see complications ahead of time. I could really *help* people!"

"There are *burdens*," Mama repeated. "And there's also danger. Yes, your sight could help . . . or it could be a disaster. You know nothing is set in stone."

"I'd be careful! You taught me to be careful. I know how."

Mama relented, but only a bit. "I understand how you think it could help, but could you imagine seeing illness and death all the time? Walking the lines just for that?"

Naya squared her shoulders. "I want to at least try. Medicine and science, they're important."

"Why do you like it so much?" Mama peered at her.

"The human body is amazing and . . . and I can see it." She struggled to describe what biology meant to her, how *right* it felt. "It makes sense to me, the patterns and the layers and the systems. It looks like a mushy mess, but it all works together to make up a whole walking, breathing, *thinking* person. It's beautiful. It's a lot like our weavings."

"It's nothing like our weavings!" Grandmother stood stiff in the doorway, glaring.

A cold wash of adrenaline swept over Naya.

"You think art is the same as some dirty, sweaty man who spits in the street?" Grandmother sneered. "The murderers, the criminals—do you want to help them too? Art is better than people! You don't know yet."

"I do know!" Naya struggled to keep her tone reasonable. She had wanted to convince Mama first, have her on her side. Now she had to start over! "I know I'm not grown-up yet, but I'm not a kid either. Art is important. But helping people is just as important."

"You haven't even finished your training! If you were really grown, you'd know better!" said Grandmother.

"Without people, there would be no art!" Frustration bloomed inside her, spiky and sharp.

"Art is a calling. And you shouldn't squander gifts like ours."

"Medicine is a calling too!" She wanted to yell, but Naya wrestled it down. Having a tantrum would only convince Grandmother she was right.

"You're turning away from your heritage!"

"I'm not! Did you know I could study our heritage through genetics? Through science?" She tried sounding as reasonable as she could. "Maybe even . . . even trace our people through DNA! Didn't you say a lot of us were lost?" There! That should warm Grandmother to the idea.

If anything, Grandmother looked less convinced. She looked almost . . . alarmed.

Confused, Naya shook her head. She turned to Mama, pleading. "You want me to be more responsible? I'm trying to plan for my future." That was the wrong tack; she knew it as soon as she said it.

Mama's jaw tightened almost as much as Grandmother's.

"Or at least," she said quickly, "one option. Science is an option. You know there are artists who specialize in medical illustrations."

Mama brightened. "Is that what you would like to do? Illustrations for science?"

Naya's throat clenched. She dropped her eyes to the floor, tried to make herself say yes, but she couldn't do it. "Maybe. I want to see . . . you know . . . the options."

Grandmother sniffed. "She's already made up her mind. Fourteen, and already decided her heritage isn't good enough! Fourteen, and she's planned out her future! For now. Let's see if next week it'll be something else, an astronaut or a trapeze artist. Oh, but if she paints the signs at the circus, it'll be okay!" She directed the last comment at Mama with a sneer.

Mama frowned, a shadow of hurt crossing her face.

Naya's temper snapped. "It's just a science camp! You're the one making it into a big deal." She waved her hands wildly at Grandmother. "You make everything into a big deal. You're such a drama queen!" Naya blanched as soon as it popped out of her mouth.

Grandmother's eyes narrowed to slits. She breathed heavily, like a bull about to charge.

"Fine. I'll make a *deal* with you." Her finger pointed with a sharp jab. "You start weaving your soul wrap . . ."

"Mother!"

Naya's eyes widened, but she tried to keep her face from changing. Her grandmother was offering her a deal! A thrill worked its way through her anxiety. Grandmother might be mad, she might regret it later, but if she set a bargain, she wouldn't go back on it.

Grandmother kept her gaze firmly on Naya. "And if you finish it, then we'll talk about summer camp."

A soul wrap was a big deal—an art project that could be any shape you wanted, but often it was clothes or a tapestry, something woven. It used to be tradition to make a cloak if you were a traveler, or a rug or wall hanging if you meant to make a home. A soul wrap was like a personal coat of arms but more than that. It was your story, your life, your dreams. Mama always said it was to set intention.

"She's too young!" Mama protested. "I didn't start mine until I was much older."

Making a soul wrap was hard. Sometimes it took a long time. But she was good at weaving. Grandmother had said so. And . . . all their people made one eventually, so why shouldn't she do hers now? She just had to finish it before the deadline for science camp.

"She's not too young to decide she wants to be in medicine! She's not too young to throw her gifts away!"

"I'm not throwing my gifts away! Can't you see? They could help!" Without meaning to, Naya raised her voice.

"If you try to walk the lines that way, to predict disease, you could go mad! At the very least, it'll break your heart, seeing death over and over!"

"Mother, calm down. I—" Mama started.

"Or, if it *did* work, if she could become some sort of miracle doctor, people would *notice*," Grandmother barked back.

Mama stiffened in her chair.

Naya's heart fell. She knew that look, the one when Mama got her most protective.

"She's right," Mama said to Naya. "There are different types of heartbreak in this world, my love. Heartbreak can wear you down, break your spirit, or make you so desperate you get lost in the lines trying to prevent it. It's happened before."

Naya wasn't sure what they were even talking about, but she felt science camp slipping away from her.

"I can handle it! I won't go crazy!" she cried out desperately.

"Naya—" Mama started.

"If she's strong enough, mature enough, to make her soul wrap, then we'll know she's strong enough for the lines," Grandmother pointed out to Mama.

Naya saw something strange crawl over Mama's face—emotions too quick for her to follow, a war of indecision.

Whatever it was, Grandmother must have seen it too. She turned to Naya in triumph. "Will you take the deal? A soul wrap to discuss your camp?" she needled at her.

"Not *talk* about summer camp! If . . . when," Naya amended. "When I finish it, I *go* to summer camp. For science." There. No loopholes. No wriggling out of anything. She held her breath.

Grandmother smirked at her.

"Fine. You finish your soul wrap, you can go to the science camp," she agreed.

"I'll do it!" Naya said before Grandmother could change her mind.

Mama threw her hands up in the air.

"I wasn't done." Grandmother fixed Naya with a steely glare. "If you don't finish it . . ." She paused for a long moment. "Then you'll give up all this science nonsense. And I mean, *all* of it! We'll pick your college. With the appropriate areas of study!"

Naya sucked in her breath so hard it hurt. This was exactly what she didn't want! She knew Grandmother wouldn't back down about picking her college either. But if she could make her soul wrap . . . if she could make her soul wrap, it wouldn't matter.

"No!" Mama said, sharp for once. "You two are being ridiculous! A soul wrap shouldn't be made for a deal. It's not a bargaining chip."

"You heard her! She's planned her future." Grandmother made flourishes with her hand. "If she knows so much, then she's ready to make her soul wrap too!"

"You are being too hard on her!"

Grandmother turned on Mama. "And you are being too soft! We've indulged her enough! She needs to get serious about her art, her heritage."

"I"—Mama glared at Grandmother—"am her mother!"

Grandmother looked away, quiet, but her jaw was still set stubborn hard.

"Naya." Her mother turned to her. "You know a soul wrap is important. You don't make one for deals or whims. It's for when you're grown, when you really know what you want in life."

"But I want to, Mama! I *know* what I want to do. I want to be a doctor!" She'd never said that seriously to them before. Her body vibrated with conviction.

Mama studied her face. The frown between her eyes made curious shifts, from worried, to frustrated, to mad, to an emotion Naya couldn't name. Naya waited, her breath hitching fast and shallow, as Mama turned it over in her mind. She could still very well say no. To the deal. To science camp. To everything.

Please, she begged silently, *please, please.*

"All right then. You can *start* one."

Grandmother huffed in triumph, and Mama shot her a glare so fierce, Grandmother picked up a pair of her reading glasses off a shelf and sailed out the door, her head high and satisfied.

Mama turned on her. "Naya, you listen up good! This is serious, and you have to take it seriously. A soul wrap is not a slapdash affair. There's no rushing! No picking a color because it's a boy's favorite or you're inspired by a trendy band or a video game!"

Naya stiffened in offense, but Mama didn't stop. "You think long and hard before you begin, you make plans, and then you sit with those plans. You can start collecting threads, but you *do not* start until you know!" Mama's eyes burned.

"I know it's hard, Mama, but I can do it! I know I can. I know how to weave, and knit, and all the other skills you've taught me."

"Naya! The 'hard' in a soul wrap isn't about hard to *make*; it's about another type of work. It's about taking a deep look inside yourself." Her voice was fierce. "When you make your soul wrap, you put all your dreams and wishes and plans for happiness inside it, yes, but you also figure out your fears and doubts and the darkness that will block you. Sometimes it's too much! That's why most of us start a soul wrap when we're older."

Naya had never seen her like this. The alarm must have shown on her face, but Mama didn't let up.

"This is about you. Your soul! That's where the hard comes in. You need to walk the lines while you're planning too. There are consequences to everything, Naya. Remember that."

A tendril of anxiety crept through her.

Mama started to say something else but caught herself, studying Naya's face again. She sighed and stroked Naya's hair. "Just remember, you can stop at any time," she said gently.

But that's what Grandmother would want . . . for her to stop.

Mama walked out of the room after Grandmother. Their voices echoed strangely down the hall, harsh and hushed and urgent.

The house was too crowded all of a sudden. She needed to be alone. Naya ran into the backyard, blinking back tears. She didn't know why she was crying. She'd won! Well, almost.

She inhaled deep and flushed at the shakiness of her breath. Naya dug her fingers into the dirt. It felt dry and cool and crumbly. She imagined her fingers growing, elongating, wiggling through the brown soil. They brushed past rocks and burrowing insects and animal bones. She said their scientific names in her head. Her fingers branched out and grew deeper and deeper into the earth, just like the roots of the great mother oak tree in the lot. Oak trees could live three hundred years, some even older. That tree had been here longer than Naya had been alive, and it would most likely be here after she was gone. The peace of that cycle seeped into her, making the fears of the present seem small and silly.

She could be a tree. She could be anything she wanted.

She could make her soul wrap too. Mama was just worrying again.

CHAPTER EIGHT

The memory flowers recorded everything, everywhere. All the mundane details and the big events. Every time someone walked down a street feeling all alone, the memory flowers remembered it. Every time a couple broke up, or someone whistled a tune, or someone made a big scientific discovery, it all went on record. All the life-changing histories and the personal mundane events, the memory flowers were there, without judgment. Nothing was ever forgotten. Often they disguised themselves as some other plant, ordinary and innocuous: a plain-Jane daisy, an innocent morning glory. But Naya could always tell the memory flowers. No matter what they looked like, they always had a certain glow, a particular yellow, at their edges. She was glad for them. In their seeds, you could find the whole universe.

One thing she knew: more of them showed up when something big was about to happen. Maybe the biggest she'd ever seen.

❧

The sun rolled in through the open window like honey creeping over her comforter. Naya stretched her back and wiggled her toes but didn't make a move to get out of bed. Sundays were usually quiet days. Sometimes Mama and Grandmother hustled them off to church, but not every week. Sleeping in had to be the best feeling in the world! Especially those mornings where everything was warm and soft and any worries of the day were still far off and hazy.

But as the room brightened, her sleepy thoughts began to churn over Grandmother's deal.

Naya rolled her eyes to the side without moving. A spool of plain white thread sat on the nightstand. She had crept out of bed the night before, after the whole awful argument with Grandmother and Mama, and pulled it from the weaving-room shelves.

She buried deeper into the covers, trying to recapture the drowsy happiness. Maybe she would even go back to sleep. Then her eyes opened wide.

Mama had shown her *how* to make threads for a soul wrap when she learned how to weave. She remembered Mama held the plain thread in her hand, and a moment later it turned green. But except for a practice thread or two, Naya had never actually made one that meant something. Now she had to make enough threads for a whole weaving!

Should she . . . start?

Anything was better than thinking about the fight.

Her hand snaked out from under the blanket and grabbed the spool of thread. She bit a piece off with her teeth and wound the string around her wrist. Then, just like Mama had said, she felt energy running along her spine, energy that was sort of like the lines but was just hers alone. The energy moved up and down with her breath, but once she concentrated, she could move it, down her legs, or high up her head, or to her hands—specifically, to the hand holding the thread, just a bit more of *her* pulsing in her palm. Then she nestled into her pillow and closed her eyes, thinking about how lovely Sunday mornings were. Spring and early summer were the best, when it was warm but not too hot yet, and you could smell flowers and coffee drifting in. Sometimes she read a book instead of getting out of bed, or stared up at the shadows playing on the ceiling. Those were her favorite mornings.

She must have drifted off after all, because she found herself startled awake. Had she done it?

She blinked the sand from her eyes. The thread wrapped around her wrist had turned the deep golden color of honey.

When Naya walked into the kitchen for breakfast, Grandmother gave her a severe look over her coffee. Naya knew she was still mad then, not mad enough to say anything (maybe), but not about to let their argument go either. Naya's jaw tightened. But then she thought about her honey-gold thread, and she held her head high. She made herself oatmeal and cut fruit and perched, her back straight, across from her at the kitchen table. She could play regal just as much as Grandmother could.

Mama bustled in carrying her work planner.

"Naya, we'll have to do practice early today," she said, peering at her notes. "I need to finish draping a dress this afternoon."

Naya suppressed a groan. Most Sundays and Mondays, the boutique was closed to appointments. It gave them all time to catch up, Grandmother said. They were also training days for Naya, time to practice walking the lines. But usually they practiced in the evenings, not first thing in the morning. And to be honest, she just hadn't felt much like practicing lately. Especially now . . . she would rather start making threads. But if she said that, she *knew* Grandmother would launch into a lecture about responsibility and probably rehash the arguments from the night before. Naya really didn't need to give her any more ammunition.

She raised her chin. In her most responsible voice, she said, "I'm almost done with breakfast. Do you want to do it now?"

Mama shot her a surprised look. "Sure, my love. Let's sit on the couch."

Ignoring Grandmother's suspicious look, Naya put her dishes in the sink and glided into the living room. She arranged herself on the couch, ladylike, as Mama set aside her planner and sat beside her. Naya raised her hands, and the lines came into focus. Mama placed one of her hands on Naya's wrist, linking their sight, and raised her other hand to the lines.

"Even your breath, ground your energy, still any extra images," Mama said, as she always did, a type of mini-meditation for walking the lines. "Now . . . relax your eyes."

But Naya was already in the lines. She hadn't had to breathe and ground in ages.

"Let's start by zooming out," Mama murmured. "Can you find the library?"

Naya followed her instructions, zooming out to find the lines at the library in less than a moment. She'd been there a million times. She could practically find library lines in her sleep.

"Let's start here," Mama said in a slow, patient voice, picking a line. "Zoom out again. See how bright it is? This person is used to routines. Now zoom in. Show me your finger work. Good!"

Naya sighed inwardly.

"Now follow the line . . . See, this man's line breaks into new lines soon . . ."

They had practiced this last time. And the time before that.

"The brightest line is the most likely outcome," Mama continued. "Or the decision he's most leaning toward . . ."

Naya dropped her hands, frustrated. She knew this already! She flopped back against the couch and rubbed her head.

"Do you have a headache, my love?"

Naya started, guiltily. "No. No, I . . . I was just thinking about homework."

"Do you have a lot of schoolwork to finish?"

"Don't let her off the hook!" Grandmother called from the kitchen. She stood and leaned on the doorframe with her arms crossed. "It's important to practice. There are still things you need to learn."

"I know that!" Naya grumbled. Mama said that too, that her training wasn't finished yet. But then why did they show her the same things over and over? "But . . . didn't we trace lines from the library last time?"

"Oh, so this is all old hat for you? You know how it's all going to turn out?" Grandmother sniffed.

"No!"

"Mother, there's plenty of time for training. Years yet! If she has homework, she has homework." Mama peered at her.

Naya remembered too late she was being responsible. She straightened up again. Grandmother narrowed her eyes.

"No, I don't have too much." Naya smiled to show she was fine. "Let's keep going."

"Okay. Want to see where his line crosses others instead?" Mama asked. "Let's see if he's a social butterfly or a lone wolf."

"Why don't we . . . why don't we practice threads?" suggested Naya.

"Threads?!" Grandmother interjected. "But you already know how to do threads, don't you? Being so grown-up and ready for your soul wrap?"

The phone rang, a buzzy, sharp sound, and all three ladies jumped. Mama answered the call. It must have been a client on the other end, because she immediately started talking about hem lengths.

Naya fidgeted on the couch, before Grandmother shooed her off.

"Go do your homework. We'll finish practice later. But first"—

Grandmother gave her a steely look—"let me clarify one thing. The deal is you have to do your soul wrap *on your own*. No extra help. Including help with threads."

Naya flushed, half with nerves, half with anger. "Fine."

She could do it on her own anyway.

❖

She took spools of thread everywhere with her. She'd have to make a lot of threads to win Grandmother's challenge. She didn't have to use *all of them* in her soul wrap, but she liked having the options, especially since she might mess up some threads before she got the hang of making them.

She made one when Short Shorts was telling jokes at the lot. That laughter sounded like a bubble of pink-gold happiness.

Lying under the oak tree made a soft, tawny thread.

Another robin's-egg blue thread captured the brisk feel of a wide-open, no-chores afternoon.

She made ones accidentally too. Those threads weren't always as pretty. Around the side of the house, memory flowers climbed and trailed along a windowsill. Naya pressed a spool to the flowers, trying to capture the energy of knowledge, the mystery, the excitement. She wasn't even sure what—just the special feeling she got when she saw the memory flowers.

A rustling from the window drew her head up. Mama was on the phone, murmuring to someone. She had that tight sound in her voice, the one that crept in when she was especially worried. Naya froze. Bits and pieces of the conversation floated through the window, but not enough to follow. Not enough to know if Mama was talking about her.

When the guilt of eavesdropping was too much, she tiptoed away. She snuck up the stairs to her room as if she had been there the whole time and put the spool on her desk. That's when she noticed it. The entire spool had changed color, not just a length of it. The thread was a mottled green-gray brown, with pink running through the brown in uneven splotches: the color of worry, and the color of care. Naya stared at it in her hand. It wasn't an ugly thread, but something tugged at her when she stared at it.

She shoved the spool in a drawer and went downstairs to pick out a fresh one.

◆━

Mama was in the kitchen with Cecilia, her best friend. Naya smiled to herself. Mama had been stewing for days, ever since the fight over science camp.

When Mama got quiet, Naya knew it was because her mind was moving fast—designing art in her head, playing with ideas, worrying too, her thoughts like a bird flying this way and that around the sky. Grandmother was the opposite. She spoke her ideas out loud, becoming brighter and brass, like she couldn't contain the creation inside her, all sun.

Cecilia was quiet too, but in a way different from Mama. She was solid and measured and determined, like the earth to the birds or the sun. Mama worried less when Cecilia was around. Cecilia had a stubborn streak too, Mama said, but most of the time she couldn't be ruffled to the point of invoking it. Cecilia worked at a foundry, casting metal, and she always had a classic car she was tinkering with. Naya loved when she would roll by with her newest restored beauty. Then Naya and Mama and Grandmother would put on fancy clothes and all pile in the car to go to dinner. Except Cecilia always would wear the plain pants and shirt she'd worn that day.

"Why don't you ever dress up?" Naya asked.

"I like simple clothes. Besides," said Cecilia with a sly grin, "I can only wear cotton when I'm working. If synthetic fibers catch fire, they can melt onto your skin." Then she'd eyeball Naya's fancy dress.

"The very idea! As if we'd traipse into a forge in evening wear!" Grandmother would huff.

Naya would laugh at the ritual teasing, old and familiar.

But sometimes just Mama and Cecilia would go out. Sometimes when Mama was real worried about something, fussing and fretting until she was worn around the edges, Cecilia would roll around the corner in one of her half-fixed cars. Most likely Mama had called or texted, but sometimes Naya swore it was like Cecilia just knew.

Naya asked her once, while she waited by the car as Mama got her purse, "How did you know to come by today?"

Cecilia smiled. "The ground told me."

"The ground?! The ground can't talk."

"Sure it can. The ground knows everything, 'cause we're walking around on it all the time, see? We're not paying attention, but the ground pays attention. And it rumbles right up through your feet. All you gotta do is listen." Then she laughed.

Cecilia wasn't one of theirs, but Naya thought she was pretty special all by herself.

❧

Naya pressed a thread to the hood of Cecilia's latest project, a rusty Ford Lincoln, half of it primed for painting. She kind of liked the cars when they were in progress, half-finished. Full of possibility, like the lines. Like a thread before it changed color.

Cecilia bounded out the front door.

Naya wound the thread around her hand. "Are you and Mama going out?"

"Yes, ma'am." Cecilia grinned.

"That's good." Naya wrinkled her brow. Mama probably wouldn't be so worried if the house wasn't so tense. "That's good," she repeated softly.

"I heard you have a project you're working on. You want to go to science camp, right?" Cecilia asked. "How's that going?"

"Good! I mean, it's okay so far. But . . ." Naya bit her lip. "Grandmother only made the deal because she doesn't think I can do it."

"Well." Cecilia stayed quiet a moment, her eyes thoughtful. "I don't think your mother would let you try if she didn't think it was good for you."

A bright bubble grew inside Naya's chest. "Yeah, you're right." *Grandmother might not think I can do this*, she thought, *but Mama knows I can. That's why she agreed to the deal!* "I can handle it."

<hr />

A bus went right past her school to the hospital. Grandmother and Mama didn't know, but sometimes she went to watch. She could get to the hospital in ten minutes, visit, and then be back again in not much more time than when she stopped by the lot after school. She wished the hospital had those observation rooms for surgeries like you see on TV. Once she asked the nurse if they had one. The nurse said no. Then she said those were just for medical students anyway. Then she gave Naya a pointed look. Naya was disappointed, but she bet if she got into the summer camp, they'd let her see some surgeries then, or they would have something similar. What would be the point of exploring a life in the medical sciences if they didn't get to see anything?

Naya walked into the emergency waiting room. The front area was crowded with patients, but all the action was behind the security door.

Around every decision was a humming pulse of energy. More than that, the energy was not just decisions but sort of the essence of a person. Someone who was very dedicated—that commitment tended to color the choices they made, steered them in certain directions. And that energy became part of the lines.

There was a doctor here. She'd seen him before when she came in with Mama for an appointment. Of all the people who worked in the hospital—nurses, doctors, administrators—he was her favorite. He was younger than the other doctors, and his eyes shone as he helped a little boy with a broken arm. The doctor cared so much about healing people that he vibrated, a hum of purpose and caring that could fill a room. It practically leaked out of him. She wanted to be just like him. She wanted that feeling for her wrap.

She loitered near the security door, holding a flu-prevention pamphlet, until a family was buzzed through. She slipped in behind them as soft as a wraith. She craned her neck around like she was looking for someone, just another kid coming to visit. Then she ducked into a curtained partition that was cluttered with crash carts. She crouched, leaning against the cool metal of the cart. Naya blurred her eyes to see the lines.

A place like this, a hospital or a police station or a government building, a place where things *happened*, had layers and layers of lines. So many weighted decisions left a resonance. Old emotion and energy piled up. A place like a hospital should be too much, too chaotic, too heavy for people who were sensitive, even without a gift like Naya's. But for Naya, the energy pumped her up. It made her feel alive. The energy, the decisions made there—they were important.

There he was, the young doctor. He frowned at a chart as he hurried down the corridor. He wasn't as cheerful as the last time she had seen him, but his energy was the same. Several lines shot away from him, more connections than most people had day to day. The lines were most likely his patients' lines crossing his, as well as other hospital staff. If the doctor didn't turn, if he kept walking straight, he would pass right by her.

Naya hid behind the curtain. She closed her eyes and brushed her hand lightly over that humming energy as he passed. The energy gathered around her fingertips like static. She skimmed just a little off the doctor's line, just enough to feel his purpose, his conviction a shining glow. She pulled the spool of silk thread out of her pocket and wrapped the energy around the whole spool until it pulsed and hummed.

The silk turned vivid blue green as it absorbed the energy. It was gorgeous! More vibrant than she could have imagined.

She hugged the spool to her chest.

This thread would be at the center of her wrap.

◆◆

She tried to make a thread for the Internet, that magic place where you could learn anything, see anything, talk to people at any time. She scrolled through videos, and photos, and people's feeds. She watched her favorite surgery videos. She texted people and wrapped the thread around her phone. She tried, but it didn't work.

CHAPTER NINE

There was a new kid in the apartment building next to the lot. He'd moved from one of the fancier suburbs after his parents had gotten a divorce. He stood at the edge of the lot, shy and determined, shuffling cards between his hands. Eventually, he drifted toward the group of boys, who nudged each other.

"Who's that?"

"He's in my English class. He's okay." And on Max's word, the kid was folded into the group.

"What's your name?"

"Nicklaus with a *K*."

"But we'll call him 'NK' for short," declared Max, "because he's the new kid. Get it?"

"And," said Tiggy, "he's a little bit of a tourist, so we gotta teach him about city life." Hoots burst out of the boys. NK smirked ruefully, unruffled.

Naya could tell he was going to fit right in.

She leaned against the cement tube with Short Shorts. The sun was warm, warmer than it had been, almost like summer. Naya twisted a thread in her pocket, hidden from view, around and around her finger. She hadn't started weaving her soul wrap yet, but she thought about it all the time. She had to be done before the science camp deadline. That gave her a little more than two months. Without thinking, she'd angled toward the path by the fence, ready for home, where she could pull out her threads and play with ideas again. She'd kind of hoped to talk to Tiggy, but he was busy with the boys.

The twins and Arnie marched across the lot, their faces flushed.

Arnie announced, "There's going to be a meteor shower Saturday night! My parents said we could come out here to watch it. I'm going to bring a telescope and everything!"

Marisol and Sarai swung their hands in excitement. "It's supposed to start at nine o'clock. You should all come too!"

A jolt of excitement ran through Naya. She tended to focus on biology more than astronomy, but she'd love to see a meteor shower!

"We should have a picnic!" Short Shorts chimed in. "A nighttime picnic."

"Ooh! Yeah, let's do it!"

The kids danced in place, shouting out suggestions. Even the new kid got in the game.

"I can make sandwiches."

"I'll bring fruit salad."

Longing bit sharp at Naya's heart. It sounded like all of them planned to go. She imagined the picnic, could almost taste the night air. But out by herself at night?

"Are your parents coming?" she asked Arnie.

"No, but my aunt lives in that building there." He pointed to the apartments overlooking the lot. "And she said she'd keep an eye on us from the balcony."

That might not be enough for Mama and Grandmother to let her come.

Short Shorts must have seen the worry on her face. "Maybe," she offered to Naya, "a few of us can walk you over and then walk you back home."

"Yeah!" said Marisol. "You're right around the corner. We'll come get you."

Naya brightened. She forgot sometimes that the other kids knew how protective Mama could be. If some of the girls came, then she could probably go. She hoped. "That would be great. Thanks! I can bring a picnic blanket and napkins." Naya thought hard. "I'll bring something else too." She hadn't learned much cooking yet.

"As long as it's not eggs!" Remembering the story about tapeworms, everyone groaned and laughed and clutched their stomachs.

"What's wrong with eggs?" asked the new kid.

Tiggy exchanged a sidelong glance with Naya. "Tourist."

•—

She looked small and unpromising through the lens of glass. The man studied her and the other children carefully. She was lighter of frame than the others, perhaps younger, easier to handle. None of them looked particularly special. But then again, that was part of their defensive mechanisms, their camouflage, so to speak. He should know. He had made the study of people his life's work—especially their kind.

Rumor had brought him to this city, like it had countless others. Then it was a matter of surveillance and patience. If his hunch was correct, the girl was a likely candidate. He hadn't seen any visible signs yet, but he could see the rebellion stirring in her. And that, well, that provided some opportunities.

•—

As soon as she walked in, she could smell the spices. Mama was making her special dish, a mix of chickpeas, basmati rice, and artichoke hearts stirred together and flavored with cumin and garlic. The dish was one of Naya's favorites, Grandmother's too. Mama must be trying to ease everyone's mood. A rebellious, squirmy part of her was irritated, but the dish smelled so good, her mouth watered. Mama always knew how to use food to spoil righteousness.

She didn't know how to bring up the meteor shower now that they were all mad at each other. Well, Mama clearly wasn't angry, but Naya didn't think a meal was going to settle anything between her and Grandmother. Not enough.

She drifted around the room before finally settling on the couch. She had some homework to do, but not much. And no hem orders for once. A basket of knitting sat next to the couch, an unfinished scarf tucked into the top. Naya pulled it out and studied the pattern before setting the needles into motion. Their scarf supply had been low lately. Sometimes they knitted for clients, but scarves were also simple projects to add to the shop, easy to make pretty with colors and patterns. "Add a bit of flair," Grandmother would say. The scarf had a lovely, slight metallic shine running through the cashmere yarn. Soft clicks from the cooking and the needles filled the room.

Naya's hands flew. She'd always been a fast knitter.

"Mama," she said, her eyes on her work. "I'm sorry about . . . well, you know."

"I know, my love," Mama said. "Maybe I'm not the one you should apologize to."

Naya stayed silent. She was still angry. Grandmother was always lecturing her to be more responsible, to think of her heritage and her future, but then she dismissed Naya's ideas, her dreams. She made them sound . . . stupid. If she tried to talk to Grandmother, they might just fight again.

Mama looked at her over her shoulder while she stirred the rice. "Remember, you can stop at any time."

"I know." She wouldn't stop, though. Grandmother didn't have to set that deal. She thought Naya couldn't do it.

Grandmother came in with paperwork and sat at the kitchen table. By the set of her shoulders, Naya knew she was still mad too. With a flash of guilt, she remembered calling her a drama queen. That was mean. And it probably hadn't helped any.

Her fingers flew faster and faster. Naya *could* make her soul wrap. Then Grandmother would see. The scarf was almost to the right length. Just a few more minutes and she could cast off.

Naya frowned at her fingers. Still, if they kept picking at each other, she'd probably never get to go out. Grandmother got stricter when she was mad. They all had a stubborn streak, the women in their family, but Grandmother was the *most* stubborn. Maybe Naya should just apologize and get it over with.

She cast off the last few stitches on the scarf and studied her work. The scarf was a beautiful variegated crimson with that hint of gleam. Naya fished in the basket and found some left-over bright, metallic gold. Quickly she crocheted, adding a pretty edge to the ends, a bit more shine, and suddenly it elevated the scarf from day to evening. She beamed at the piece. Funny how something as simple as a scarf could make someone feel special.

Naya got up from the couch and quietly laid the scarf next to Grandmother at the table before going to her room.

Grandmother could take that as an apology if she wanted. And then Naya didn't have to say a thing.

CHAPTER TEN

What should her soul wrap look like? Naya squinted at the art magazine for ideas. A soul wrap could be almost anything that could be made out of thread. Some people made wall hangings, or fiber art, or clothes. In olden times, they made ceremonial robes, and lots of women traditionally made formal dresses. But since almost all of their kind were creative, they often came up with inventive soul wraps, especially in modern times. Mama once went to an art show where an artist had made their soul wrap in sections as part of a huge mixed-media canopy hanging from the ceiling. Mama didn't know that artist, but she knew what the soul wrap was as soon as she saw it. She said it was a little shocking to see it on such public display, but it was beautiful.

Sometimes people kept their soul wraps simple: an everyday dress, or a comforter for the bed, even a woven box if you used thick enough threads. Grandmother said one of her cousins long ago made his soul wrap into a hat!

"He was mad about hats. He *did* have a really big head," laughed Grandmother. "And not much in it!"

Naya had heard the legend of the first soul wraps since she was small. Long ago, a group of their people were trapped by an evil ruler. Even though this ruler had his own city with mines full of rubies, he was greedy for more. He rounded up their people from the temples and their homes, and he stranded them on an island with no way off. Then he ordered them to weave his life in a tapestry, showing how he could win all his battles, and expand all his territories, and collect all his riches, so he would always know what steps to take in life. Anyone who refused was locked away and starved.

Every week, the ruler would visit the island and demand to see his tapestry. But the people told him it took time and patience to unravel the lines for the best path. They said the lines foretold he would be a man of great importance. They said his tapestry would be glorious. But they needed rope for the looms, and wood for the tapestry frame, and a flock of sheep to have enough thread. Pleased, the man agreed and sent them what they asked.

Seasons passed as the people tended the sheep, and prepared the looms, and built the giant tapestry frame. Guards were set on the island, and they kept the people from teaching their children, or talking too much, or doing anything but work on the tapestry. So the people wove messages to each other in a secret code that only they could read and hung them on the tapestry frame. Then they wove their stories into soul wraps so their children would never forget. Over time, the guards grew lax watching people do nothing but sit and walk the lines all day. The guards often fell asleep at their posts. Then the people built boats from the wood for the looms, and packed rope and dried meat and other supplies, and they hid it all under the tapestry frame.

The ruler came to check their progress, and the people said it was finally time; his promised tapestry would be ready in three days! However, they needed a night of solitude and prayer to see the last lines of his fate. They said they foresaw great riches, more than the ruler could dream, if only they could unwind the final knot. The ruler, his greed fed fat on the promises, agreed, and he instructed his guards not to disturb their people during their night of holy solitude in their great weaving room. On the night before the deadline, the people moaned and fell into ecstasies of prayer while the guards shivered outside in the night air, so the guards fell back to their own cozy guardhouse. Soon the lazy guards fell asleep. Then the people quickly unpacked all they had hidden away. They tied the guardhouse doors closed with strong rope and carried their wood boats to the shore. They stitched their soul wraps together into sails, all of their history and all of their stories catching the wind, a rainbow of memories. And in the dead of night, they left the island for good, sailing until they were beyond the ruler's reach.

Left behind was a small tapestry. Not nearly as big or grand as they had promised the ruler, but the tapestry did show glorious scenes of conquest and treasure. The ruler was so excited, he forgot about pursuing the people and set to work right away on his first campaign. Following the tapestry step by step, he invaded the next city over.

What the tapestry failed to show was the huge army that protected that city. Their people had seen that the ruler would never achieve his goals, no matter how long they walked the lines for him, so they only wove what he wanted to see. The evil ruler died in battle, clutching the tapestry around him, and their people never had to worry about him again.

The weight of the story hit Naya. Imagine having to leave home with only a few supplies and a cloth of stories? With nothing but the clothes on their backs? She had never really thought about that expression before, but it wasn't just an expression, was it? To protect their secrets, their people had had to move around a lot, traveling from one country to the next. Suddenly, Grandmother's endless stories about their people made a little more sense. Even if she was annoying about it.

Naya rubbed her fingers along the hem of her sweater, hand-crafted by Mama like those people long ago had crafted their sails. What if she had to carry all her history, all her essence, on her back? No wonder a soul wrap was important. It was a marker of their very existence, wasn't it? An art piece that told not only their past and present but also their future. It wasn't like Mama had knit "future doctor" and "lover of science" into her sweater. Mama barely knew those things about Naya yet.

But Naya wanted her to know. Her soul wrap could tell her. Some people kept their soul wraps private, as secret as their gift of walking the lines. Naya didn't want to keep hers private.

She thought about the blue-green thread from the hospital.

She wanted hers to shout to the world.

＊＊

The night of the meteor shower, Mama forced a flashlight on her and reminded Naya three times to make sure her phone was charged. Then Grandmother made her promise to take a lot of pictures so they could see the meteors too, but Naya knew that was just her sneaky way of making her text them while she was out.

Right on time, Short Shorts and the twins showed up on her doorstep. Naya grabbed her basket for the picnic, gave Mama and Grandmother hugs, and rushed out the door before they could ask the kids a million nosy questions. Mama tried to hold on a moment longer, squeezing tight, then let her go with a sigh.

The setting sun painted long shadows across the ground, like a world dipped in indigo. She'd never been out like this, at night, without her family! A nearby clump of blossoms, wide open four-o'clocks, sang the evening in, but Naya could tell they were memory flowers undercover. She'd seen similar clumps all over the neighborhood, growing out of cracks in the sidewalk or crowding flowerpots. They were here for the something big she'd seen in the lines, for sure. If it were to happen at all, it must be getting close. A thread of new excitement curled through her.

When they reached the lot, Tiggy rushed up to Naya while the twins giggled behind her. He helped her spread the blankets she'd brought.

"Out in the middle, where we can see best," Arnie directed. He already had his telescope set up and was fussing with a star app on his phone.

Naya handed out paper plates and napkins while the other kids unpacked food. Sandwiches and fruit salad and cans of soda were passed around. Down at the bottom of the basket, she discovered some fudge. Naya couldn't help a squeal of delight. Grandmother must have cooked it while she was at school. Fudge was her secret specialty. She'd sworn to only give the recipe to family, no matter how often people asked her.

Naya's cheeks flushed warm. That was just like Grandmother. She didn't apologize much or admit to being wrong, but she put special treats and little surprises where people could find them, just because. Naya was glad their fight was smoothing over. She should have given them both longer hugs when she left. She'd hug Grandmother extra hard tomorrow.

"Here, Naya, try this." Someone pushed a sandwich at her. She piled food on her plate. There was so much to try, and it seemed like everyone had brought a little extra. Excited talk filled the cooling air as they ate. They talked about meteors, and favorite recipes, and whether there was life on other planets. They traded gossip from school and shared plans for summer. Jokes flew back and forth, until they laughed so hard they had to take a break from chewing so they wouldn't choke. Naya hadn't spent this much time with all of them before, outside of school. She couldn't believe how much fun she was having!

The sunset gave up the sky, and stars appeared in ones and twos as the color melted away. She pulled the fudge out last, and everyone cooed over the little squares. It felt strangely adult to be serving dessert, like she was hosting an event. Well, it was really Arnie's event. He was the most excited she had ever seen him. He'd put on a plaid button-up shirt with a duct tape bow tie like a little professor. He kept checking the telescope and showing kids pictures of constellations.

"Twenty minutes, everyone!" he announced.

Naya flopped backward on the blanket and groaned at her full stomach. "I'm going to watch the shower just like this!" she said.

"Good idea!" said Short Shorts. She tidied up discarded wrappers and paper plates to make room.

They scooched until as many of them could fit on the blankets as possible. Tiggy lay right next to her, and she suppressed a shiver of nerves, suddenly shy.

It was a perfect night. The shooting stars shimmied and shot across the sky above them, like the best party ever. She could practically hear the stars singing. She felt bigger, and it wasn't just from the food.

Tiggy turned his head and grinned at her, jubilant for no reason. Her mood twinned his, and her smile felt a little giddy when she met his eyes. They both burst into laughter.

In her pocket, she wrapped a long thread tight, tight around her finger, willing the energy into it, wishing it would never end. How did you top a night like this?

Eventually, Arnie's aunt shuffled down from her apartment and asked everyone when they needed to be home. More than one phone lit up with parents checking in on their kids. Groans rose up around the lot. Naya's phone buzzed in her pocket. She texted a thumbs-up without bothering to read the message from

Mama and reluctantly sat up. She shook the blankets out and folded them, making cleanup last as long as possible.

"Thanks, Arnie!" she called to him where he was packing up his telescope. "This was a great picnic!"

Even in the dark, his smile shone bright.

Arnie's aunt offered to drive the twins home.

"Wait! We have to walk Naya back," the girls explained. "She's just around the corner."

"Come on, Tiggy!" Short Shorts called. "Never let a lady walk alone in the dark."

Naya hid her grin as he jogged over to her. They trailed behind the group down the alley. "That was amazing!" she whispered to him.

"Yeah," he said, and fell quiet.

She squinted at him in the dark.

He reached out and pulled on her arm as they reached the corner of the house, and her breath caught in her throat. The long shadows wrapped around them like blankets.

"So . . ." Tiggy looked down. "Do you want to meet me after school on Monday? I'll walk you home."

"Yeah, okay." She hugged herself and danced from foot to foot, pretending she was cold.

She knew she couldn't see her own line. But maybe she'd sneak down the lines, just for a peek at Monday. Maybe this time she'd see something.

The man sighed, putting away the binoculars. The last remnants of the meteor shower danced unnoticed above him.

She had been trained well. The other one, the boy—she clearly liked him. The man had hoped, in the party atmosphere of night and no supervision, that she would be careless with her gift. But she hadn't slipped, and he still was unconvinced that she was the right one at all.

Something big, the man mused. *Something big would be needed to push her over. Something where she wouldn't be able to help using her talent.* Then he could be sure.

CHAPTER ELEVEN

I n the morning, Naya's skin felt tingly, her legs longer, like she had grown three inches in one night, her head floating high. She took the stairs two at a time, taking unnecessary trips up and down between her bedroom and the weaving room. The thread from last night had come out midnight blue. She wanted a bit of silver to compliment it, but it had to be the perfect shade.

And, she thought triumphantly, she had managed the night out just fine, despite Mama and Grandmother's worrying! She had even stood out a little; she'd gotten lots of compliments for the blankets and the fudge. And nothing bad had happened! Nothing at all.

This is the first step, she thought, a thrill working through her again. *The more Mama sees how I can handle myself*, she thought, *the more she'll have to loosen up the rules!* There was no reason to be so protective. Naya just had to show them she wasn't a kid. She planned the next outing in her mind. Maybe a night movie with her friends? Maybe all day at the mall? Maybe camping! Ooh, she'd never done that before.

The more opportunities she had to go out on her own, the more proof she'd have not to hide. And the more proof she'd have for the science camp too! Well, at least if she finished her soul wrap.

A surge of confidence flowed through her. She could do it. She knew she could.

She clattered loudly downstairs again, jumping the last few steps. Grandmother gave her a disapproving look, but it couldn't squelch Naya's mood. She trailed her fingers along the shelves of threads and picked out a shimmery spool. She had only tried making her threads with the plain white spool. Could she use colored thread? Would it change the color, or just enhance it? She started to call out to Grandmother, then stopped herself.

Grandmother said she couldn't have any help. Her mouth twisted in thought. She should find out on her own anyway. Experiment, like a scientist would. She smiled to herself. Like an adult.

One thing was certain: after last night's meteor shower, Naya didn't want to go back to playing it safe.

❥

In the kitchen, Mama was humming at the stove while Grandmother squinted at customer bills scattered across the table. The room was warm and rich with the scent of cooking. Naya put her homework in her backpack. Any moment now, Mama would gently suggest that *someone* set the table. Then Grandmother would tut and scramble to gather up her paperwork as Naya got the plates. Mama and Grandmother did it *every time*, like they didn't even notice. Naya smirked to herself. If she could look at their own lines right now, she bet they would all be in loops and circles. On impulse, she reached into her pocket and wrapped a thread around her finger, waiting.

"Did you know," Naya said to the air, "that the definition of insanity is doing the same thing over and over again and expecting a different result?"

"Did you read that on one of your meme things? I think there's a little more to mental health than that," Grandmother declared.

Mama looked over her shoulder. "I think it's almost time for someone to set the table," she murmured.

"Oh now, already?!" Grandmother's hands flew across the table, organizing the bills into piles.

Her eyes gleaming, Naya marched to the cupboard. While her back was turned, she caught the energy, rushed and routine and familiar, and let it soak into the thread in her hand. She had to subdue the smile on her face before she turned around.

She didn't know why she'd done that. The thread didn't really fit her soul wrap, but she'd keep it just in case.

◆━

Grandmother had made her get up extra early. It was a *time change*, and Grandmother always made a fuss over those days. Not like a "set the clocks back" sort of time change, but an older event, timed to celestial changes or the seasons or something. They weren't on a calendar or on the same date twice. Naya didn't fully understand when they happened, but she didn't really have to know, because Grandmother kept track of that sort of thing. *Time changes* were almost like holidays for their kind. Mama would cook something special, and Grandmother would make cake. Sacred days, Grandmother called them.

Naya, yawning, didn't understand why sacred days had to be so early. It wasn't even light yet! The edges of her pajamas were soaking up dew from the garden flowers. Grandmother had wanted her to get dressed, but she just shoved her feet into shoes and stumbled out after her. She'd have to change before she went back to bed.

Grandmother had put on the dress that made her look like the priestess of an ancient sun cult, shimmery white silk with gold lamé rays radiating down from her shoulders. Mama had opted for a simple but flowy dress in sunset colors, with a sweater thrown over it. She and Mama and Grandmother huddled around the aging apple tree in the back corner. Naya yawned again, and Grandmother shot her a stern look.

"We celebrate the changing of time and are thankful for all that is," Grandmother intoned.

They linked hands.

She liked this part. When they walked the lines together, she could feel Mama and Grandmother with her. They couldn't see each other's lines, but when more than one of their kind were in the lines at once, you could feel the others near you, likes auras or ghosts.

She liked this part too, when the sunrise crept up the sky like great globs of honey sweetening the day ahead.

The time change grew closer, like the dawn. The lines' glow grew more intense, and then each line thickened, the strands widening, becoming the size of ropes, then cables, then more. The glow grew until the lines spilled into each other, their lights merging. For a brief moment, the lines were all one, everything a wash of light and potential and warmth. Naya could feel Mama and Grandmother breathing deep beside her, and she did the same. The peace of the light lit her from the inside out.

Then the glow receded, and the lines shrank back to their normal size.

Naya smiled. She'd never admit it, but that was worth getting up early.

After the time change, Grandmother slipped off her shoes and fussed with her flowers while Naya slipped off back to her room. Grandmother always said it was good to wiggle your toes in the dirt. For someone who took such care with her appearance, Naya thought it was funny to see her walking the garden in her bare feet, with her fancy skirt or pants hiked up. Grandmother was at her quietest when she was out in the garden, as if her spirit slowed down, as if the very air around her paused and focused.

Mama said for people like them, those who walked the lines, it helped them to "ground." Naya still wasn't sure what that meant—not entirely, even though she did the grounding exercise with Mama. Mama explained it was to remember that they were part of the earth, connected to it, not floating among the lines.

Naya thought that was silly. Of course they were part of the earth. It was right there. How could you forget you were part of an ecosystem?

◆━◆

Mama was at the cutting table, her eyes unfocused, walking the lines. Her hands strummed the air restlessly.

"Mama? What are you looking for?"

Mama jumped. "Oh! Naya! Nothing, baby."

"Are you looking at that big thing that's coming?" Naya realized with a start that she hadn't checked the lines for the something big in a while—after being so obsessed with it! But then, that was before she knew about the medical camp and had started her soul wrap. Now she wondered, was the something big closer now? Were there more clues in the lines?

"No, actually, I wasn't looking at that. But speaking of which . . ." Mama smoothed out a piece of fabric on the table and then patted the chair next to her until Naya sat. "I know it's tempting to walk the lines, but no amount of checking will change a person's mind once they've set a course. I want you to remember that."

Naya frowned. "But sometimes you can change things," she protested. "Like that time Grandmother saw the car crash in the lines, so she didn't go to the store that day. Or how we prepared for the storm."

"Yes, but those were all events that were going to happen

anyway all on their own. We just got out of their path. Like checking the traffic reports before you get on the highway. You seem like you've been walking the lines a lot. I'm concerned that you might be thinking you can change things. Are you trying to steer events?"

"No!"

But Mama was watching her steadily, with that worried look that tugged at Naya.

"I'm not trying to *change* things. I guess . . . I guess I'm just curious."

Mama sighed and patted Naya's shoulder. "Curious is okay, but don't get too caught up in the lines. It's very difficult to make changes. Sometimes sorrow comes despite your best efforts."

Naya felt even more confused. This was all stuff she knew already. "I don't understand. Why are you asking . . . ?"

"Lots of our young ones go through a spell where they think they can change the lines, manipulate them even. It doesn't usually end well. I just wanted to check in with you."

"Okay." Naya couldn't help but wonder if there was more to it.

Mama, a line between her eyes, studied Naya's expression. She said, "I had a cousin once. He was a sweet kid, but he was . . . awkward. He got the idea that if he could stay ahead of the fashion trends, he would get more girls. It worked for a while. He turned around his image and went out on some dates. He got a nice girlfriend, and he got a big head about it too. Then he saw a trend coming that he knew he couldn't pull off, started by another boy at school. My cousin thought he could change the future by influencing the boy." She shook her head, but a small smile twisted the corners of her mouth.

Naya didn't think any of that sounded so bad. It was just fashion. Fashion changed all the time. It wasn't like the world was going to end. "What happened?"

"He started hanging around that kid all the time, trying to

steer him in new directions. He was almost a stalker! As things went on, he became downright pushy with everyone. Until finally the boy lost his temper and they got in a fight. Remember how I said my cousin was awkward? Well, he was better with computers than his fists. He ended up with a broken nose. His girlfriend dumped him in front of everyone and started dating the other boy right on the spot! And in the end, that other kid still started the next trend."

"What was it? The fashion trend?"

"Oh. Fedoras. Everyone wore fedoras for two months!"

"Well, that could be unfortunate on the wrong head."

Mama snorted despite herself. "You see what I'm saying? Do you think all that trouble was worth it?"

"No, ma'am."

--

"Want to share some chips?" Tiggy tried for gallant but spoiled the effect by nervously shuffling his feet. He waved at the vending machine outside of a mini-mart.

"Sure." True to his word, Tiggy had waited for her after school on Monday. Her stomach felt like it had a glowing sun inside it, both warming and uncomfortable at once. Without saying anything, they took the long route to walk home, away from the lot and past neighborhood shops.

Tiggy dug a worn-out dollar from his pocket and carefully smoothed it against his jeans. He straightened each corner, casting shy grins at her the whole time.

"What's your favorite?" he asked.

"Salt and vinegar," she answered, because she knew it was his.

"That's my favorite too!"

"Really?" She smiled at him.

He inserted the dollar and some change and triumphantly

pushed the button. The spiral metal rolled forward, and forward, and forward, but the chips just hung there, caught by one folded edge. Another pack sat right up behind it, like they were hugging.

Tiggy was trying hard not to show his disappointment. He swore at the machine instead and shook it experimentally—not too hard, or the store owner would yell at them. While he was messing with the machine, Naya let her eyes blur, just for a minute. Then she caught herself, Mama's and Grandmother's words echoing in her head. *Don't be seen. Don't walk the lines for a lark. Don't try to steer events.*

The chips refused to budge. Tiggy swore louder and checked for the owner.

But why could her people see the lines if they weren't supposed to use what they saw? To help in the day-to-day?

Tiggy shot her a glance, frustration etched on his face. With a pang, she realized he was embarrassed. She didn't care about the chips; she just wanted to help him.

Naya blurred her eyesight. She could look without anyone knowing. She didn't even have to use her hands.

He swung his leg back for a good kick.

"Wait!" Naya barked, and he jumped. She lowered her tone and put a hand out to him instead. "Wait, hold up." She drew him to the far side of the machine, off the sidewalk.

Tiggy frowned. She nudged him with her elbow. "That guy over there? Watch the apple," she said.

"What? Why?"

"Just watch."

Tiggy screwed his eyes up at her but then turned to look at the man walking down the sidewalk toward them.

The man wore a rumpled suit, folded papers sticking out of a pocket. He walked with the rambling procrastination of a man who needed to be somewhere but didn't really want to go. He threw an apple up as he walked, caught it, threw it again. He seemed pleased with the simple game, but he was paying too much attention to the apple. He sailed past Tiggy and Naya, and three steps later, he stumbled on an uneven patch of sidewalk just as he tossed the fruit. The apple popped up high, banging into the sign above the shop. The sign board jolted, one side coming loose from its nail. With a groan, the sign swung down and hit the vending machine's side in a terrific crash. Three packs of chips fell into the slot.

Tiggy gaped at her with wide eyes. He grabbed the chips and hurriedly scooted away, Naya on his heels. Behind them, the shop owner came out, yelling and waving at the man with the apple.

"How did you *do* that?" Tiggy whispered. "That was so cool!"

Naya shrugged, smiling, her heart beating hard in her chest. Sweat beaded along her neck too, but she ignored it. *Where's the harm?* "I didn't do anything. I was just standing there."

"Yeah, but you *knew*!"

She shrugged again. "That sign has been loose forever. It was bound to fall sometime. Lucky guess."

He snorted. "Guess, my ass." He looked pleased at the phrase. She couldn't help laughing.

➤

The house was quiet and soft. Mama had gone out with Cecilia on a fabric run. Grandmother was meeting some of her artist friends for coffee. Naya was glad for the space. She had lots of homework, after all.

Tiggy's smile hung in the room with her. She'd close her eyes and there it was. When he smiled, these lines appeared around his mouth, like an old man's but not. And his nose would crinkle, just a little, when he laughed out loud.

She hugged herself and imagined he was hugging her. She never thought she could like someone so much.

CHAPTER TWELVE

Mama had her hands up in the air, the dust dancing around her in the sunlight.

"There's still that dissonance down the line," she murmured to Grandmother, probably hoping Naya wouldn't hear.

Naya's ears pricked up. She dipped her head over her book, pretending she was buried in schoolwork.

"Well, that could be anything," said Grandmother. "Might not affect the shop at all."

"Still . . . it wouldn't hurt to pad business a little, just in case."

"We could hold a Spring Tea. We haven't had one in ages!"

Naya's head popped up.

"Yes," said Mama slowly. "That might do nicely . . ." Her hands skimmed the air, and her eyes narrowed.

Naya loved Spring Teas! Mama and Grandmother would invite other businesswomen in the area, usually artists. Then those women would invite five other women, either clients or other business owners. Everyone came in fancy clothes and accessories that showed off their art, or they contributed something that did the same. Attending a Spring Tea was like being at a walking art gallery. One year, a local glassblower lent an entire set of dishes for food, and each one looked like a miniature stained glass window! Mama and Grandmother hadn't hosted a Spring Tea in a while, even though they attended one every year. But everyone said that the Intertwine Boutique's were always the best teas.

"How many people do you think? If we keep it to five, food would be easier to manage," said Mama.

"Six has always been a good number for us, if we want to be sure of buzz and new clients."

"Then that would be thirty-six on the outside," Mama said. "Someone always shows up with an extra or two. I'll need to make more cake."

"*Mmmm*, cakes. You should invite Mrs. Chen!" Naya didn't really think about it before she spoke. She just pictured the soft yellow-green icing Mrs. Chen used on her princess cakes. Mrs. Chen was a baker who had moved to the neighborhood about a year ago and hadn't attended a Spring Tea before. But there was a shiver in the lines when she mentioned her name. Grandmother and Naya put their hands up at the same time. They couldn't see their own lines . . . but there were ways around that.

Naya skimmed her fingers across the lines and zoomed in on images of their street. That let her see around the shop, without being so close that she got the blank spots when she tried to see her own line. It was a tricky sort of dance. Every time one of them left the house, some of the street images blanked out, holes where one of them would be, but it could be done. She sorted through potential futures quickly . . . until she saw ladies walking up the street in fancy hats and beautiful dresses, art pieces delivered outside . . . Was anyone carrying cake?

Mama's and Grandmother's hands flew even faster.

"Well!" said Mama, after her hands had stilled.

"I guess that settles that!" Grandmother agreed. "Good idea, Naya."

Naya didn't know what they had seen, but she couldn't suppress a shiver of delight.

"I'll call Mrs. Chen after I've sent the invitation. Maybe we could work out catering together." Mama pulled a notebook onto her lap and started writing notes. "So it looks like Jane is a must, and Lacy Fenton and Beauregard. How about that sculptor Amelia? You know, the quiet one? Her pieces are amazing."

"And precious Portia of course," Grandmother snarled.

"Are you sure?" Mama lowered her pen.

Portia Sinclair was another clothing designer and one of their bigger competitors, but most importantly, she was one of Grandmother's oldest rivals. Naya swore Grandmother looked forward to their conflicts almost as much as she complained about them.

Grandmother still had her hands on the lines. "Yes, it looks like we won't want her to miss it. Besides, she won't be as hard with company."

"I'm sure Sylvia will come along too. That should be fun," Mama said to Naya.

Naya sighed internally. Sylvia Sinclair often accompanied her aunt Portia to fashion events around town. Sylvia was also queen gossip at school, spreading the type of nasty rumors that really hurt people. Naya wouldn't go so far as to say that Sylvia made up the rumors herself, but if the gossip was appalling and juicy, she always, always passed it along. Naya had never had a problem with her directly, but some of her friends had gotten in her crosshairs before. "Could I invite someone?" She chose her words carefully. "Sylvia is a bit hard all on her own."

Mama tried not to show it, but Naya could see her smile. "Yes, that would be fine."

━◆

Naya kicked the dirt in front of the oak tree. The Spring Tea was coming, and she hadn't invited anyone yet. She didn't really hang out with any of the girls one-on-one. When she was younger, her best friend, Lindsey, came over all the time, just the two of them. But after Lindsey moved away in fifth grade, Naya would just go to the lot for company. She couldn't invite Marisol without inviting Sarai, and vice versa. If she invited Tiggy . . . well, that put some extra weight on the event, almost like it was a date, and she wasn't ready for that. Especially with Mama and Grandmother there! Besides, what if she asked him and he said no?

She tried to watch the kids on the lot without them noticing, weighing the pros and cons of who she should invite. She remembered the large group of girls walking her home after the meteor shower, a lot more than she expected. A few had been girls she didn't even know, friends of friends who had come for the party. But Marisol and Sarai had been there, as good as their word, along with Short Shorts and Tiggy. In fact . . . Tiggy probably wouldn't have come if it hadn't been for Short Shorts.

Suddenly, Naya knew who to invite.

"Hey, Short Shorts! Can I talk to you for a minute?" Naya sidled away from the group and then walked toward the cement tube until they were out of earshot.

"What's up?" Short Shorts caught on quick, lowering her voice.

"So . . . my mom and grandmother are hosting a Spring Tea. It's this event where a bunch of artists and clients get together. Have you heard of those?"

"Like an English tea? Like *Alice in Wonderland*, with crumpets and stuff?"

Naya had never thought about it like that. "Well . . . yeah, I guess so! But ours has art and less madness." She paused, thinking of some of the more eccentric artists. "Maybe a little madness." She shook her head. "Anyway, it's this Saturday afternoon. I get to invite someone this year. I was wondering . . . would you like to come?" She found herself holding her breath.

"To the tea?" Short Shorts beamed. "Sure! That would be fun!"

She smiled, suddenly relieved. "Great! It starts at two o'clock at my house. But it's like, you know, a little fancy." Naya bit her lip. "Fancier than shorts."

Short Shorts put a hand on her chest and feigned offense. "Shorts are my signature look."

"I know, but . . ." Naya cast about for a compelling reason that wouldn't hurt her feelings. "Sylvia will probably be there too, and you know how she is."

"Oh! Miss Fancy Pants herself?" Short Shorts smirked and looked thoughtful at the same time. "She's not so special."

"I know."

"Okay," she said finally. "I think I've got something in mind." Then she grinned in a way that was a bit more evil than Naya expected.

She couldn't help but grin back.

◆━

Mama walked the lines again the day before the event.

"What is it?" asked Grandmother.

"You know . . . it just seems like a lot of people coming down the street. Double-check me."

"Hmmm." Grandmother dropped her hands a moment later. "I think you better ring Mrs. Chen again."

Naya wanted to check the lines too, but her arms were full of bolts of cloth as she helped clear out the front room. Her legs felt like they would fall off from running up and down the stairs. The Spring Tea was more work than she remembered. Or maybe Mama and Grandmother were giving her more work now that she was older. She didn't mind. It was fun being part of the planning.

"Get more cake!" she gasped, as she hurried by them. "You promised!"

"We did not promise you cake!" Grandmother called after her.

Naya dropped her load and raced downstairs. She swatted at the sweat on her forehead. "If I'm going to maintain a civilized conversation with Sylvia, I need cake!"

Grandmother opened her mouth to snap back and laughed instead. Mama looked up, surprised, and joined in.

—◆—

The day of the Spring Tea it felt like even the flowers were showing off extra pretty for the event, blooming in bunches next to the shop.

Cecilia had come by to help, unloading bags of ice from one of her cars. She didn't normally go to the Spring Teas, only the ones Mama and Grandmother held. She never dressed up or brought clients. She wasn't in the same world of art that the other women were, but she was an artist when it came to restoring cars. She'd park a classic car ready for sale out front while she helped with food and getting ready. Usually, the car sold pretty quick after the tea.

Naya's dress swished around her knees as she set out plates and wine glasses. The dress was soft rose, with a full tulle overskirt that was split asymmetrically so it showed off an embroidered, shimmery underskirt in unexpected ways: here a glimpse of a butterfly, there a peek at vines and flowers. Traditionally the embroidered skirt would be on top and the tulle underneath, before Mama had the idea to reverse the layers. Mama called it her hide-and-seek dress. Naya felt like a princess in it.

The shop looked a bit like a castle too! She and Cecilia had set up long tables in the front showroom, with beautiful lace tablecloths. Grandmother had decorated the chairs with white organza and hung shimmery fabrics along the ceiling in drapey swooshes. Naya had helped her pick the colors. Along with white, they chose the palest pastels—cream, peach, lavender—in fabrics that would catch the light but wouldn't detract from the art pieces. One of the artists had come by with blown glass vases full of flowers. Mama was putting out food with Mrs. Chen on fancy silver multitiered platters. And of course, art from all the artists was displayed all over the first floor of the house. Mama and Cecilia and Naya had even moved furniture upstairs to make room.

"Naya, your friend is here!" Mama called behind her. "What was your name, honey?"

"Isabelle, ma'am."

"What a lovely name, young lady!" Grandmother exclaimed.

Naya put down the rest of the wine glasses before she turned. Her jaw nearly hit the floor.

Short Shorts wore a seafoam-green chiffon tea dress that glowed against her brown skin, a white wide-brimmed hat, heels, and white gloves. Gloves! She looked like a lady—a lady who went to lunches and church and maybe someplace extra fancy, like an opera.

Naya felt herself walking over in a daze. "Wow! Short Shorts! You look fantastic!"

"Thank you!" She beamed. "I thought I'd give this a whirl, even though you know shorts are my signature look."

"You look so grown-up! And your figure!" Naya glanced down at her nearly flat chest. "I still look like a kid."

"Are you kidding?" Short Shorts laughed. "You're always the best-dressed girl in the room! Your clothes are so sophisticated. Most of the girls at school are green with envy. Even some of the high schoolers." She cocked a hand on her hip. "But what do you think? Will it put Sylvia to shame?"

Naya gave a wicked grin back. "Absolutely!"

"Oh, for goodness' sake!" Mama rushed over. "A reporter from the *Herald* is coming with Lacy! Naya, get another set of dishes, and could you bring in that bistro set from out back? I'm sorry, but I think you'll have to sit there, or we'll run out of room. There's extra tablecloths and flowers in the kitchen."

Naya exchanged a look with Short Shorts.

"I'm sorry. We're still setting up." She flushed with embarrassment. "You can sit down if you like, or look around or . . ." She craned her head for a seat that was ready.

"I don't mind helping!"

"Really? You don't have to. You're my guest."

"Not at all!" Short Shorts, grinning with excitement, turned to Mama. "We're on it!"

Mama leaned in close to Naya. "Don't let your picture be taken by that reporter if you can help it," she whispered.

Naya rolled her eyes. "Yes, Mama."

Short Shorts turned out to be an enthusiastic worker, bringing in the extra table and helping Naya decorate quickly while they moved place settings around, so much so that Grandmother said they should hire her to help with the next tea too. Short Shorts beamed with pleasure.

"Sometimes I help where my uncle works," she said. "I go with my cousins when they need to do inventory. Just to earn a little money."

Naya thought about all the times Short Shorts waited for the older kids. "Is that where you go in your trendy tops?"

Short Shorts laughed. "Sometimes. Other times I'm just hanging out with my cousin." She stroked the threads of a weaving lightly. "Your house is so pretty, Naya. There's so much color! It fits you. You must feel so at home here."

"My mom and grandmother always say a home is about family, not about a place." When they said that, Naya got the feeling there was something more, a level underneath the words they weren't saying, but she wasn't sure what it was.

"Why do you spend time down at the lot when you could be around this all the time?" Short Shorts said, sounding wistful. "All this art?"

Naya peered at her. "Short Shorts, do you like art? I didn't know that! Do you draw or paint?"

"No, I'm not good enough. But I sure like looking!"

"Anyone can learn," Naya said encouragingly. "I could show you. It just takes practice. I have to practice all the time too. I made part of that one," she explained, pointing at a weaving. "But I really like science and biology. I think that's why I like the lot— it's outside and open." She thought about the freedom of being at the lot, of the night of the meteor shower. Then she hastened to add, "Besides liking you guys too. Hanging out."

Short Shorts laughed and would have said something, but the door to the shop swept open. The girls hurried forward to take coats as guests entered.

When Sylvia arrived, she took one look at Short Shorts in her fancy dress and gloves and her face tightened in envy. She wore an eyelet cream sundress, and it was pretty enough, but not as nice as Short Shorts's dress, in Naya's opinion. Sylvia must have agreed, because when Naya gestured toward a seat at the bistro set, she looked a bit sour and opted to sit at her aunt's table instead.

"Oh, my aunt would rather I sit with her." Sylvia nodded toward the biggest table and flipped her hair. "I help with her business, you know."

"Oh, we understand," Short Shorts said. The two girls smiled fiercely at each other until Sylvia spun away. Naya hid her laugh behind her napkin.

She didn't mind having the bistro table just to themselves. The smallest teapot was also her favorite, and she had snagged them extra pieces of cake when all the guests were seated.

Short Shorts paused when she saw who wore the largest hat of the tea. "Who is that?" she whispered. "I thought this was just for ladies."

Naya didn't blame her. Beauregard and Grandmother always competed to see who could make the most stunning entrance. Since Beauregard topped Grandmother by a good six inches and would wear evening sequins at nine in the morning, she usually won. "That's Beauregard. She works in clay." At Short Shorts's expression, Naya added, "My mom says we have all types of ladies here."

Short Shorts nodded, unfazed. "Good to know." She took a sip of tea, her face thoughtful. "So . . ." she said at last. "You didn't invite Tiggy because this is a ladies' tea, right?"

The cake made a lump in Naya's throat, and she had to swallow it down quick. "Um . . . yeah. And I wanted to invite you."

"But . . . you could have invited him. There are a few men here. That lady brought a man with her, and there's the reporter."

"Well, it's not a strict rule . . ." Naya said, hedging. "If someone has male clients, they can bring them, or wants to invite a friend . . . but it's mainly for women who run art businesses."

"Is that the real reason?" Short Shorts asked, her tone sly.

Naya played with the napkin in her lap. "Um . . . what do you mean?"

"I know you like him, Naya!"

"Shh!" Her face flamed with heat, her head whipping around to see if Grandmother was nearby. She could only imagine what she'd say!

"All right, I do!" she admitted. "But I don't know what to do about it. And I don't want to make it into a whole big thing, you know? I really like being friends with him. I don't want to mess it up." She shrugged. "Besides, I don't even know if he likes me that way."

Short Shorts's eyes went big and she tilted her head, like she wanted to reach over and pat Naya on the back, a little astonished, a little kind. "Um . . . I think he does, Naya. He always makes an excuse to come over, even when he's having fun with the boys. When you're not there, I see him looking at the path. I think he's looking for you."

"Really?" Naya could barely breathe.

"Yeah, really!"

Naya tried to keep her face from breaking into a smile, but it felt like she was glowing from the inside out.

Short Shorts could tell anyway. She gave a big wink as she took a bite of food.

It was, Naya thought, the best Spring Tea ever.

✦

She sighed, happy she was full of cake. The aftermath of the tea was always a lot of work. First the cleanup, which seemed to grow exponentially from the setup. Then later would be all the extra work in the boutique as new clients came in, lured by posted photos and social gossip.

Naya hung her dress up carefully on the rack for cleaning. She started to turn away, then she remembered: she had tucked a long strand of thread in her pocket before the event, a blue thread, to see if it would change color. Halfway through the tea, she had willed energy into it, but she hadn't pulled it out to check. Reaching into the pocket, she chided herself for not putting a plain thread in the other pocket. A real scientist would have set up a control group and would be marking up stats and notes. She should be keeping a journal, she thought—start taking herself seriously as a scientist. But mostly, she chided herself because it was such a wonderful Spring Tea. The first one where she felt like a grown-up—an actual organizer and guest both! She should have used the plain thread just in case the blue one didn't work, so she could have this moment in her wrap. *Next time*, she thought, as she opened her hand.

The blue thread had changed to such a deep, vibrant purple, it almost glowed.

CHAPTER THIRTEEN

Grandmother had reading glasses tucked all over the house. "I don't need full glasses," she insisted. "My eyes are still as sharp as a snake's in the grass."

"You know a snake can't actually see that well. They rely on their—" began Naya.

"It's an expression!" she huffed. "I only need readers to help when my eyes get a little tired, is all."

Of course, since it was Grandmother, she couldn't have just one or two pairs. She needed enough to coordinate with *outfits*.

"Eyes are the windows to the soul, and glasses are an accessory for the spirit!" she said. "They just happen to be useful too. Now, have you seen my purple leopard-print ones?"

For someone so meticulous about everything else, Grandmother was a little silly over the glasses and a bit forgetful. She would practically coo when she spotted them at a store. Then she would pose and try them on and ask complete strangers how she looked. Naya usually tried to sneak away to the next aisle. She had pairs in every color and trend. Often she'd buy a pair, insisting she didn't have that style, and then Mama or Naya would find glasses in the same color sitting on a shelf or next to the phone.

Grandmother spent one whole winter buying readers from the drugstore and adding her own flair: gems and enamel paint and woven cords to hang them on. Naya asked her why she didn't just leave them plain. They were already in pretty colors.

"What's the point in wearing something, if you don't want to be *seen*?"

She made more than she could possibly wear. Eventually Mama convinced her to sell some in the shop. They were flamboyant and over the top and sold surprisingly well. Then Grandmother did a series of coordinating tops. Those sold even better.

Even with all those reading glasses, Naya still got stuck picking out stitches and most of the other monotonous tasks that needed good vision.

"Your young eyes are made for this," explained Grandmother as Mama nodded agreement, trying not to laugh.

Several orders had come in the day after the Spring Tea, surprising them all. Naya got roped into helping finish old orders to make room. She sat on the couch, half watching the news while she picked apart hems. She'd been at it for hours and it was getting late, that weird in-between time when it didn't feel like evening and it didn't feel like day. She didn't mind helping out with the shop most of the time. Usually she worked a couple of hours a day, and when it was more, Mama bumped up her allowance as pay. But she didn't want to hem clothes all her life, and after all the work from the Spring Tea, she had looked forward to having a break and working on her soul wrap. If she didn't finish up soon, she wouldn't have any time to herself at all.

The longer she pulled apart seams, the more bored and tired and grumbly she felt.

When I'm an adult, I won't have to hem anymore, she thought, picking out stitches one by one. *Well, except for surgery stitches.*

She remembered laughing with Short Shorts over cake, the gorgeous decorations she helped put together for the tea, and a surge of pleasure made her smile. The glowing memories battled the vexation of tiny stitches.

"When I move out, I'm going to eat cake all the time!" she declared to the empty room. Mama and Grandmother were downstairs at the sewing machines, rushing through orders. She'd need to get this next batch of clothes to them soon.

A duplex had caught on fire. It was all over the news. The sky darkened into a shade of gray that almost looked like rain clouds. But Naya knew better. There was no rain predicted for days. An older man hadn't gotten out of the duplex in time and was in the hospital in critical condition.

Naya twisted a thread in her hands. *Walking the lines could have prevented that*, she thought. *If I were a firefighter, I would check the lines all the time to do my job better.* She pulled at stitches until they broke. *When I'm out on my own, I can make my own decisions*, she continued in her head. *I can set my own schedule. No one will nag me all the time. I'll move into the dorms so I can study medicine, or whatever else I want.*

She couldn't wait to see a college library—all those books, *real* medical texts, science journals! Not like her school library, or even the city library, which had mainly fiction. After she graduated college, she'd get a job, maybe at a research lab or a hospital. She pictured herself in a lab coat, smart looking and polished. She'd get a teal clipboard, though. That would be her signature piece, so people would know it was her.

And then I'll get my own apartment and . . .

Naya's thoughts faltered. She could see herself at school, in the classroom. She could see herself in a hospital . . . but when she tried to conjure her future home, she couldn't quite see herself living anywhere but within the brightly painted walls of the shop.

All the threads were there, but she couldn't see the tapestry.

She sighed, and her jaw clenched.

Her soul wrap would change that. She knew it—once she set her intention, as Mama would say. Her collection of threads was growing, but she still needed a lot more. She had gotten the hang of them quickly, without any help after all. And she would keep experimenting. Maybe start a journal with notes, like the ones Mama and Grandmother used for customers, but more scientific.

Of course, if she ended up pulling apart hems all night, she'd never get to start!

She gathered up the bundle of clothes she had finished and floated down the stairs slowly, one step at a time. She should have made more threads at the tea. She should have made a whole spool! But a tea didn't really fit with being a doctor, did it?

Naya was so preoccupied that, for a moment, she didn't register the words drifting out of the sewing room.

"You know she's too young for a soul wrap," Mama argued.

Naya froze on the bottom step, out of sight.

"Of course I do!" came Grandmother's reply. "But some people only learn by failing."

"No mother wants her child to fail . . ."

"But she needs to fail!" Grandmother interrupted. "And this lesson will be twofold . . . it'll show her she's not ready, and it will also make her concentrate on art for a change. She's never really immersed herself in art the way we do. Maybe she needs that. She loves weaving; you know she does. Maybe she needs to see how much she loves it to refocus her energy. She's talented!"

"This is about more than ability," came Mama's soft voice. "You know she's . . . young . . . for her age."

What did Mama say? A funny feeling went through Naya—like a flush in reverse, cold instead of hot, until it settled frozen and spiky in her stomach. Was Mama saying she was . . . immature? More than the other kids?

"Well, she's never had to struggle, thank goodness!"

"It's more than that. I'm worried that she doesn't understand the consequences," continued Mama.

But she did so well in school, and she worked in the shop! She was working for the shop right that moment! She had more responsibilities than lots of kids her age.

"A soul wrap will certainly show her state of mind," said Grandmother. "Show her it isn't the right time too."

Sure, she got mad sometimes, or stubborn like Grandmother, but she didn't fuss or pout or cause trouble like other kids at school. Not really.

"You're right," Mama said. "Maybe failure is the only way."

"Better something small now than . . ."

Suddenly, Naya couldn't stand to hear any more. She backed up the stairs to the living room, her footsteps light as whispers. At the top, she stared blankly at the couch, trying to get enough air around the tightness in her throat. They thought she was still a little kid. A baby. She'd expect Grandmother to say she was a child, but not Mama. Then another thought struck her like a punch to the gut.

She thought Mama believed in her, but Mama didn't think she could make her soul wrap after all.

Tears prickled her eyes, and Naya clenched her jaw until her teeth ached.

She placed the finished clothes, neatly folded, on the coffee table and retreated toward her room. Then she stopped. There was still a small pile of garments to finish. It would be immature to leave them undone. Naya blinked rapidly as she picked them up and went into her room. She closed the bedroom door softly behind her. As soft as a breaking thread.

CHAPTER FOURTEEN

S hort Shorts was out of school with the flu. Marisol and
Sarai had gone by her house with her homework, and her
mother said it would be at least a week before she would
be back. A vicious rumor spread that Short Shorts had been poisoned. Naya only half paid attention to the gossip, as ridiculous
as usual. It wasn't until Sylvia made sure to talk about it near
Naya's locker that the full weight of the rumor hit her.

"I'm not saying it was on purpose. I mean, food poisoning
can happen anywhere when you're not . . . hygienic. It's a wonder we aren't all sick!" Sylvia looked around before adding in a
stage whisper, "It just seems kind of suspicious to me. Holding an
event like that? Great way to take out your competition."

Shock coursed through Naya. What? The rumor was Short
Shorts had been poisoned at the Spring Tea? They would never
poison anyone, accidentally or otherwise! Wait, was Sylvia saying
they were dirty?!

Her head shot around, and she gaped at Sylvia. The girls
were laughing. At her. At Short Shorts. But worse yet, a number
of other kids were giving Naya suspicious looks.

Her cheeks burned like fire.

"But, you know, maybe it will do some good, help Short
Shorts lose some weight," Sylvia snarked.

The shock turned into an anger so thick, Naya's vision blurred. The lines popped into focus automatically, and she battled through the images and a narrow tunnel of black until she found Sylvia's sly face. "You're just jealous!"

Heads turned in the hall at her shout.

"Just because she looked better than you, doesn't mean you have to be such a rotten bitch!"

Sylvia's face pinched tight with anger, but she smirked at Naya.

"You *would* try to deny it. It was *your* house, after all." Then she snickered with her friends.

Naya started to stomp off, then whirled back. "You know what? I'd be real careful of rabbits if I were you!" she hissed.

The confused looks on the girls' faces was worth it.

◆━

She was still mad when she got home. Naya walked into the kitchen and threw her backpack on the table. She tried hard not to, but she knew she was pouting a little. She could feel the corners of her mouth turned down, felt the tightness in her jaw. It was stupid, really. There wasn't an ounce of truth in what Sylvia had said! Clients had called after the tea, and no one had gotten sick. She shouldn't get so upset.

But she *was* upset. She was furious! And . . . and offended! For herself. For her family. For Short Shorts. She'd never thought Sylvia was that smart, but somehow she'd come up with a rumor Naya couldn't escape. Either they had poisoned Short Shorts on purpose, or it was an accident because they were dirty! Even if Short Shorts denied it when she got back to school, Naya knew Sylvia would twist it.

Mama walked in with an armful of fabric. Grandmother

must be using the table downstairs, so Mama needed to cut her pattern in the kitchen.

Naya buried her face in the fridge. She could tell Mama. Then Mama would tell Grandmother, and Grandmother would tell Portia, and then Sylvia would probably get in trouble. Her chest ached to tell *someone.*

But she wasn't sure she wanted Mama to know. She was still trying to wrap her head around the meanness, decide how she felt about it, whether it was worth talking about. Would repeating it out loud make her feel better? Or would she just be passing on the hurt?

And . . . somehow . . . she also felt ashamed. As if she had done something, something to make people think she was dirty or would poison her friends. Sylvia's comments churned in her gut. What if other people saw her as the type of person who would do stuff like that? What did they see that she couldn't see?

Also . . . there was what Mama had said, about her being young. Did other people think she was immature too? How do you fix something if you don't know where it's broken? She leaned farther into the fridge, hoping Mama would finish her cutting quickly.

Mama could tell, of course. She always could tell. She had a way of listening to silence the way other people listened to conversations. "What's going on, my love?"

It's because she worries so much, Naya thought miserably. *Every bad thing that could happen is already in her head. Well, maybe not this one.*

"Nothing."

"It doesn't sound like nothing. Was someone mean at school?"

Damn it! How did she know?

Mama's warm embrace wrapped around Naya from behind. She turned and hugged her back. Mama's hugs felt like the whole world was glowing, a warm bubble where all the bad stuff got just a little less . . . bad. For a minute, Naya let the day fall away, like she was five years old again with a skinned knee, like she could tell Mama anything. The story trembled on the tip of her tongue.

Then Naya stiffened. She wasn't a little kid anymore, and she didn't want to be treated like one! She needed to figure things out on her own.

She pulled away abruptly. "I've got homework," she muttered, and rushed to her room.

◆━◆

Her homework was all done, but the anger wasn't. It had only dulled to a bitter ache in the back of her throat. If Sylvia wanted to come to the next Spring Tea, she was going to be sorely disappointed. Naya *would* tell Mama. Rumors being spread about their business were important. Just . . . not yet.

The day was waving its way out, dusky and glowing outside her window. The sky turned gold, and brilliant coral colored the upside-down clouds. Naya blinked, and a ribbon of red appeared, streaking across the blue velvet growing from above. Some timelines changed so quickly . . . even sunset skies that looked like they would stretch on forever. The cool night dropped in, and she shivered as it soothed away the harsh outlines, buried the disappointments of the day into rest.

"Hello, stars. Hello, moon," she whispered.

One time, a long time ago, she saw Grandmother in the garden late at night. Naya had crept out of bed and through the house and into the wet grass. She curled her seven-year-old hand into the edge of Grandmother's dress where she stood by a flower bed.

"What are you burying?" Naya peered at the softly turned soil.

"These are old bothers," Grandmother said, wiping dirt from her hands.

"What's that?"

"Yucky thoughts. Worries. Old scares. I'm giving them to the ground. It'll take all the bother out of them so they won't keep me awake at night anymore."

"Oh." Naya thought that over.

"What's bothering you, honey?"

"Johnny says I like to eat glue. He told all the other kids."

"That does sound like a bother." Grandmother squinted at her in the dark. "Do you like to eat glue?"

"No!"

"Then you know it's not true, don't you?"

"Yes, but . . ."

"Johnny can only bug you if you let him, if you let the lie become a bother. How about we let it go? Find a rock. Pick a good one."

Naya bent over the garden path until she found a smooth, round stone, smudged and pale in the dim light.

"Oh, that is a good one!" Grandmother praised. "Now hold it in your hand, close your eyes, and think about the bother. Think about how it makes you feel: worried or angry or hurt. Give it a shape."

"A shape?"

"Yes. I always imagine mine like slimy gunk. I can picture it better that way. Understand?"

Naya nodded.

"Now take those shapes, all that feeling, out of your heart and head and put it in the rock."

Naya screwed her eyes tight and thought about the mean things Johnny had said. She imagined sharp invisible spikes going into the rock. She knew it worked because when she opened her eyes, the stone lay cool in her hands, the spikes poking at her already fading.

"Good," said Grandmother. "Now pick a spot to bury it . . ."

Naya's fingers dug into the crumbly dirt.

"And as you cover it up, say, 'Bother, I release you.'"

"Bother! I release you!" Naya pounded dirt over the stone.

Grandmother nodded in approval. "One last thing, and this is important: Don't dig it back up. Leave it there. The ground needs time to do its work. Okay?"

"Okay."

"Now"—Grandmother guided her toward the house—"anything Johnny says is not going to bother you anymore, all right, honey?"

And after that, it never did.

"Grandmother?" she asked as they walked through the house. "Have you buried a lot of bothers?"

"Oh, I've had my share."

❧

The school hall buzzed days later. A buzz that crawled under Naya's skin and nibbled with sharp teeth.

"Did you hear? Sylvia's cousin has a rabbit. Well, I guess Sylvia was holding it, and it kicked her in the chest! The scratches are so bad, she doesn't want to come to school."

Naya tried to look like she was surprised. But she wasn't. She wasn't at all.

"Do you think she'll have scars? Sylvia will flip out! Can you get plastic surgery for accident by rabbit?"

Naya felt sick to her stomach. She shouldn't have said anything about the rabbit. Mama would be so upset. The image had popped up, crystal clear, when her vision was swimming from the anger. She had never had that happen before, seeing someone's possibilities without trying, having an emotion so strong it pulled in the whole line.

She had never sworn at someone before either, much less in the middle of the hall at school. She didn't swear much. It was one of the things Grandmother called "uncouth." But Mama swore if she cut her finger or something. She did it real quietly under her breath. Naya assumed she didn't want to hear Grandmother's comments either.

Grandmother would have a fit if she knew about the rabbit.

Actually, Grandmother would be even more mad about the poison comment. She might forgive Naya for using the word "bitch" and defending them. Maybe.

Or they could get into another fight and be angry all over again.

Maybe Naya should just keep the whole incident to herself.

CHAPTER FIFTEEN

Naya rarely went to the mall. What with all the custom clothes Mama and Grandmother made, she didn't have to. She didn't know her way around like the other kids. She knew every fabric and notions store in the city inside and out, not to mention the specialty places, like that place that sold the alpaca fleece. Her nose wrinkled. Just thinking about it made the back of her neck itchy. Washing out stinky fleece was her least favorite chore.

She followed the twins and Arnie into the maze of Abercrombie.

"We have to wear a plain black skirt for the orchestra performance," Sarai explained. "But I don't want it too plain, you know?"

Naya was only too happy to help. She sorted through the racks, pulling out skirts for Sarai to try on. They'd been wandering around the mall for an hour. After how well the meteor shower had gone, Mama hadn't flat out said no, but it had taken a bit of wheedling before she said yes to the mall trip. Naya had used her most responsible-sounding arguments to convince her. Mama wouldn't let her take the bus after school with the other kids, though. She dropped off Naya and insisted she'd pick her up when they were done. Naya had waited anxiously for Mama to pull away, half expecting her to wait in the car the whole time.

She couldn't help but grin when Mama left. Then a strange mix of hurt and determination chased it away. She had won another victory in the war for freedom. Only now, she worried she had been fighting the wrong war the whole time, that she was being immature when she thought she was growing up. But was she really young? Or did they just want to keep her a baby?

She shook the thoughts away and focused on the clothes in front of her.

"I'm going to take guitar lessons next year," said Arnie, as he flipped through clothes. "If Marisol learns drums, we could form a band."

Sarai looked doubtful. "I play the cello, Arnie. That's not exactly popular."

Arnie shrugged. "So we'll be eclectic. Indie, even."

A pencil skirt caught Naya's eye, and she ran her fingers down the fabric. The crepe was on the cheap side, but it had a small topstitched design in silver along the hem—not enough to break the rules, but enough to be interesting. She held it up. "What about this?"

"Oh!" Sarai reached for it. "That would be perfect!"

"Go try it on!" Marisol urged. She turned to Naya and said in a lowered voice, "I knew you could help. I'm not good at shopping. I get bored. Arnie is better."

"I totally am," agreed Arnie.

Reemerging from the dressing room, Sarai posed, twirling in the skirt. The skirt fit her perfectly, flattering, with just the right amount of shine. Sarai beamed, and Naya beamed right back. Helping someone was the most amazing feeling in the world!

After the cashier rang up Sarai's purchase, they left the store for the food court, sliding into seats around a table.

Naya couldn't help looking around to see if anyone else from school was there, if anyone else noticed her *out*. She sat straight and regal in her chair as if yes, she came to the mall all the time. It was practically her second home. She was worldly that way. Mature. Then Arnie made a joke, and she ruined her careful posture by collapsing into giggles. But the giddiness felt free too. She could laugh and be loud and tell dirty jokes as much as she wanted, behave in a way that wasn't allowed at school or at home or in the shop.

There was that itch on the back of her neck again. Naya frowned. That wasn't from the thought of scratchy alpaca again. It was almost like feeling a vibration on the lines. Maybe . . . she should check? Just in case. It could be the something big.

She looked around the crowded, noisy food court. This was the worst place she could possibly be to check the lines! She stared at a menu sign over a burger counter and let her eyes blur. Several lines were glowing brighter than others, almost buzzing. She'd have to raise her hands to walk those lines, but one was lower. Maybe she could reach it? A light sweat broke out on Naya's arms. She knew she shouldn't, not in public. She could wait until later to trace the lines. But it was right there! She dropped her hand below the edge of the table and touched the line.

A woman was looking through receipts, a confused look on her face. She was at one of the stores in the mall! But why did Naya feel that buzz on the lines? Because she was so close? She walked the line backward to see more detail.

Naya struggled to keep her face blank. It was that man again, the one she'd seen around the edges. She hadn't noticed him in a while. She still couldn't make out his face. He never seemed quite in focus, but the images also showed him never doing much either. Like one time, she saw an argument, two men shouting at each other in front of a bank, and the blurry man was standing off to the side. He literally stood at the edges.

On this line, he was walking out of the store.

"Naya?" Marisol squinted at her. "You there?"

Naya dropped her hand to her lap and blinked back to the table. "I'm sorry, what?"

"You want to get ice cream or pretzels?"

Naya grinned. "Ooh, let's get ice cream! My treat!"

＊＊

It was just chance that he spotted her. His usual surveillance time wasn't for a couple of hours yet. He had wanted a new set of clothes, something that looked official but forgettable, with snappy socks. You could always do something interesting with socks, no matter what you wore. He caught a glimpse of storm cloud hair turning a corner. Startled, he hurried to follow, but no one was there. The timing seemed off—weren't they supposed to be in school? Still . . . he looked for the stores most likely to lure in teens. He drifted in and out of shops, glancing down aisles. Iron-ically, it was often the coincidental moments that were the most advantageous.

He spotted another group of teens and wandered after them, adopting their meandering style, flipping idly through racks. Mim-icry was its own form of camouflage, and it usually flushed out the behavior patterns he needed. Ah! The store they entered had mul-tiple entrances. That would explain the sudden disappearance. He patiently followed the teens until they left the store, and a hundred yards away was the food court.

There she was, sitting at a table, spooning up ice cream, chat-ting with friends. He almost laughed out loud.

At a bench, he flipped through his phone, watching her over its edge the whole time.

＊＊

At the library, Naya ran her fingers over the book spines on the shelf. She'd have to study a lot if she wanted to be a doctor. The thought made her smile. In science that day, they had looked through a microscope at different organisms. Her breath had caught in her throat as the high buzz of discovery pulsed in her. It was amazing, what you could see with science! What scientists could do, once they learned enough. She barely had to push to put that energy in a thread, turning it a rich turquoise. She already missed class. She wanted to feel that sense of discovery all the time.

That had given her an idea too. She wanted to capture the books' essence in a thread. But books were different from people. Their energies were based in a concept, the promise of knowledge, of wisdom, and, very faintly, the energy of the people searching for that knowledge. It was a wily energy, hard to hold on to. In a weird way, a book's energy was more about potential than actuality—sort of like the lines.

She pulled a length of thread out and held it in one hand. She dragged her other hand along the books again and thought hard about learning from them, remembered the thrill when a new idea clicked. She felt the concept gather around her fingertips. She couldn't grasp the energy, but it did follow after her hand like the tail of a comet. Close by, a group of students from the community college had gathered to study. She held up the thread, dragging the energy with her, and she walked by the table of students, passing through their energy as they shared notes for an upcoming test. There—knowledge potential, plus their studying, plus her thrill at a new idea. Maybe that would do it.

The three energies combined and attached to the thread with a little ping. Naya held it up triumphantly. It worked! Well, sort of . . . The thread only held two colors, green and pearly white splashed haphazardly along the string. The energy wasn't as strong as it usually was either, and as she watched, the green bleached away and the pearl faded.

She frowned. Maybe she had to try this another way. But how? Naya wandered around the library, musing, until her feet found her favorite aisle, nonfiction science. Her face lit up. On the "New Releases" shelf was a book about DNA! Naya grabbed it and sat down in the aisle, her back to a shelf. She lost herself in the miracle of genetics.

Half an hour later, her phone alarm beeped, reminding her it was time to go. She looked up and sighed. The book on DNA was fascinating, but she couldn't check it out until she returned the books she had at home. She slid the book back on the shelf, and she noticed she still had the thread wrapped around her wrist. The color from before was completely gone, but a new color had taken its place. A bright, joyful yellow pulsed to the same rhythm as her heartbeat.

It has to be personal, she realized. *The energy has to be tied to me. It can't be someone else's energy, snagged up and slapped on a string.*

But the young doctor's energy had worked! Hadn't it? His was one of the first threads she made! She frowned as she left the library. The more she thought about it on the walk home, the more a feeling deep inside her whispered something different. She had *thought* it was the doctor's energy—his passion, his commitment. But maybe . . . maybe it had always been *her* energy she had captured in that thread, so similar to his that she unconsciously recognized it. The young doctor's energy let her see the passion inside herself.

She walked down the street, grinning like a maniac, her cheeks stretched so wide they hurt. Maybe she was just like the doctor already.

Her dream felt closer than ever.

When she got home, she made a list: all the things she wanted to try, all her plans for the future, and which ones she could accomplish and capture in a thread in time to finish her soul wrap. She couldn't get them all done, of course, but she bet she could make threads that were close enough. For example, visiting the local college was *almost like* being enrolled at college, right?

CHAPTER SIXTEEN

Tiggy's older brother, Brandon, was in juvie. Everyone at school was talking about it. Naya heard about it from three different people before she even got to first period. The spiteful kids were swooping around like birds, looking for the juiciest pieces of gossip. Apparently, Tiggy's brother had started hanging out with these kids from his high school who got in trouble every time they were bored, and everyone said Saturday night was pretty boring. Those boys set an abandoned car on fire. They said Brandon had already left and was walking home. They said he didn't even know what was going to happen, but he got picked up by the police all the same.

Naya spotted Tiggy on the far side of the school, near the yucky bathrooms no one liked. Her heart went out to him. He slunk through the halls like he wasn't sure whether to be ashamed or brag. She walked over slowly so she didn't spook him.

"Hey," she said softly. "You okay?"

"Oh yeah! Yeah, I'm good!" He puffed up his chest, but his smile was weak.

She eyed him, her face solemn. "If you want to talk . . ."

He gave up all of a sudden. "It's so embarrassing! Brandon knew they were going to do something dumb, so he left. Not ten minutes later, they set that car on fire! They thought it would be funny. It was a stupid prank." Tiggy put his hands over his face.

"I'm so sorry."

"My parents are coming down on me hard. They put me on a curfew, want me to check in all the time. I'm practically grounded. It's so unfair! I didn't do anything. My brother didn't even do anything!"

She wondered, with a guilty twinge, if that was really true. She could go back and look, walk the line backward. She couldn't see how they would have picked up his brother so quickly unless he was still close by. Just thinking about it made her feel disloyal. She didn't think it would help Tiggy knowing either way.

"How's your brother doing?" she asked instead.

He dropped his hands with a shaky laugh. "Worse than me, that's for sure. He says juvie sucks. He won't get out until his detention hearing. Then there might be a trial . . ." He trailed off. "It's so weird, him not being there. I'm used to talking to him every day, you know?"

He sounded very lost.

"Things will get better," she said. "Just wait."

"I'm glad we got to see the meteor shower." He smiled at her. "I probably won't get to do anything like that again for a long time."

❧

The rumors at school turned ugly, saying Tiggy's brother was in a gang now and that the car fire was part of his initiation. They said he wasn't walking home at all. They said he held up someone at a gas station for the gasoline. That he danced around the fire like a wild man, and the gang was coming for Tiggy next. The rumors were just ridiculous. But Tiggy got mad and punched a garbage can. Naya gripped a thread in her pocket without realizing it, and when she pulled it out later it was a horrid color, gray brown and pulsing with anxiety.

"I'm not surprised. I mean, look at his brother."

Naya buried her head in her locker like she was searching for King Tut's tomb. But she was listening. She had found, time and again, that if she held really still, sometimes people didn't notice her at all. She'd slide into her locker sideways if it would let her hear more.

"I heard they were going to send him home, but he asked for after-school detention instead. Who asks for detention?"

The girls were talking about Tiggy.

"*I* heard that his parents don't want Brandon around anymore. They might send him to military school or just leave him in jail. If Tiggy starts following in his footsteps . . ." Sylvia let the thought dangle for their imaginations.

Naya held her breath against the surge of anger.

"No?" chimed the other girls. "Really?"

"Well, if the worst happens, I'm sure they'll let the brothers bunk together at juvie," she finished in mock sympathy.

Laughter barked next to Naya's locker. "You're terrible, Sylvia!"

"Hey, I didn't set a car on fire."

Sometimes, if people say something often enough, they can narrow the possibilities of the lines. Like if a dancer enters a contest, but she keeps telling herself she won't win, then more lines appear where she doesn't win. Even if there are lines where she was successful, the dancer might unconsciously choose actions that lead her down the lines where she fails. Because, ultimately, the dancer doesn't really believe in the best outcome. She still has a choice, but she puts out such a strong intention of failing that the lines react. Grandmother called it a "self-fulfilling prophecy."

Naya had seen it happen to people from the outside too, though—an outside-fulfilling prophecy, and that really scared her. One time, a rumor started about an older man in the neighborhood . . . labeling him a sex offender because he liked to go to the park and talk to the kids. He wasn't actually a sex offender. Mama had checked his lines when she heard, but people believed it anyway. He got yelled at on the street. People called the cops when he went to the park. He stayed indoors more and more. He had been a postal worker before he retired; it was hard on him to stay inside all the time. Naya watched as there were fewer and fewer possibilities on his lines, until he gave up and moved away. Everyone else had created his future for him. Naya would hate for that to happen to Tiggy and his family.

Maybe . . . maybe she could help him somehow. Maybe if she took a peek down the lines.

She traced the line backward. She didn't know Brandon very well, so it was harder to find him in the lines. She'd only seen him coming or going, at a distance. It was easier to find someone, or something, if she had a clear picture in her mind. It was almost like she called them, and then their line would come to her. In any case, she could get to their location if she knew what someone looked like and their name. She found it *much* easier to trace the lines of people and things she didn't know anything about, like randomly surfing the Internet. She'd just pick a line and follow it to see if anything interesting happened. Then once she knew a person's line, she could find it again. Naya blew her breath out in an exasperated puff. She didn't have as much practice tracing specific events, especially backward, the way Mama and Grandmother could.

Grandmother always told her to practice more.

"But I already know how to walk the lines. I just see them. We all do!" she had protested.

"Any talent you have can be improved with training and practice! *Life* can be improved with practice! It comes down to seeing the street, or seeing the colors of everyone's shoes on the street. Sometimes the fine details lead you to big movements on the lines."

Naya would roll her eyes and watch a video instead. She didn't know why anyone would want to see the color of someone's shoes. Practicing was just one more thing for Grandmother to lecture about.

Now Naya wished she had paid a little more attention to the tips.

She *could* trace Tiggy's lines to find Brandon, but she felt weird about that. It wasn't implicitly against the rules; sometimes they had to look for people they knew in the lines, and all the times she was with him would be blocked to her sight anyway. But he was her friend, and it felt like spying. What if she accidently saw Tiggy in the bathroom or something embarrassing?

She needed another way to find Brandon. What if she started at the car they set on fire? The car in question, a rusty green Honda Civic, had sat abandoned at the edge of the mini-mart's parking lot forever. Everyone knew it. A car doesn't make choices, doesn't have a timeline itself, but it was part of time, just like everything. If she zeroed in on the location, she could watch what happened around the area.

She concentrated on the image of the car in her head. She didn't usually walk the lines this way, through an object instead of people, but Grandmother talked about it, so she knew it could be done. As she concentrated, the lines shifted to a new angle but . . . not really. It felt like when she watched TV lying upside down on the couch. Naya blinked rapidly, and the car snapped into focus, black with fire damage, the lines of multiple people running around it. Good. Now all she had to do was trace those lines back until she found Brandon or one of his friends.

It took longer than she thought to find the right one. She had to get to the correct time, and a lot of people had been out to the mini-mart that night. Then a bunch of people had stopped to stare at the fire's destruction afterward, adding more lines. Most of the strongest lines were from the firefighters and police at the scene. Finally, she caught an arc of light from one of the police officers.

Arcs showed up wherever two people, or animals, or things had an interaction. Since interactions happened all the time, the arcs happened all the time too. Stopping on the street to say hello to someone would form an arc, a bright curve connecting their lines together. But the arcs were temporary and faded quickly. Naya usually didn't pay any attention to them at all. The only time an arc lingered was if it had a strong emotional attachment or if it led to a significant event in a timeline.

The arc from the policeman was still showing days after the fire. On a hunch, she traced the policeman's line, and a short while later, she found out why it lingered. He was one of the arresting officers.

Brandon's face was terrible to watch as the police questioned him. Denial, feigned innocence, anger, belligerence, shock, and finally fear passed through his eyes before he was put in the back of the police car.

Naya almost stopped then, her hands hovering in the air. But she had his line, so she traced it back.

Her stomach clenched in a sick twist.

Tiggy's brother wasn't part of setting the fire. But he was a lot closer than he let on, just down at the other side of the parking lot, yelling encouragement and laughing. He watched from the sidewalk, his face alight, as the first flames licked the frame of the car. He didn't even leave until someone down the street started yelling. Then he sauntered slowly away.

He didn't even look worried. He looked sort of . . . proud.

Naya wandered, dazed, into the painting nook. Mama was painting night skies and blackbirds.

"Mama," she whispered. "What if you knew something . . . that you didn't want to know about a person? But you kind of feel like it's important that someone else who also knows that person should know what you know." She wasn't sure if that made sense. "Do you . . . tell them?"

Mama squinted at her, her forehead pinched, her paintbrush floating over the canvas.

"You've been looking at the lines. For what?" Her voice sharpened. "What are you planning?"

Naya jumped. "Nothing! Nothing, I just feel really bad for Tiggy's family."

"Oh, that mess." Mama's face cleared. "It is a shame." She thought for a moment. "Will what you saw help his case? Or help anyone feel better?"

"No. No, I don't think so."

"I'm not sure there's a point to saying anything then, my love."

"I just feel bad," she repeated wretchedly. How was she supposed to face Tiggy at school knowing what she knew?

"Hey." Mama's hand was gentle on her cheek. "You don't have to hold guilt for other people's choices. He's young, and we all make mistakes. Maybe he'll get a second chance."

Should he get a second chance? Naya wondered. He didn't actually do anything. But he didn't seem innocent either.

Maybe she shouldn't say anything at all.

"He's a good kid, a good kid."

Naya kept hearing it whispered—at school, at the store, anywhere the grown-ups gathered.

Well, not all the grown-ups. Some of them were outraged mean.

"Thank goodness the fire didn't spread. Can you imagine? These damn kids think they're being clever. Never thinking about the consequences."

"They got what they deserved."

"Just plain stupid. Good thing they were arrested. I don't want idiots at school with my kids."

That was something Sylvia would say. But it hurt more, hearing it out of an adult's mouth. Naya couldn't decide what was more disappointing: what she saw in the lines, or the petty things people were saying.

Tiggy came to school late, right before the bell rang, so he could run to his locker and then to class without talking to anyone. The only place she could find him anymore was in the yucky bathroom. He even ate lunch in there. She had to knock three times on the boys' door, their secret code, to hand him a banana from the cafeteria. Then he might talk for a minute or two. But there were times when she knew he was in there and he never answered the door.

◆━◆

Naya had been staring out her bedroom window for an hour. She'd given up on homework. Tiggy's worried face kept floating through her mind. Mama's advice was right; saying something would only upset Tiggy's family more, but it gave Naya an idea. Maybe she could find something else in the lines that would help. When a thread snags in a sweater, sometimes if you pulled threads in the opposite direction, you could smooth the snag out. She had looked at the past. Now that she knew how to find Brandon, she could walk his future lines.

That meant she'd probably see his time at juvie. Naya bit her lip. When she imagined prison, all that came to mind was dark and dirt, bars on windows and black bars on clothes. She knew bad things happened in prison, like people getting beat up or stabbed. Would juvie be like that too? She didn't like cop shows much—too violent. Now she wished she'd watched a few, just to know what to expect.

Wait, they didn't even wear striped prison clothes anymore, did they? It was all about orange jumpsuits. Orange could be a difficult color to wear.

Naya shook the distractions out of her head and squared her shoulders. No matter how nervous she felt, if she could find something that would help, she had to try. Shifting in her seat to a comfortable position, she narrowed her eyes and put up her hands as the lines snapped into focus around her.

She found Brandon easily. He was sitting on a bunk bed, in a white-and-gray room full of other bunk beds. The room wasn't nearly as dark as Naya had imagined, more like a small gym or a large classroom, with tile floors and fluorescent lights. Brandon wore baggy khaki pants and an oversized khaki polo shirt with a gray long-sleeve shirt underneath it—almost like a school uni-form, but ill-fitting and uglier.

Naya waited for Brandon to move, but he just sat on the top cot, staring off into space. She traced the lines with her hands as they split.

Most of his lines only had small variations, which made sense, considering he was in an enclosed space under lock and key. She zoomed out until she could see around the time of his trial. Naya frowned. She couldn't see many options. He looked belligerent in a lot of the lines, angry and put out. He yelled at people, or he was huddled with other boys in juvie, looking like he had a chip on his shoulder.

The judge ruled against him every time.

One time, he was limping and he had a tight, frightened look on his face. She zoomed in on that line. The judge didn't rule against him then. In the courtroom, his mom's eyes welled up with tears; his dad's hands clenched and unclenched. Brandon looked small as he walked out of the room with his parents. But at least he got to go home.

She didn't have it in her to walk farther down his lines.

━◆━

"It's so unfair! He didn't do anything!" Tiggy raged. "He wasn't even there when it happened!"

They were sharing lunch outside the bathroom again. Two other boys were eating with them, listening to Tiggy's rant. Naya stared at the floor. Tiggy thought he knew what had happened, but she knew better.

"They've got the other two. Why do they need him?" agreed one of the boys.

"They just have it out for us. It's racial profiling. I heard they're trying to clean up the gangs." The other boy made air quotes around the word "gangs." "Like every brown kid is in a gang," he said sarcastically, and slurped his chocolate milk. When he was finished, he dunked the carton into a garbage can and nudged Tiggy. "Hey, we're going to play some basketball before the break ends. You wanna come?"

Tiggy glanced over at Naya. "No, I'm good."

As soon as the other boys left, Tiggy sagged against the wall next to her. He ran a hand over his head in a bewildered, forgotten way—deflated.

"They need scapegoats. That's what it is," he said, more to himself than to her.

He sounded tired, and he looked miserable, utterly miserable. Naya wondered if it was normal for her heart to hurt this bad.

"I don't know what I'll do if he doesn't come home." His voice caught. He covered it with a cough.

"Tell your brother . . ." It came out as a whisper. She swallowed and tried again. "Tell your brother to act extra sorry at the hearing. Maybe even a little scared."

"What?" Tiggy looked at her, astonished.

"He can't act tough. Or angry! Tell him to hang his head and apologize, even if he doesn't feel like it."

"Is this . . . is this like that guy with the apple?"

Naya pressed her lips into a line. "Do you want your brother to come home? Just tell him. Okay?"

"Okay," he said, hope blooming in his eyes.

◆━◆

Something was wrong. She wasn't sure what it was. It wasn't the something big trembling on the lines. But there was something . . . down deep at the bottom of her stomach and then shivering up through her heart. Like an ache for a blow that hadn't come yet.

The lines didn't show her anything at all.

CHAPTER SEVENTEEN

A crowd of teenagers she didn't know, high schoolers she thought, stood in front of the shop in clumps, eight or nine of them at least. Naya slowed her walk and frowned. Occasionally they had teenage customers, especially around prom time, but most of the Intertwine Boutique's clothing was too pricey for kids shopping after school. Anyone who could afford their clothes had to make an appointment. Why on earth would they be hanging out here?

"There she is!" A tall teen pointed at her over the heads of her friends.

Naya stopped dead on the sidewalk as the crowd engulfed her.

"I need your help!" A girl pushed her way in front of her. "I need you to tell me if Bobbie is going to ask me to the prom!"

"What?" Naya stared around her.

"That's stupid!" a boy shouted out. "Everyone knows he's not asking you! I need you to tell me my SAT scores. I'll pay you!"

"Yeah, me too!"

All the kids spoke at once.

"What are you talking about?" Naya gasped.

"We heard about you," said the tall girl. "You're psychic."

"You helped Brandon escape jail."

The world crashed down on her head. Naya felt blinding hot and then so, so cold. Her mouth moved without a sound while the kids continued to hurl questions at her.

"He didn't escape!" she choked out finally. "He went to court!"

"Here, read my palm—tell me what it says."

A dozen hands were shoved in her face.

Naya batted them away. "Stop. I'm not psychic! I didn't do anything." The lie twisted her stomach.

A thin, quiet boy stepped so close, panic flared in the back of Naya's throat. He grabbed her arm. "I really need your help. It's important," he whispered. "I need you to tell me where my dad is. My mom is sick. We're going to get kicked out of our home." The desperation was thick and final in his voice.

Naya gaped at him. "I'm sorry. I can't help you."

"Come on, just answer our questions!"

"No! Leave me alone!" She pushed through the crowd into the shop. She locked the door with shaking hands before anyone could follow her in.

Mama stood at the bottom of the stairs, her arms crossed. Naya had never seen her so livid. "Upstairs, now!"

Naya bolted up the staircase.

Mama said, "They started showing up an hour ago. They seem to think you have psychic abilities for sale."

"I don't, Mama! I'd never do that!" She put her hand to her mouth, and her fingertips came back wet. She didn't remember starting to cry.

"Then why do they think you can? Have you been telling people what you can do?"

"No!"

"Well, you must have done something! Showing off, or dropping hints, or . . . Have you been looking at the lines where people can see?!"

Naya stood tongue-tied, her face flaming. She had done all of those things but only in tiny ways. No one should have noticed. She didn't think anyone had noticed.

"No," said Grandmother. She sat in a kitchen chair, so quiet Naya hadn't noticed. Grandmother's hands were up in front of her.

Naya's stomach flipped over again. *She can't see my line,* she reminded herself.

"That boy Tiggy." Grandmother ran her fingers through the air. "The lines shifted around him recently, a big shift. You said something to *him,* didn't you?"

"It's not his fault!" It burst out of her before she could think to deny it. "His brother was in trouble!"

Mama sucked her teeth, anger wiping out all traces of the worry usually in her face. "What did you do?"

"I . . . I . . . looked at the lines, but I didn't tell him what I saw! I swear!"

"But?" Grandmother's eyes were sharp, boring into her.

"I just said that Brandon should look sorry in court. For the judge. But I didn't say anything about the lines!" She swiped at the snot running from her nose.

"You told that . . . ?" Grandmother got up quietly and left the room. Her bedroom door closed with a final-sounding click. Naya stared after the door, her cheeks burning like Grandmother had slapped them.

Mama's voice cracked like thunder, and Naya jumped.

"That's it, young lady! You are grounded! You will come home straight after school. You will not be hanging out at the lot. And you will certainly *not* be hanging around boys that make you irresponsible."

"What? No, it's not like that!" Naya had never seen her so angry.

"I don't want your excuses! You are also banned from the lines." Mama counted out each restriction on her fingers. "And you've lost your phone privileges too!"

Naya stared at her, appalled. "For how long?"

"Until I decide! That's how long!"

◆━◆

A fuss was centered around the girl. He watched through binoculars, deliberating, then hastened to the street. A small group of teens, two girls and a boy, were turning around the corner. They looked put out.

He sidled up to them, close enough to hear the boy grumbling about being turned away. "So," the man tried, "that was rude, wasn't it?"

"Yeah, it was!" agreed a girl with pink tips in her hair.

"We just wanted her help! It was a compliment!" said the other girl. She flicked dark hair behind her shoulder.

"There was definitely no reason to be rude about it." The boy rolled his eyes.

"Wanted her help for what?" the man probed.

"She's a psychic. She can talk to dead people," explained the boy. "I think I'm being haunted."

"No, she's a white witch," Pink Hair protested. "She broke Brandon out of jail. Like, she does rituals and spells in the empty lot at night! In one of those fancy dresses she wears, but all in white. People have seen her!"

"Either way, she still could have helped us!" the boy argued, and a small squabble broke out.

"Really." The man's mouth twisted ruefully. He should have listened to his first instinct and dismissed this as teen drama. He'd been quite diligent in his surveillance of the lot. Still, there might be an opportunity here.

"She sounds like quite the talent!" He beamed at the teenagers. "I'm sure she'll share her gifts with you if you're persistent."

"Yeah, maybe we should go back."

"Not today, though. Her mom was pissed."

"Another time," the man encouraged, until they nodded their heads at him and slipped away.

✦

The dust kicked up behind her as she wandered the house, trailing her fingers over fabrics and books and art supplies. Whenever she heard Mama or Grandmother coming, she'd move to a different room. She had too much time now that she was banned from her phone. She hadn't realized how much time she spent watching videos. And she didn't want to touch her soul wrap. As upset as she was, she was afraid she would ruin the threads. Instead, she drew designs, planned the patterns she wanted, but that only took so long.

She knew it would be boring.

What she hadn't expected was how her fingers would itch to walk the lines. She hadn't known she'd made it into a habit. How she relied on her gift for little things—glimpses of where people would be, or what the weather was like, or which teacher would be late for class so she could linger in the morning. She hadn't recognized how much she walked the lines just to relieve boredom.

A pile of gray built up on her fingers as she dragged them along the top of a clock. She moved on to the tops of picture frames to see how much dust she could collect. Maybe she could collect a tower's worth. A city of dust before the buildings toppled over.

She had been grounded only one other time. That time, she understood now, had hardly counted. In third grade, she'd gone through a stubborn streak. That's what Mama called it. Not for any particular reason either—just because. She'd sneak an extra cookie because Grandmother said no. Or she'd turn the light back on and read after she was supposed to be asleep—silly things mostly.

Until the paint incident. The paint *and fabric* incident. Naya had wanted to draw birds. After she drew them, she wanted to add colorful paint. Then she thought how great they would look with some feathers from the notions cabinet. She wasn't supposed to be in the supply room or the notions cabinet, and certainly not with a full pot of open paint in one hand as she tried to climb the cabinet to the feather drawer. When she fell, she splattered paint all over a stack of expensive fabrics specially ordered for a client.

Mama and Grandmother had come running when they heard her fall. They screamed when they saw the fabrics. The screams had scared the daylights out of Naya, more than the grounding she got afterward.

She had been grounded from art supplies for a whole week, which was just about the worst punishment Mama and Grandmother could think of. That's when she started helping in the shop regularly too.

"Once you see how much work this is, you'll respect our business supplies," Grandmother had said.

She rolled her eyes at the memory and destroyed her dust city with a swipe across her skirt. Then she paused, Mama's voice echoing in her bruised heart: *irresponsible, excuses, young.* She picked up a rag and beat at the gray smear on her skirt, then ran the rag over high shelves and picture frames, wishing she could clean the words out of her head as easily as the dust.

Her wandering trail took her into Grandmother's bedroom, where a bookshelf almost filled one whole wall. Once she found a photo of her grandfather tucked inside an old book. Its corners were brown and bent, and it looked like it had been carefully placed so that no more damage would come to the thin edges. There was a photo album with other pictures, but this one was different, like Grandmother held it special. In the picture, her grandfather was young and had wild hair and looked like he would laugh at any moment. *Carefree*, Naya thought. Grandmother stood in the background, camera shy and serious, but with the smallest lift at the corners of her mouth.

Something had happened to her grandfather. He had died when Mama was still a child. Naya didn't know the details. When she asked, Grandmother would get stiff and stern and tell her not to bother with the past. But her eyes looked so, so sad.

Sometimes Naya would sneak into Grandmother's room to look at that photo.

An old crumbly book caught her eye, one she hadn't looked at in a while. She pulled it from the shelf and slowly turned the pages, feeling the fine texture of the paper. The gilt on the edges was flaking away. The book was full of myths and fairy tales. She carried it to the empty living room and her favorite spot on the couch.

She remembered one of the stories was about Arachne. Little webs were drawn in a border around the text. She supposed the webs were easier to illustrate than the weavings Arachne and Athena had made, but whoever had drawn the webs had made them intricate and fine, and she loved to gaze at them, study them, as if hidden messages might be there in the language of spiders. She'd always wondered about the story. Maybe they had gotten it wrong. Maybe Arachne had been one of them, and she had said too much about walking the lines and that's why she was punished. Naya's mouth pinched. That sounded like something Grandmother would say. But in one of the pictures, Athena and Arachne were sitting at their looms, and they both had their hands up in the air. You could argue that they were gesturing at each other, but it reminded Naya of something else.

Every once in a great while, one of their "family" would come to town and stop in for dinner. Grandmother would make something special, and dinner would last so long with everyone talking, it would turn into a sleepover and carry on into breakfast, almost like a holiday. Sometimes they were actual relatives. A great-aunt came to visit, and one time a distant cousin, and sometimes they were just people like her and Mama and Grandmother. The conversations were always full of laughter and gossip and walking the lines as they traded stories. Everyone's hands in the air as they laughed and ate. Mama said it made communicating faster because there was always a lot to catch up on. Critical news, she'd say. Then everyone around the table would laugh even louder.

Another time, a woman had come for help. Mama canceled their boutique appointments, and Grandmother moved three cushy chairs in the living room so they formed a triangle. Then they shut the door on Naya. When it had gotten quiet enough that Naya knew they wouldn't notice, she peeked around the crack of the door. All three women sat with their knees touching and their hands up, murmuring to each other. They were tracing the lines, looking at something so complex it took three of them to make sense of it.

That's what Arachne and Athena looked like they were doing. Looking at something the rest of them couldn't see. Something big. Naya flipped through the book to find the right page. Naya got the sense that a long time ago, when Grandmother and her grandfather were young, visits with family were a lot more frequent. She wondered why they had stopped.

Mama walked into the living room, her back stiff, and organized papers on the kitchen table. Naya's whole body froze.

Mama was trying not to show it, trying not to keep talking over a thing they had already gone over, but she was still angry. Naya could tell—still really angry.

Naya flushed and looked away from Mama's tense frame. Her lip quivered. Mama had never gone this long, this angry, before. Grandmother, yes, but not Mama. It wasn't really in her nature.

Well, I'm mad too! Naya told herself. She tried to come up with her own list to be mad about. *I didn't tell anyone about the lines*, she said in her head. *I didn't show anyone the lines, or tell anyone's future. It's not fair to blame me for other people's stupid rumors.* A pang twisted her gut. *It's . . . it's not like I killed someone! They're acting like I broke the law or something!* Instead of rousing an answering anger, guilt twisted her gut and tears sprang into her eyes. She buried her nose in the book before any tears could escape and tried to control her snuffling.

When Mama finally left, Naya crept to her bedroom and eased the door shut. Then she curled up on the far side of the bed where no one could see her.

━◆━

The teenagers showed up one more time. Mama met them at the shop door and said a few words, and they never came around again. Even though Naya was relieved, she couldn't help feeling a little sorry for them when she listened from the upstairs window. Mama had used her best sarcastic, skeptic voice. Mama didn't pull that voice out often . . . but when she did, it made you feel like the dumbest person on the planet.

━◆━

She was changing books out of her locker when she felt Tiggy over her shoulder. Naya stiffened, the crash of school noise dimming around her. Someone must have blabbed, and the only person she had talked to about Brandon was Tiggy. She couldn't decide whether she was mad at him or not. She was mostly mad at Mama and Grandmother. But her anger kept circling around, and sometimes it got mixed up with frustration and blame and something like sadness, even though she didn't know why she should feel sad about anything. But the point was, Mama should never have even found out!

"Hey, Naya," came his quiet voice behind her.

She tried to remember if she had told him not to tell anyone.

"So . . . um . . . want to walk to class?"

But wouldn't not telling be obvious? She slammed her locker closed and turned.

Tiggy's eyes were large and alarmed. "Hey, I heard . . . um . . ." He dropped his gaze to the floor. "I noticed you haven't been at the lot. I was just wondering if everything is . . . okay?" He shuffled nervously.

"I'm grounded."

"Oh, really?" He looked almost relieved. "Parents are such a pain. What did you get in trouble for? Homework or something?"

Naya's anger flared again. She had been expecting an apology or an "I miss you" or at the very least a thank-you! Something! Did he really not know what this was about?

"I got grounded about Brandon!" she hissed. "Because you told someone!"

"What? I didn't! I swear I didn't tell anyone but Brandon!"

"Why did you tell him *anything* except to look sorry?"

"I . . . I had to tell him about you, like that apple incident, or he wouldn't do it. You were right—he was being stupid! He had all this attitude. He was going to blow it. But why would you get in trouble about that?"

"Why?! Because . . ." She stopped herself. She couldn't very well tell him that walking the lines was a secret when she had never told him about the lines in the first place.

Tiggy gaped at her, bewildered.

Naya was trapped. She couldn't explain without revealing her family secrets, but the assumptions people were making about her were almost as bad. She couldn't feed any more rumors—she just couldn't!

"Because kids came to the house!" she finally said. "They interrupted business, and my mom and grandmother were pissed! They were practically stalking us!"

"I didn't know that! I . . ." Tiggy flailed his hands, then dropped them. "You're right. Brandon, he must have told people. I'm sorry you got in trouble."

"Well, tell him to stop! Whatever he's saying! My family is very private. Those kids said all sorts of crazy things. And anyone who's watched *Judge Judy* and with any sense would know that you're supposed to look sorry in front of a judge!" There, that might throw Brandon and the other kids off. She hoped.

"I . . ." He stopped. "I didn't think about that."

He looked sorry. He did. But not *that* sorry, and he had never said thank you, and all the frustration of being grounded settled into her jaw and clenched teeth. She arched her eyebrows at him. "I'm not supposed to hang out with you anymore."

Tiggy looked devastated.

Naya blinked. She had wanted him to feel bad. She hadn't expected him to look like *that*. For a long minute, she watched him try to control his face, try to go blank and not succeed. With every second, guilt melted the ice she had built up around herself. She touched his arm, but it didn't slow down the pain running across his face.

She needed to take it back! How could she take it back?

She leaned in close. "But . . . what they don't know won't hurt them, right?" She could only manage a whisper.

Relief flooded his eyes, and he gave her a shaky smile. "Yeah," he whispered back. "It'll be our secret."

For science, she had to collect plant samples for a project. Naya wandered the backyard with a Ziploc bag in her hand. They were studying types of leaf patterns. There were two main clas-sifications, simple and compound leaves, but then there were all sorts of different shapes within those categories. She would have rather walked around the neighborhood—some of the other kids were doing that—but she couldn't, because of the grounding. At least Grandmother had a lot of plants.

They were supposed to find as many distinct shapes as they could. Tiggy had wanted to partner up. He said she should leave the house early before school so they could meet without Mama knowing. A flare of anger had lit Naya from the inside. She walked away, abruptly, mumbling something about helping in the shop. Guilt and anger twisted together. She didn't want to hurt him, but she was already disobeying Mama by talking to him.

She didn't know she could feel bad for someone and be mad at them at the same time.

Slipping off her shoes, she scrunched her toes in the circle of cool grass underneath the apple tree. She crouched over a patch of clover, hoping to find a four- or five-leaf clover to add to the regular three-leaf clover she'd already picked. Mr. Ned had brought in some cool spiral plants that he had found while camping, carefully dried for study. One was a familiar fern frond that curled up at its end. The other was a small stem with curved spokes radiating out from the top, just like a spiral galaxy. It was precise and perfectly symmetrical, and Naya was fascinated by it. Sometimes you saw something in nature that was so ordered and mathematical that it didn't seem like it could be real. Like some random person made it and snuck it into nature as a prank to trip everyone else up. But it wasn't! Nature was amazing, and the spiral galaxy plant was just another cool surprise. Even Mr. Ned was still trying to identify it.

She'd love to find something cool like that for class! Clover wasn't all that unusual, but four- and five-leaf clovers were caused by a gene mutation. She'd looked it up. Some of Grandmother's plants were a bit exotic. Maybe she could find something different than what normally grew in the neighborhood.

Collecting plants with Tiggy would have been fun, but she still couldn't believe he'd asked her to sneak out after getting her in trouble! Besides, she already knew he would rush through the project. Mama and Grandmother might think she was just a kid, but at least she took the time to do her assignments right.

She reached for an apple leaf, spring green and new. Way up high, a frog was clinging to the branch. It was green, like the leaves around it, but white lines down its back contrasted sharply against the bark. The frog didn't look very secure. Naya frowned up at it. It was in its natural environment. Why did it look so shaky, walking along the branch? Like it would fall at any minute.

She slipped back into her shoes and moved away to the far corner of the garden, poking through pots and shrubs along the fence. Grandmother was always adding this or that, so Naya didn't know all the plants in the backyard. Usually if she lingered out here too long, Grandmother would put her to work weeding. She loved nature, but she definitely did not like weeding.

A plant caught her eye. She waded farther into the crowded corner. She moved a pot out of the way and then squeezed around a shrub. In a large pot near a sunny spot along the fence was a smallish tree-looking plant. Its leaves were spread out in a fan, but the ends changed shape from the main leaf, scooping in and then out so the tips looked like little spades from a deck of cards. She'd never seen leaves like those before! The tag around the trunk said "*Manihot grahamii*," then underneath in Grandmother's neat hand was written "tapioca plant."

Naya shivered. It was perfect! She looked for the prettiest, most symmetrical leaf she could find before carefully picking it. The leaf almost didn't fit in the Ziploc bag. She had to hold it flat so the edges wouldn't crumple. This was sure to impress Mr. Ned! Maybe he'd talk about it in the letter he was going to write for science camp!

She wondered how many plants Tiggy had found yet. She scowled. Her brain just wouldn't leave her conversation with him alone, wouldn't leave the thought of *him* alone. Despite everything, she still liked him, and somehow that made her even angrier.

When Mama said she didn't want Naya hanging out with Tiggy anymore, it didn't sound like the kind of anger that would blow over. She sounded like she *meant it*. It would be tricky enough staying friends with him after the grounding was over—she certainly wasn't going to push it now. Didn't he get that?

CHAPTER EIGHTEEN

Naya had woken up snarly.

Everything was irritating. Grandmother kept sniping at her about this hem job and that client order. Mama was worrying over their supply inventory, even though the shelves were perfectly stocked like they always were. Naya tried to control her temper, but really, she didn't want to. She wanted to yell at both of them to knock it off, but she just rolled her eyes behind their backs and schlepped through her chores. In fact, she rolled her eyes so much, they were starting to hurt.

Sore eyes were also annoying.

It felt like her grounding would never end. She was being unfairly punished, that was for sure. She really missed her videos. And going to the lot. She saw the other kids at school, but it wasn't the same. It wasn't like staying home was teaching her life lessons or anything.

She had just finished folding towels at the kitchen table when the screechy buzzer went off on the dishwasher, right next to her ear.

"Mama, the dishes are done!" It felt good to yell. Like she was getting even with the dishwasher. Maybe . . . she was getting even with Mama and Grandmother too.

"For heaven's sake, Naya! I'm right here." Mama shook her

head so her hair flew in quick jerks. "I've got my hands full with this. Unload it, please."

Naya's hands flopped to the table. She stared into space, fuming. She had just gotten her chores done! Was the universe going to crash a car into the shop and ask her to clean that up too?!

Grandmother sat on the couch, going over their client checklist. As Naya continued to sit, Grandmother slowly raised her head to give her a glare.

This time she couldn't suppress her eye roll. Naya pushed back from the table and unloaded the dishwasher, rattling each dish and banging the cabinets. Mama and Grandmother ignored her. She slammed down the last of the dishes.

When she safely escaped to her room, she reached under the bed and pulled one of their small handlooms out from under the bed. She scowled down at her soul wrap. She'd only started a few rows, just to play with ideas, but she didn't want Mama knowing. Not yet. And certainly not Grandmother.

Naya picked up a blue thread and wove it in. The thread kept catching and pulling. The threads were so pretty, with their energy and bright color. She'd thought they would look wonderful together, but when she wove them, they didn't work. The threads wouldn't lie flat, or clashed horribly. The pattern she had in her head didn't match what was coming out on the loom. The piece didn't even look like a beginning; it just looked like a mess. She picked another thread and held it up against the weaving. Then another. Nothing seemed to go together. This was her life—how could they not work? She worked! She'd never get her soul wrap done in time if she couldn't even start!

This was all Grandmother's fault! All her comments had got inside her head, and now she didn't know how to weave. Naya stood up abruptly, kicking her loom in the process. She turned on the radio at full volume and then grabbed a pillow and screamed into it.

"Will you knock off that racket?" Grandmother shouted. "What has got into you?"

When she got her breath back, a thread was still clutched in her hand. Half the energy was gone, and the emerald green had muddied to the color of old peas.

◆━

The man scowled behind the binoculars. The children poured into the empty lot after school, but once again she wasn't there. He'd gotten used to her routine. The change was highly irritating. Perhaps . . . the earlier fuss with the teenagers had resulted in the girl's schedule being . . . curtailed? What was that called again? Oh yes—"grounding." He rolled the term around in his mind. He remembered it vaguely from the many foster homes he had lived in. Grounding had been one of the lesser and more manageable threats thrown around.

He had never allowed himself to be grounded.

Well, she had to resurface at some point. The shop was as busy as always. He could change his focus to the local school, but that was hardly an ideal location for their introduction. The teaching staff could be . . . problematic.

The man decided to move forward with the next step. He still needed that nudge.

◆━

Naya didn't know anything about her father. Anything at all. She wondered if Mama had a picture of her father somewhere that Naya had never seen.

It was strange, but when Naya was small, she never wondered about her father. Mama and Grandmother had been everything. More than enough, especially with Cecilia and kids at school and all the other art ladies and customers thrown in. Lots of kids only had one parent or grandparent. And she also had art and science and books.

More and more as she got older, she wondered about her father. But she had never asked about him. She didn't know why. Maybe it was that sad look in Grandmother's eyes when Naya asked about her grandfather. Her throat tightened just thinking about it. Maybe she was afraid of seeing Mama look like that.

Now she felt funny about asking. Like she had missed a window. And she wondered, with all their secrets, would they even tell her? Naya always felt like they were holding something back.

She poked through the bookcases whenever she thought they weren't looking.

◆━

One of their loud clients had come into the shop for a fitting. She wasn't loud in the fun way Short Shorts was, all infectious exuberance. This client was loud like she thought everyone was hard of hearing. The woman spent a lot of money on clothes, but she always patted Naya on the head and talked at her like Naya was five. And deaf. A deaf five-year-old who could serve endless drinks. She snuck away to the bathroom, even though Grandmother was giving her the stink eye to stay and help. Naya made a slight face and rubbed her stomach, like she was feeling gassy but was *much* too polite to say so, but she didn't think that fooled her.

Naya shut the bathroom door firmly and stared into the mirror. She tilted her head, pursing her lips. Her fourteen-year-old face was changing. She didn't look like an adult yet—her underdeveloped body was proof of that—and she was shorter than most of the other kids, but she didn't look like a child anymore either. Naya's shoulders fell with a sigh. She could be mistaken for one, though, especially if she was standing next to the other girls.

Out of habit, her eyesight blurred and her hands drifted up. Then a pulse of adrenaline froze her. She was banned from the lines. Mama said so. She'd almost forgot!

Anger heated her cheeks. Why shouldn't she look? No one would be able to tell! But she'd never not listened before. Her heart pounding, she let her vision go blurry again. The lines came in, bright and shiny. Her fingers hovered over a line next to her cheek, a few millimeters from touching it.

Naya slowly let her hands fall. She didn't have anything to look at. She could look for the something big again, but what was the point? She could see what her friends were doing at the lot, but that felt like spying in a way her normal walks down the lines did not. They were her friends, not just random strangers. She had already spied on Brandon, and where did that get her? It wasn't like she needed to look at the lines. Not the way Mama and Grandmother needed to sometimes, to help with their live-lihood, or for safety reasons. Or the way she might walk the lines when she was a doctor, to save people's lives. Why was she really doing it? Just because she could?

Her own life couldn't be that boring, could it?

━◆━

Cecilia came by and brought Naya a big stack of books.

"How's prison treating you?" she said with a wink.

All the books were science related! One was about Marie Curie; another was an autobiography of a doctor who traveled to different countries. The last few, though, were novels. Naya read a lot of nonfiction books about science, but she had never read nov-els about medicine before. She skimmed the back covers: a Civil War midwife who wanted to be a surgeon, a teenage girl training to be a vet, a group of nurses and doctors in World War II. There was even a fantasy story about a healer who was also a witch! Well, that was just intriguing.

"Thank you!" Her cheeks hurt from smiling.

Cecilia nodded. "Your mom said you've been looking through the bookcases. I figured you needed something new."

Naya flushed, thinking about the photo. "Um . . . these are perfect. Thank you," she said again.

Mama was a little easier after Cecilia came by with the books. The line of her back was softer, and smiles came more often. The cloud of anger that weighed on Naya didn't feel so dark and heavy. Or maybe she just didn't notice as much with the books to distract her. She started with the book on Marie Curie but soon moved on to the novels, getting lost in the battlegrounds of the Civil War, or the green rolling landscape of the countryside. Neither Mama or Grandmother eased up on Naya's workload, but they didn't say anything about the teenagers anymore. She snuck away, as soon as her homework and chores were done, to read, curled up near a window where the sun could cast her in its yellow glow.

◆━

Once, when she was younger, she and Mama and Grandmother had driven to the coast. They arrived late and stayed the night in a motel that had seashells on the wall. The next morning, Naya had run down to the beach without her shoes, Mama yelling behind her. The sand was cool and slightly damp under her feet. When she reached the water, it churned cold around her toes, stole the sand from under her heels and then danced, laughing, away. The ocean was the biggest thing she'd ever seen in real life. The lines, crisscrossing each other like a web, were bigger than any ocean, but Naya was small then and could only see a little bit of the lines at a time. She could see more as she got older, but still.

The sea glittered in the sun, stretching farther than she could see, even on her tiptoes. The water murmured to her, endlessly moving—feeling like a welcome, feeling like a wave hello. Naya had ducked down and whispered, "I like you too," so close the spray made a crown in her hair, before Mama pulled her back, fussing and worrying.

The ocean made her feel like she was part of something huge and beautiful. It was too bad she couldn't capture past memories. Naya wished she had a thread just of that moment. She wished she had threads for lots of memories. There weren't nearly enough threads right now for a soul wrap! Unless she made it very small, and she thought Grandmother would have something to say about that. She wished she had known how to make threads her whole life. Then she wouldn't be short anything now.

✦

It was two weeks before Mama relented and Naya got her phone back. The phone felt solid as a weight in her hand. The relief she felt when she got it back was almost disturbing. Almost. She clutched it to her chest as she scrolled through the texts she had missed.

She still had to come home right after school, and she wasn't allowed out with friends or at the lot. But Naya thought that was mainly because they needed her help with orders coming in, at least she hoped.

Mama didn't say she couldn't, but Naya was afraid to go back in the lines yet.

✦

Naya borrowed some of Mama's paints to paint figures along the frame of her bedroom door. She'd picked a style that was more ambitious than what she usually painted. Really, she wanted something art related to talk about that wasn't her soul wrap. She needed advice, but she couldn't let Grandmother know how hard it was making the soul wrap. A new project always piqued their interest.

Over dinner, right on cue, Mama asked, "How is your painting coming, my love?"

"I can't get the pattern quite right. But I've had a lot of practice painting before! Why is art so easy sometimes, and then other times it's hard?"

"When you understand, truly understand, responsible commitment," Grandmother said with an arched eyebrow, "training hard, understanding priorities, focusing on your craft . . . then your art will come easier."

Grandmother wasn't very subtle, in Naya's opinion.

"It's about experiencing life," Mama countered. "I think great art comes from deep emotion: joy, love, pain. But who wants their child to experience pain? Don't be in such a hurry to grow up, Naya."

"I've experienced life!" Naya protested. She thought about everything at school, and helping customers, and all the medical stuff she had learned on her own. She had done lots of things other people hadn't.

"You've experienced a child's life," said Grandmother. "Sheltered, serene, I'd even say idyllic."

Naya groaned inwardly. When Grandmother started talking like poetry, she could go on for a while.

"I'm really having a problem with the colors clashing in a way I didn't expect," she said, trying to distract Grandmother.

"Have you introduced a neutral color?" Mama asked.

"Well, yes . . ."

"Try a different neutral, one either warmer or cooler than what you have," Grandmother said.

"Or add another neutral to break up the pattern," added Mama. "You can also mix that neutral into one of your brighter colors if you need to tone it down."

That last idea was for paint, not threads, but the rest were good ideas. Naya had been so reliant on the threads she'd made that she hadn't thought about adding in some regular thread to anchor the pictures.

"Hmm . . . that might work," she murmured, pretending to think it over. It wouldn't do to give them big heads, after all. "I'll give it a try. Thanks."

◆

She didn't feel like doing anything. Or thinking about anything. Just the idea of working on homework or her soul wrap or any of the stuff she usually did made her whole body feel like it was dragging to the ground—a giant Jell-O person. A sloth. She didn't even want to watch surgery videos; they would take too much concentration. But she kept feeling like she *should* do something. If only she could find the right thing.

Maybe she should eat something. Chocolate pudding would be perfect. She dragged her feet over to the fridge and stared into it. There was no chocolate pudding. She could make some, but that seemed like entirely too much work. Naya groaned and shut the fridge. She pulled Cheerios out of the cabinet and ate them right out of the box.

What was wrong with her?

From downstairs came a huge thump. That was probably the shipment of notions Mama had been expecting. Naya sighed and almost sank to the floor. She couldn't think of anything worse than doing notions inventory. Even hemming was better. In fact, if she was hemming, they probably wouldn't ask her to help unpack the shipment.

From the top of the stairs, she could see Mama and Grand-mother moving back and forth. When the hall was empty, she skittered, quick as a leaf, down the steps and into the sewing room. She slid in behind her favorite sewing machine, checked the needle and thread, and started on the hem of a blue taffeta skirt. Taffeta could be tricky, but it would also look like she needed to concentrate.

The steady thrum of the machine actually felt nice under her hands. She still didn't feel like doing anything, but at least if she was doing *this*, she didn't have to think too hard. Measure, fold, pin, sew. She could do this in her sleep, even the slippery fab-rics. In the other room, the thump of boxes stopped. She thought she felt someone's eyes on the back of her head, but no one said anything. Relieved she wasn't getting dragged into inventory, she finished the hem and started the next job, a pair of slacks that also needed taking in at the waist.

Two hems later, sudden and sharp cramps needled her stom-ach, like a kitten biting her from the inside. Naya stopped the sewing machine and bent over, holding the material steady with one hand and her stomach with the other.

"Oh, honey." Grandmother came in behind her and cut the thread on the piece she was mending, putting it to the side. "Come on. Go sit on the couch."

Naya stumbled up the stairs to the couch and curled up with a throw blanket over her like a hood, as if it could block out the yucky feeling inside her.

"Why don't boys have to feel like this? It's not fair," she muttered.

"Don't compare victimhood, child—it's gauche." Grand-mother swept into the kitchen.

Naya pulled the blanket over her head and groaned. She didn't know what "gauche" meant. Not that she was going to tell Grandmother that.

Grandmother came back to the couch with a hot pack and a cup of tea. "This will help. Boys have their own trials. Everyone does. Pain means that you're alive. And if you're alive, you can feel everything else too . . . love, joy. We know better than most that this too shall pass."

Naya groaned again.

Grandmother took pity and stopped the lecture. She rubbed Naya's back.

"I can make you some soup. Would you like that?"

Naya looked up at her with her biggest puppy dog eyes. "Pudding sounds better. Chocolate pudding."

Grandmother laughed. "Well, then I'll make you chocolate pudding. See? Sometimes with pain also comes enjoyment!"

That was a roundabout way of saying "I told you so," but since Grandmother was making the pudding, Naya decided to let it go.

—◆—

The green thread wove in and out of the blue like a leaf against the sky. Naya was amazed at how well the two threads meshed together. What's more, the soul wrap was finally starting to *feel* right.

Before, Naya couldn't see her life in the weaving, no matter what scenes she tried. She had started with basic pictures: herself at school, being at the library, her room. Then she moved on to what she wanted in the future, how she imagined her life at college and in a hospital. But none of those pictures really turned out. Somehow the threads would fray or tangle, but when she pulled the weaving apart, the string looked fine. Or, if she got everything woven right, the threads clashed or the picture would go flat on the loom, no life in it at all. And certainly not *her* life.

In exasperation one day, she unwove it all and started with a tiny swatch, almost a practice piece. She wove a leaf from the big oak tree at the lot. The leaf had glowed on the loom. Naya stared at it, stymied. That tiny piece felt more right than all the scenes before. Without really thinking too much, she set up her bigger piece again, and rewove the small leaf. Then, pulling threads by instinct, she started weaving symbols instead of scenes. Piece by piece, as they came to her—working at it, without working at it.

Now she could see herself in the colors and patterns, like little pieces of her soul made physical, made into beautiful art. She hugged herself as she looked it over. Now she understood why it was called a soul wrap. She wondered if other people would recognize the pieces of herself when they saw it, the way she could. Maybe that was just for the weaver to see.

The soul wrap wasn't nearly finished, though. It was barely begun! The deadline for the science camp was awfully close.

❖

The man was enjoying the cheeseburger and chocolate shake. Not the fanciest of food, but it afforded him a chance to learn the neighborhood better while he scoped out possibilities. The perfect candidates are the ones that don't know themselves.

A young man, barely into adulthood, slouched into the fast-food restaurant and stood, irritably, before the menu. The man curled his lip at the youth's dirty brown hair, hanging far longer over his ears than the man would ever allow. The youth's jeans looked like they had been washed but still clung stubbornly to dirt as if it were a point of honor.

The youth stepped up to the counter and ordered the cheapest hamburger they had and a glass of water. Then he asked if they were hiring. When the girl behind the counter said no and asked him what type of toy he wanted with his kid's burger, the youth could visibly barely control his temper.

The man smiled. Candidates with strong emotions, like frustration or greed, rooted into their soul were ideal. Or this gentleman—the man laughed to himself at the description—who had vines of desperation wrapped around him, and anger was the soil it fed on.

Yes, he would do nicely.

CHAPTER NINETEEN

She still wasn't technically allowed to hang out with Tiggy, but she could go to the lot again. As long as she asked and kept her phone on and told them what time she'd be back and blah-blah. It was enough to make her scream . . . but not before she got out of the house. Turning into the lot after school, seeing the other kids trickle in, feeling the dust scuff under her feet, she felt her chest loosen.

Naya marched to her favorite tire, sat down, and flopped backward to stare up through the oak tree. Her clothes would probably get mud stains. She couldn't find it in herself to care about that. She was free!

"Hello, tree," she whispered. "I missed you."

The leaves shook their laughing hello. She breathed deep and long and let her muscles fall loose and looser still. *I'm definitely grinding dirt into my clothes*, she thought. She drooped an arm over the side of the tire. After a while, it felt like she was breathing in time with the oak. The tree was so big, compared to her. The sky was huge past the tree. It made her feel quiet inside but expansive too. Out of habit, she groped in her pocket, pulled a thread out, and wrapped it around her finger. *Part of an ecosystem*, she thought. When she looked down from the leaf canopy, the thread had turned a rich mahogany brown.

Then she frowned. She had been sick of being in the house, but she was worried about being at the lot too. The science camp deadline was coming up, and her soul wrap wasn't close to done. She was running out of time.

She needed more threads. A lot more. But they had to be special. She racked her brain for ideas. Could she use more than one of the same type of thread? Like . . . if she visited the hospital again? Would the thread turn out the same color as the first time, or would it be different? Could she do a whole spool at a time? She wanted more threads about science, but she knew the conceptual ideas wouldn't take; it had to be personal. Otherwise, she'd lay threads in all her favorite science books.

The threads were supposed to be about her future, her hopes and dreams. She knew she wanted to be a doctor—it burned in her—but unless she thought about a particular surgery video or being at the hospital, her vision of the future was hazy. She could picture herself in a doctor's coat, walking the halls of the hospital with a stethoscope, but it stopped there. She didn't know how she would talk to patients or what medicine she'd specialize in—not yet anyway. She tried imagining her own apartment, but it kept tangling up with the crowded art house she lived in now. Her vision of college looked a lot like her classes at school.

Naya's jaw clenched. This would be so much easier if she could see her own line!

She tucked the brown thread away and pulled out another. A song had played the night of the meteor shower, sounding tinny and small from the phone. But everyone had chimed in until their singing rang out under the stars. The memory of it made her smile, how wobbly some of the singers sounded, how they all cheered at the end of the song. Naya sang it again under her breath, as she curled the thread in her hand. The tree shook its leaves and breathed with her. At the end of her song, the thread had turned the same midnight blue as the one from the night of the meteor shower.

She bolted upright and gaped at the thread. A tingling thrill worked its way through Naya, starting small in her toes and growing until it felt like sparks shot out of her head. Memories worked! She couldn't believe it. She'd have enough threads now! She could duplicate the important ones for her soul wrap. And she could capture old memories too! She just had to start weaving, and she could make new threads as she went.

She clutched the thread close, letting it bask in the sunshine of her smile. She'd win Grandmother's challenge now. She knew she would.

➤◆

She remembered.

She remembered the first time she had found the hidden picture of her grandfather. The thread she held turned silver gray, like cobwebs on precious metal.

She remembered the ocean, and another thread turned the perfect shade of pearly pink and promise.

She remembered painting with her fingers like the only thing in the world was a bright orange spot dancing on a page, and the thread rippled into that sunset color.

She remembered the first time she helped Grandmother with a weaving. Her heart lurched in a weird shift, and a ruby thread waved in her hand.

She remembered the first time she wanted to be a doctor. A boy had fallen down some steps at school. He was younger than she was, just a little first grader to her fourth. The lines whipped around her, but she couldn't take her eyes off him. He lay so still at the bottom of the steps. It was like he was getting smaller in front of her, shrinking inside of himself, while a teacher bent over him and the recess guard kept the other kids back. The principal had rushed outside holding her cell phone, and in the distance, a siren sounded. No one knew what to do, except wait. If Naya was a doctor, she would know what to do. The lines whipped around her, bright and frenzied, but they couldn't tell her enough. They couldn't tell her how to fix him. She had to learn that. She needed to learn that so he could get up again.

The ambulance arrived, full of shiny equipment and medical devices. The EMTs were calm and efficient as they unpacked their bags and checked on the patient. A wave of relief had rolled through the playground.

The thread came out a confused swirl of anxious muddy beige and brilliant jade green. Looking at it, Naya's heart sank. The thread captured what had happened, but it wasn't pretty. There was too much childhood fear in it, and it wasn't what she wanted in her soul wrap. She brought up the memory again and concentrated on how impressed she was with the EMTs. She held a thread in each hand, just in case . . . and the colors separated, one green, one beige.

She wrapped the green thread carefully around and tucked it with her other threads.

She left the muddy beige one on the floor. The color would fade in a while if she didn't use it. She knew it would.

◆━

It was time. On a whim, the man had procured a cake for future congratulations. The man thought it never hurt to lean on the side of optimism.

He leaned against the side of the bakery, licking frosting off his fingers, as the grubby young man he'd seen at the fast-food place entered a nearby mini-mart with a Help Wanted sign hanging in the window. Soon after, the youth left, frustration simmering in his expression.

The man's timing was perfect, as always.

PART II

"Said the Spider to the Rose"

Said the rose to the spider,
"I have one eye, most creatures two . . .
Tell me now, tell me true,
What do you see with all those eyes,
When one is as good as two?"

Said the spider to the rose,
"One eye is for looking forward,
One eye is for looking back,
One eye sees all directions,
And one is blind and black.

One eye sees this moment,
One eye measures growth,
One eye sees the distance,
And one just peeks up close."

"That's too many eyes," said the rose.

"One eye sees geometry,
One eye sees the art,

One eye views the surface,
And one eye captures heart.

One eye observes the heavens,
And one eye watches earth.
One eye spies all love unbound,
One eye spies the hurt."

"That's too many eyes," said the rose.

"One eye saw the center
And all its many parts.
One eye witnessed consequence,
And one eye saw its start.

One eye is for the darkness,
Where all creation grows.
One eye is for the brightness,
Where no one with breath can go."

CHAPTER TWENTY

Spring was shaking off the last of the wet season, all Naya's homework was done, and she was glad to be out of the house. She had no mending orders today either. Or, at least, she didn't have any when she left for school that morning. She might have some new work waiting for her when she got home, which is why she had stopped at the lot first.

She kicked her heels against the cement tube and smirked to herself. She was supposed to go straight home. She just didn't feel like it, not after being at home all the time from the grounding. A few minutes wouldn't matter.

She needed to keep working on her soul wrap, but she also needed a little bit of a break. The deadline was coming up, and she figured she was about halfway through. But Naya had a plan, and she was confident she could get it done on time. Not only that, her ideas for the rest of the wrap were sure to knock everyone's socks off.

She couldn't wait to see the look on Grandmother's face! Her mouth twisted to the side. She wanted to be right, to show everyone she wasn't a child, but . . . she also, sort of, wanted Grandmother to be proud of her work too, which made her feel like a little kid. She shook her head. It wasn't like Naya was waiting for a grade or anything. Her soul wrap was all about her dreams, being an adult, her *life*. Grandmother would see *her* in her soul wrap.

But being right *and* doing great work? That would be the best feeling in the world. She bet that's what adults felt like all the time. Although Mama had been right about the soul wrap being a lot of work. But not as much work as she had made it out to be.

I've got this, Naya thought.

Besides, it was just too nice to go inside yet. The air held the crisp smell of growing plants. Bees swarmed the memory flowers that climbed up over the lot's fence and up one side of an apartment building. They looked really pretty against the sky. The little kids weren't at the lot yet, so Arnie was doing a silly dance in the dirt circle, a combo of flailing arms and legs that made the twins giggle. When Short Shorts joined in behind him in an equally hilarious parody, Naya couldn't help but laugh.

Naya squinted behind the dancing kids, her furrowed brow easing away the laugh around her lips. That was an awful lot of memory flowers. She tried to remember an event where she had seen so many . . . maybe the last presidential election, or that time a carnival came through? Nothing came to mind, and she shook her head. Those flowers were more than she had seen in one place before. She took a half step toward the tire hill for a better view.

"Gun! Gun!" someone shouted down the street. "Run! Go, go, go!"

Arnie paused in his dancing, a quizzical look in his eye. Short Shorts turned her head, frowning.

A sharp crack broke the air.

Naya stood frozen. All the lines shifted hard at once, shocking her to the core. Images flooded over her, and she stiffened—so many images from the lines, she couldn't sort through them at first. She barely noticed when the twins grabbed her and dragged her behind the tire pile.

This was it—the something big. It hadn't solidified until now. She battled through the images until she could find the cause, the source of the shot: a young man, maybe college aged. All his lines had merged for the moment. He must have only just made up his mind. She could see him.

He slouched through the streets like an uncaged tiger, turning his head side to side, like he was listening to something only he could hear. The gun was a heavy-looking piece, awkward and overly large, the metal gleaming ugly. He held it like a club. Naya jerkily skated up and down the line to see what he would do next.

His line felt ugly.

The anger of it poured over her. But the other lines in the area were worse, heavy with fear and adrenaline. The young man's anger and fear merged with the others' emotions, and she lost his line. Images overwhelmed her again. People were scrambling out of the way. Or hiding. Or considering fighting. Someone grabbed a baseball bat. Someone ducked behind a shelf. Someone held their phone. There were shouts and tears and silence. The lines branched and merged, branched and merged. She was lost in the pictures.

A bright, bright light burst behind her eyelids, and for a split second, she saw herself from high above, crouching in the dirt, saw the streets around the lot . . . then it was gone. The vision dazzled her, and her head ached. All the other lines reappeared around her. Everyone in the lot was in the gunman's path.

"Naya! Naya!" someone said. "What's wrong with her?"

She concentrated to find his line again. The lines shifted and shifted again. It was almost too much to follow. Another crack rang out, and a cry followed it. Emotion tinged the lines in explosions.

"He shot out the mini-mart," Naya whispered.

"What?"

"What she's saying?"

"He's going to keep shooting," she said. "He's committed now. He doesn't care who."

"Is this . . . like that thing with Brandon?"

"Willow! He's on Willow Street," Naya hissed. "He's coming this way."

"That's so close!"

"Naya, which way do we go?"

A hard jolt shook her. She looked up startled, the lines dimming, the images swimming to the edges of her vision. She was sitting on the ground, her hands held up stiffly in front of her. Arnie peered anxiously at her, holding her shoulder. Behind him, the twins and Short Shorts crouched low.

She dropped her hands. "Where are the boys?" Naya asked.

"Those fools are standing by the tree!" Short Shorts's voice was harsh with fear. "Out in the open!"

Naya scooted forward to see around the edge of the tire. The boys were shuffling uncertainly by the oak tree, posturing tough and unwilling to be the first to break. The trunk didn't give them any cover at all. Short Shorts was right—they were acting like fools, full of street cred they didn't have. More disturbing was seeing Little Ben there. He wasn't more than eight, holding onto his older brother, Max, and trying not to cry.

"Okay," Naya said. "Okay. We've got to get out of the lot. We've got to get to the fence behind the boys."

"There's no way through on that side!"

"We'll make one." Naya thrummed with tension.

"Can't we go out the path by the cement tube?"

"The shooter will see us. We've got to hurry."

She crouched in a sprinter's stance, staring at the others over her shoulder until they nodded and bent to run too. Naya took a breath, and then another, counting in her head. "Now!" She sprang forward. Short Shorts passed her with five big steps, but the others were close behind. They dashed across the empty lot to the fence line. As they passed the tree, the boys broke their posturing gratefully and scrambled to the fence with them.

Someone started screaming down the street, a long, heart-wrenching wail. The sound pierced through her, and she froze for a moment, images flooding through her again, before her panic broke her out of the daze. She couldn't lose any time! The others were clustered around her, staring toward the street side of the lot, their irises ringed in white. She knew what to do, she knew . . . but she'd never had to act and filter images from the lines at the same time. She'd never been in the middle of events unfolding, been part of them. In front of everyone, she put her hands up and walked the lines until she found the rest of the path she'd seen by the tires. She scrambled at the fence posts until she found the one that was missing a nail at the bottom.

Naya picked up a jagged brick and banged it on the low end, hard and fast.

"Stop! That's too much noise!"

"Is she crazy?!"

"Naya, what are you doing?"

She banged it again, and the top nail loosened with the impact. She grabbed the board at the bottom and wiggled it frantically. Tiggy jumped forward. He and Max worked sticks into the gap, pulling the nail farther out of the board. The other boys leaned in to help. They weren't prepared when it popped off violently. The board hit the ground with a dull thump. They pushed the littlest kids through the narrow gap first. But the bigger kids, Short Shorts, and the older boys, couldn't fit through at all.

The voices shouting down the street drifted closer. Two sharp pops, one right after the other, cracked the air, and the kids jumped.

Naya slipped through the fence next. Short Shorts's panicked face showed through the crack. She wouldn't fit.

"I'm not leaving you! Back up," Naya said as quietly and forcefully as she could. She kicked low to the ground at the next board, loosening the nail.

"Tiggy, come help!" she called.

It took him a moment to work through the hole, sucking in his gut and scraping his arm. Once through, he pushed the board hard with his shoulder.

"Don't push it all the way off. Just make it swing. Like that old sign, remember?"

"Yeah," he grunted. "Leave one of the top nails in."

Max grabbed the board from the bottom and gave it a wrench as Naya and Tiggy kicked and pushed, prying the nail out of the wood. Max pivoted the board to the side. Short Shorts was the first through the larger gap. The boys squeezed after her, one by one.

Naya leaned through the hole and hauled the free board up from the dirt, balancing it against the fence. At first glance, it would look like a solid fence.

When Naya turned around, she found the other kids huddled against the alley side of the fence, staring at her. Little Ben had tears running down his face. Except for the wailing down the street and a shout here or there, it was eerily quiet, like the whole neighborhood was holding its breath. Naya realized with a start that the kids were waiting for her to tell them what to do. It was against the rules. But they'd already seen her, and the images were coming faster, coming harder. She surrendered to them, putting her hands up to trace the lines. A moment later, she blinked the images to the back of her mind.

Naya took a deep breath. "When I say go, everyone make for home. Avoid Willow and Montgomery. Stay behind the fences as much as you can, out of sight."

"But we live on Montgomery," Marisol whispered. She exchanged an anxious look with Sarai and Arnie. There wasn't any way to get to their apartment building.

"No," Short Shorts told them. "You're coming to my house."

"Get ready. Don't move until I tell you to." Naya checked the lines and pointed to each kid when it was their time to run. "Go, go, go."

The girls and Arnie dashed off.

"Wait." She held her hands up for Tiggy and the older boys, counting in her head. "Now the rest of you." She grabbed Max by the elbow. "Don't go in your front door, go to the back."

Tiggy was lingering, watching her.

"I'll be fine," she said in a firm voice. "But you have to leave now."

He spun without a word and hurried away from her.

Naya felt exposed and jittery. The images were still coming, and it made her feel undone around the edges, ragged and blurred. She heard another crack and couldn't tell if it was an echo in the lines or if the gunman had shot again. From far off, sirens wailed, and she jumped. That was good, though; the sirens would cover sound. Did she need to be worried about sound? The lines shifted hard, but it was from the police, the cars tearing down the streets. So many of them. She pushed the images back as best as she could and stumbled home, half blinded.

Mama caught her at the edge of the path and wrapped her arms around her like a blanket.

⊷

That was it then. The man lowered his binoculars and chuckled, delighted, to himself. The nudge had worked to a tee. People were so predictable, even at their most base forms—especially then.

He found it rather comforting, like good socks, or macaroni and cheese.

He giggled again before snapping himself together. He needed to prepare. He pulled out a crumpled piece of paper and jotted out a list. He'd have to get some supplies, and more observation was needed. But, in his bones, he felt these were mere details. She was the one.

He should be able to scoop her up shortly.

CHAPTER TWENTY-ONE

The sirens kept going long after Naya thought they should have stopped. Maybe she just couldn't get them out of her head. Maybe they were trapped there. Maybe they were echoing in the lines, in the memories of other people, not just her own, and she would never, ever stop hearing them. She burrowed into her bed. She found a blank spot where she hadn't doodled on the wall, near the ceiling. She stared at the small, clean space through the night hours. When she woke up, she didn't remember sleeping.

◆━◆

The lines shifted back and forth for days. They pulled at her, like they needed a witness, but she didn't want to walk the lines. Naya hated the way they felt, tinged with sorrow and panic, full of changed plans and second guesses. Mama didn't let her go to school the next day or the day after that. Some of the other kids didn't go back to school right away either. Parents lingered anxiously in front of the school at pick-up and drop-off times. Kids who usually walked were driven instead. Mama walked Naya back and forth to school as many days as she could. Sometimes the shifts in the lines were so jarring, it woke her up at night, feeling the echoes of other people's nightmares.

Then there was the other thing . . . Somehow she had seen herself. Or been shown her own line, however briefly, enough to know to get out of the way. If she tried to remember how it happened, her head ached, like it had at the lot. She didn't know what to make of that at all.

❧

The first day back at school, she'd given Mama a hug and hurried away before Mama could walk in with her. Naya stepped stiffly into the school hall and braced herself for a crowd of kids—braced herself for the demands for help, the questions. She hadn't told Mama and Grandmother that she'd walked the lines at the lot. She didn't tell them that she'd helped all the kids get home. They knew she'd been overcome with images, of course. Mama and Grandmother had seen them too. But Naya had really, really broken the rules at the lot, way worse than telling Tiggy about Brandon.

What were the kids going to do now that they'd seen her? Like, really seen her? Did the whole school know already?

A group of boys from the lot were huddled in the hall, looking a lot like they had huddled near the oak tree. Naya coiled, tight as a wire, as she passed them on the way to her locker. *Here it comes*, she thought. *Here it comes, here it comes.* What would she tell Mama?

The boys quieted as she neared them. Then one smiled. And another nodded. Max reached out and patted her on the back. Then the other boys did the same. But not one said a word.

In fact, no one said anything about her all day.

❧

At school, after the initial shock passed, people pretended they were okay. Kids laughed, boys bragged and hooted again, their voices not as hushed. But Naya felt the instability of the lines. A million decisions and indecisions were happening, even if they were only in the minds of the kids around her. People were ready to bolt at a moment's notice. When a carbon monoxide detector went off in one of the science rooms because the battery was low, several kids shrieked and ducked. A girl named Melanie collapsed in the hall crying, until the nurse had to come get her. Melanie had just come back to school. When the shooting started, she had been trapped in the mini-mart down the street, her cousin hit by a stray bullet.

Naya's heart twisted and tore seeing Melanie cry like that—little whimpers like a wounded animal, her panicked eyes wide. A group of girls tried to calm her while everyone else shifted their feet, nervous and awkward.

Something else churned in Naya's gut too. She felt sick and heavy but couldn't figure out why. Unlike everyone else, she'd known something big was coming. Even if she couldn't see all the details, she'd had warning; she could prepare.

But she hadn't prepared, had she? She had always watched the lines, but she had never really felt them. Not like this.

Then it hit her, with appalling clarity. She had been a tourist.

She'd watched everything, as far as she could see, like the images were something to pass the time. Curious about *what* would happen, not the pain the events would cause. Like they were videos. Acting like she *knew*, but she didn't, did she?

She hadn't warned anyone. She hadn't done anything about it coming.

After the nurse and a teacher had ushered Melanie away, the hallway had quieted down. Kids drifted off to class. In the empty hall, Naya stared at nothing and realized her cheeks were wet.

She finally figured out the sick, twisty feeling: it was shame.

She wanted to be a doctor. She wanted to be one of the people who help.

She should have done more.

Mama was a wreck at home, worrying like the other parents on top of the worry she always had, ramped up to a million. But even more surprising was Grandmother. She'd taken a fall when the lines shifted, down the two steps from the house into the backyard. It wasn't a long fall, but she'd been carrying the water can. The lines had caught her by surprise, taken her concentration midstep. She was usually so graceful. Mama had found her sprawled in the grass, and Grandmother was still having dizzy spells days later.

Not only that, but she seemed out of sorts. She fretted and complained vaguely . . . about the evil of people, about where Naya was, about how her food tasted funny. Her ankle was swollen, but she would forget and try to stand on it. Mama made her stay on the couch, and Grandmother would flip through the TV channels almost like she didn't realize what she was doing.

Naya kept waiting for her to snap back to her bright, bold self.

"You be careful at school, honey. Come straight home, all right?" Grandmother shuffled down the hall and smoothed Naya's hair as Naya packed her backpack.

"I might have to pick up some books at the library for a project," Naya said. Which was true—she did have a project coming up that she would need books for. But Naya also wanted to leave a little space open to sneak by the lot. If she asked to go, they would only worry, maybe even say no. The lot had been deserted immediately after the shooting, but the kids were slowly trickling back. "I'm not sure when it's due yet. We might get the details today. It's a big project."

"Oh, you always do well at school."

"It's a term paper, though." Naya made a face.

"You always do so well," Grandmother repeated. "Have you seen my glasses? The green ones?"

Naya looked at her askance. "You're already wearing them. They're around your neck."

"Oh, of course." She pulled her sweater close around her and stared at the wall. "Maybe we'll have some pie tonight. Something with flavor."

"Sounds great!" Naya threw over her shoulder as she hurried down the stairs.

✦

Her whole morning had felt off. Naya scowled at her locker. She couldn't figure out what was bugging her. Maybe she was mad at something, from the past or from a dream? Once she had spent a whole day irritated with Arnie before she realized he had been teasing her in a dream. Her mouth twisted wryly. She should have known better. He was never that mean in real life.

A hard tug on the lines jolted her. Her throat closed in panic. Naya looked around frantically for someone coming down the hall with a gun. Or police officers. Or rabid wolves. After the shooting, it felt like anything could happen.

There was no one in the hall but kids and teachers and crumpled papers on the floor.

The lines settled again. She blinked a touch of dizziness away, could swear for a minute that she saw a glimpse of their kitchen floor. That was weird. But it wasn't anything like the wild whipping of the lines during the shooting. It couldn't have been anything big then, but she wondered what it was. She didn't have time to duck into the bathroom for a look before her next class. Besides, she was trying to lay off the lines for a while.

She swapped books out of her locker, tension still hovering

around her shoulders. She was being silly. She probably just woke up on the wrong side of the bed.

◆—

Words could be squirrelly. Just when you thought they meant one thing, someone would say they meant something else.

They were studying poetry. Naya groaned inside even when she heard the word "poetry."

She always had a hundred questions for Mrs. Xiang. Not the type of questions she asked in her other classes either, where she knew what was going on and wanted more information. Most of her questions in English class came down to "Why is English so hard?"

"Isn't your mother an artist, Naya?" Mrs. Xiang would reply. "I'm surprised you're struggling with this."

Yes, but that art was physical. Weavings had lines that only went in particular directions. Clothes only draped on a body in certain ways. There were limits. Some rules you just couldn't break. Words could have a rule attached to them, and then they up and *changed*.

"Okay, I want everyone," Mrs. Xiang called, "to take the next few minutes coming up with your own simile."

Naya suppressed a groan again. She bent her head over the example poem and tried to come up with an idea that didn't sound dumb or make her head hurt. She wished she was in science class instead. The lines didn't have limits either; they changed like words, but she couldn't write about those.

But . . . an idea tickled the back of her mind. The lines were made up of decisions, the decisions that people made every day. She could write about choices, choices that could become traps if you weren't careful, even if you didn't mean to. Like what happened with her helping Brandon. Like her *not* helping before the gunman came. Naya shook her head, as if she could clear it of the dark path she had started to go down. She concentrated on the poem in front of her. Choices like . . . roads or branches or sticky spiderwebs. Oh! That was a simile!

Her phone pinged, loud in the room, and her teacher frowned at her. She waited until Mrs. Xiang turned her head, then she glanced down at her phone. Naya sat up straight. Mama never texted her during class. She held it in her lap and turned off the sound before reading. *Grandmother is at the hospital. I'm getting you excused to meet me.*

Her body flashed hot and then went very, very cold.

The classroom phone rang. Mrs. Xiang picked it up and looked over at Naya. She hung up and made her way gingerly between the desks.

Naya was already packing up her books. Her hands were shaking. When did her hands start shaking?

"You need to go meet your mother," Mrs. Xiang whispered. "Don't bother with sign-out. It's already taken care of."

Her phone pinged again. *I'm sorry, love. You'll have to look up the bus line.*

But Naya already knew which bus to take. She texted back. *Is she all right?*

They're running some tests.

That wasn't really an answer. Grandmother had been fine that morning. Well, not her old-self fine, but she wasn't sick or acting unusual.

What happened?

But Mama didn't text back.

A sick dread settled in Naya's stomach. What if Grandmother was really sick or had gotten hurt? She'd been shaky lately; maybe she fell again. *Don't jump to conclusions,* she told herself. She'd talk to the doctors with Mama, get the facts first.

Whatever was going on, she was sure the doctors could take care of it. Modern medicine was amazing. Everything would be fine.

She was on the bus without noticing how she got there.

Walking into the hospital, she couldn't quite breathe. Her chest hitched shallow and fast, and her blouse pulled tight. She must be growing out of her clothes again. Grandmother would insist on making her a new shirt. Maybe Naya would tell her to make it in yellow; that was Grandmother's favorite color. She always wanted to dress Naya in yellow.

She walked down the hall without checking at reception. She knew Mama would be at the ER. That was in the east wing. She wouldn't have to slip in behind another family this time, she thought distantly. She could tell the nurse, and she'd be let right in.

Everything would be fine.

When she got to the ER, a nurse came around the desk to take her to her mom. Naya wanted to say she knew the way, but the nurse had soft eyes and was patting her on the shoulder, and all the words got tangled up in Naya's throat until she choked on them.

The door buzzer went off. The sound drew out and out forever.

"There she is." The nurse pointed down the hall.

Naya almost didn't see her for a moment. Mama's head was bent down, her arms clutching her sweater. She looked like a tired hospital visitor, just another temporary person sitting in the hard plastic chairs Naya passed by when she came to visit.

But Naya hadn't really been visiting, had she? She'd been poking around, spying on the doctors.

Was she visiting now? Her feet sounded loud on the tile floor. Usually she glided, fast and quiet. Visiting Grandmother? That didn't sound right. Naya's head spun. Grandmother shouldn't be here.

"Oh, baby, my sweet girl." Mama held out her arms and drew Naya in, but her body felt tight.

"Is Grandmother okay?" She gasped it into Mama's ear. "What happened?"

"She's all right for now. Now listen, Naya. Grandmother had a stroke. They've given her some medicine to break up the clot, and they're checking on her now. The doctors say she might have had ministrokes before this and never even noticed."

Naya's stomach dropped to the floor. She remembered Grandmother complaining about the food after her fall, acting vague and unsteady. Why hadn't she looked up her symptoms? She normally looked up symptoms until Mama and Grandmother yelled at her to stop.

"I'm sorry I couldn't pick you up, but there were a lot of questions to answer. Cecilia is on her way too. She can give you a ride home. You won't want to stay long, I'm sure."

"No! No, I want to stay!" Panic rose in her throat, threatening to choke her again.

Mama's eyes searched her face. "You can stay for a while. But you're not staying here the whole time. Testing usually takes a long time. If I can't get home tonight, Cecilia will come stay with you, okay?" Mama looked down the hall as if Cecilia would appear just by saying her name.

"Okay," Naya whispered.

"You ready to go see her?"

"Will the doctor be there?" She would feel better if she could ask questions herself, hear the diagnosis in calm, clinical details. Get all the data. Know the plan of action.

"A doctor was just here. It will probably be a while before another one comes."

Naya swallowed. They walked a short way down the hall to one of the rooms, right across from an empty nurses' station.

Naya froze in the door.

Grandmother was all wrapped up in the bed. Heavy wires were attached to her arm and her head and coming out from under her robe on her chest. She looked like a shrunken doll, pinned down by wires, in the middle of the blankets.

"Grandmother?" she called timidly. "Mama? Why isn't she talking?"

"They gave her something to calm her down, and she fell right to sleep."

Cecilia rushed through the door. "I'm here!" she called. "I'm here."

Naya had never seen Cecilia flustered before. Like she had hurried to get there. Like she was worried. But as soon as Cecilia slowed and then stopped in front of Mama, it was as if her roots sank back into the ground, steadfast. She radiated strength, and Mama looked happy to soak it up.

"Thank you for coming," Mama whispered.

Naya hung back from the bed, her eyes wide. She listened as Mama and Cecilia made plans for the next few hours and days, decided what contingencies might need to be made.

"We don't know the amount of damage yet," she heard Mama murmur. "She fell again, in the kitchen this time. We're lucky she didn't hit her head."

Naya remembered her vision of the kitchen floor earlier, the dizziness. Was that when it happened? Had she seen a glimpse of Grandmother's line?

The ping of machines, the squeak of gurney wheels, the buzz of lights combined into a constant hum. Naya wanted to look up "stroke" on her phone. She had it in her hand, but she couldn't look away from the bed. She tried to focus on only positive outcomes for stroke victims, but the machine sounds grated against her ears, distracting her, a slow saw grinding away at her concentration. Why hadn't she ever noticed the noise of the hospital before?

Grandmother woke up with a start, her eyes flying back and forth. A look of panic crawled across her face. Mama hurried to her side.

"Mother, you're all right. I'm here. You're in the hospital, remember?"

Why was Mama talking to her like that? Like she was an old woman? Grandmother wasn't old!

"And look, Naya's here." Mama waved her closer.

Naya approached the bed gingerly. She leaned over and took Grandmother's hand, trying not to dislodge any of the IVs. Grandmother squeezed her fingers hard. It made Naya feel a little better, seeing Grandmother as fierce as always. But standing there felt awkward, her legs aching at the angle. *If I sit on the bed*, she thought, *will I hurt her?* She didn't want to take the chance.

"I'm glad you're here, honey." Grandmother's speech was slurred.

Her arm wasn't moving right—not the one weighed down by wires but the other one. Naya could tell Grandmother was trying to move it, but the arm just lay there, like a piece of wood.

Grandmother rolled her eyes toward Mama. "Well?"

Mama leaned over on the other side and murmured a list of procedures and tests and which doctor had said this and which doctor had said that. There would be other specialists to see her, and guidelines for care at home and physical therapy.

Naya's heart eased a little when she heard "at home," but then she glanced at Mama, whose shoulders were rounded and tight, and at Grandmother, who was nodding because talking was too much. A hot, hard ball formed in her stomach. This was going to change everything.

Grandmother couldn't weave with her arm like that. How would Grandmother live if she couldn't weave?

Tears crept up from somewhere deep. Naya blinked them back, made herself smile at Grandmother—at Grandmother sitting in the bed of wires stringing her to this room, this hospital, this other life that was not theirs.

It couldn't be, could it?

Before Mama was through with her update, Grandmother dimmed before them, her eyes growing heavy, her fingers loosening in Naya's grip. Mama patted her shoulder, fast and for too long.

"It's okay, it's okay. Sleep will do you good." Mama stared at the bed for a moment.

When she turned, Naya couldn't control her face.

"It's okay, my love," Mama said again. "Grandmother is stable for now."

"For now?" Her voice was a croak.

"They have medicines for these things. Treatments. She's going to have some tests done. It might take a while." Mama looked lost in thought for a moment. Then she gathered herself, and her face folded into a faded-out smile. "Why don't you head home, my love? There's no sense in us both waiting. Cecilia, can you give her a ride?"

"Of course." Cecilia put her strong hands on Naya's shoulders. She almost collapsed under the weight.

"There's food in the fridge to heat up," Mama said. "I'll call you later when we know more. Get some rest."

But Mama was the one who looked tired.

CHAPTER TWENTY-TWO

The routine was off again. The man ground his teeth. He had planned an introduction, but now he had to reschedule.

Drive burned in him like venom. He'd been close a number of times. This reminded him of that boy in Dubai, before that debacle had gotten too hot even for him to handle. He had had to leave quickly and definitely not in the refined manner he was used to traveling. Unfortunately, he had succumbed to a fit of temper for a number of weeks after the incident. But once he had calmed down, the man had only become more relentless in his search. He certainly wouldn't be swayed now.

The grandmother getting sick was . . . unexpected. He'd seen the hospital ambulance take her away. However, perhaps he could turn that to his advantage.

The grandmother had always posed a problem. Now she could be dealt with.

◆◆

Home was too quiet. Cecilia had dropped her off before going back to the hospital, promising to be back later. Reminding Naya to keep her phone charged. Telling her it would all be okay.

Naya sat on the back steps and looked at Grandmother's garden, the colors blurring together. Her face was hot, almost feverish. Her arms and legs felt heavy and useless. She didn't feel like eating or sleeping, but she couldn't just sit around either. Her feet walked, without asking her, around the corner to the empty lot. But it wasn't empty. A knot of little kids scream-played at tag. Three boys from school huddled around a phone. Misty cigarette smoke trickled out of the cement tunnel. The scene looked normal and familiar, and Naya wavered, leaning on the edge of the wood fence, not sure if she could walk in.

Under the oak tree, a shadow moved. Then Tiggy was walking toward her, and the weight of her not-normal day lifted slightly. She ducked back behind the fence. When he came around the corner, his smile was like the sun.

"Hey, Naya! Why did you leave school early? I've been looking for you." He reached over and tugged playfully at her hair.

"My grandmother . . ." She bit her lip at the sudden burning in her eyes. "She's at the hospital. She had a stroke."

"Oh man! Really?" His smile dropped, but then he brightened. "That's too bad. But she'll be home soon, right?"

"I don't know." It felt like her stomach was full of pins. "I hope so."

"You 'hope.' Yeah, right." He laughed. Then he reached out and tugged her hair again, teasing.

She stared at him and shook her hair away. "Stop. This is serious."

He put his hands up in surrender. "No, no, I know! It's hard when family gets sick."

"Grandmother has always been so tough," she said slowly. "And healthy! I don't know what to do to help."

Tiggy looked at her quizzically. "But didn't you know? You're, like, psychic, right? You should have seen this was coming."

Naya recoiled, fear and denial almost choking her. "I'm not psychic!"

"Yeah, right." His laugh felt like an accusation.

"You don't understand." Guilt crashed over her. She should never have shown him the man with the apple! Then she remembered his brother, and the shooter, and realized the apple didn't make a difference. They had all seen.

"Come on, isn't that why you're so good in school?'

"What?!" She stared at him. "No! I study!" Did he think she cheated? He was making her feel worse, not better.

"Just do your psychic thing."

"My . . . what? How is that supposed to help?"

"You'll see something . . . like the right medicine, or the right doctor, or something, and she'll be fine. You can get out of anything."

"That's not how it works." She shoved away from the fence, away from him, letting her head hang so all she saw walking home was the dirt path and the dust covering her white shoes.

"Naya!" He sounded surprised behind her. "Come on, wait!"

Her stomach twisted in knots. She had been showing off because she liked him, because Tiggy made her laugh, and she felt special when he singled her out.

Had she made this happen somehow? Was she being punished for breaking the rules? She thought Mama was just being paranoid. Could there be other reasons? Mama always said there was a balance to things. But why would Grandmother get sick and not her? She should have paid more attention in training, not blown it off so many times.

Guilt gnawed at her fear until it was a sharp point. And worse, deep down she felt a terrible helplessness, because even if she had followed all of Mama's rules, she wouldn't have seen this coming.

Without thinking, Naya let her eyes go blurry and started tuning into the lines. Even if she couldn't see Grandmother's line, she could look *around* her . . . at the lines of doctors and the hospital, even clients, to see when Grandmother would be back to work.

Then she froze, terrified. Tears choked her throat. What if she looked at the lines and Grandmother wasn't there?

➻

Mama and Cecilia came home and ate dinner with Naya before Mama headed back to the hospital. Cecilia tried getting Mama to get some rest, but she wouldn't hear of it.

"Can you stay with Naya tonight?" She asked it as if Cecilia would say no, as if Mama had just remembered there were other lives going on.

Naya had forgotten too. The casserole she had reheated in the microwave sat like lead in her stomach.

"Of course." Cecilia hugged her hard.

They put the TV on and watched it blindly. Naya felt like she should say something—ask questions, be a good host. But after her conversation with Tiggy, she couldn't get any words out. What if talking to Cecilia didn't make her feel better?

Cecilia didn't say much either, but her strength rolled through the room.

Naya scrolled through medical outcomes for stroke without letting her phone fall below 80 percent, moving the charger from her room to next to the couch. She didn't want to miss a call from Mama. The first thing she had to ask tomorrow was what type of stroke had Grandmother had. She thought it might be an ischemic stroke, because Mama had mentioned a clot and ministrokes.

Cecilia kept glancing at her phone, waiting for it to ring. Finally, she went into Mama's room to sleep. "You should go to bed, Naya," she said first. "You need some rest."

"I just want to watch the end of this movie," said Naya, even though she had no idea what was on. Her voice sounded faint and faded.

Cecilia sighed. "Don't stay up too late." She rubbed Naya's shoulder as she left.

Naya waited a few minutes, enough time for Cecilia to fall asleep. Then she turned off the TV and stared into the dimness, watching the specks of darkness dance around each other—around and around, like atoms and quarks, like a midnight ballet, until she stopped thinking about anything but the spots.

◆━

The grandmother's second stroke happened around midnight. The man lurked in the hallway, watching the young doctor frown over the medical chart. The doctor seemed unsure whether he had actually administered the medicine that helped break up the clot—the medicine the man had watched the doctor pick up a syringe to inject. Then a multi-car crash had come in that sent the doctor rushing off to help in the ER instead.

The man knew the chart *looked* correct—after all, it was proto-col to write on the chart after the medicine was administered, not before. But still, the doctor squinted at the form. He was coming off an eighteen-hour shift and he swayed with exhaustion. Doctors were used to being correct, but the man found they could also be curiously stubborn. Finally, the young doctor nodded, set the chart down and checked the grandmother's vitals. The man smiled tri-umphantly and slunk back as the doctor left the room.

◆━

She was asleep on the couch when Cecilia burst in from the other room. Naya woke up screaming and fighting her rumpled clothes, the skirt tangled around her legs.

"It's okay! Easy, easy!" Cecilia planted her feet. She looked rooted as ever, but there was something moving behind her eyes. "I've got to drive you back to the hospital."

Fear squeezed the breath out of her. "Is Grandmother okay?!" Naya squeaked.

"She's hanging in there yet. But you need to be with your mom now."

"Um . . . okay." Naya walked in a daze toward the front door.

Cecilia put a hand out and steered her back toward her bedroom. "Go get changed, brush your teeth. You'll feel better. I'll grab something for us to eat."

Naya stumbled into the bathroom and splashed water on her face. The weak, watery light of daybreak glowed against the window. She tried to push her hair into shape, but she didn't want to bother. Her hair wasn't important! Then she thought about what Grandmother would say if she showed up a mess. Grandmother, who was always dressed well, if not regally, no matter what. Even when she was in bed with a cold, she wore a silk chinoiserie bathrobe and nice slippers.

"Even sniffles need a little flair," she'd say around her tissues.

Grandmother didn't have her bathrobe in the hospital. But maybe Naya could bring it to her!

She hurried to Grandmother's closet, pushing the racks of clothes aside until she found the bathrobe. She actually had three silk robes, but Naya chose the one she thought looked the prettiest on Grandmother—peach with butterflies and leaves floating down the fabric, the one most likely to make her smile. A large tote was hanging near Grandmother's bed. Naya folded the robe gently and tucked it in. Maybe she should bring her a book too, for when she felt better. She looked on the nightstand for whatever Grandmother was currently reading. There weren't any books, but there was a stack of art magazines with dog-eared corners. She added those and a pair of reading glasses to the tote.

Naya tried to decide what to wear as she hurried back to her room. It was hard making her brain care about clothing at the moment, but the least she could do was be dressed for Grandmother, show her she *listened* when Grandmother talked about appearances. Not one of her fancy dresses. Hospitals weren't places for fancy clothes, but she could still look nice. Maybe the blouse with the flowers down the sleeves? Grandmother had embroidered them herself. The blouse was getting a little tight, but it would do, paired with her yellow skirt.

Naya dressed quickly and smoothed her skirt in front of the mirror. She still looked a bit . . . disheveled. She added a yellow headband that managed to tame the wild look of her hair.

"Naya!" Cecilia called. "Hurry up, hon! Your mom's waiting."

In the kitchen, she grabbed a box of Grandmother's favorite tea and added it to the tote bag. Cecilia gave her a funny look but didn't say anything.

Cecilia was quiet on the drive over. But Cecilia was always pretty quiet.

At the hospital, Naya ran straight to the ER, leaving Cecilia behind, and squeezed through the doors with another family walking in. The nurse at reception lifted her head as Naya flew by, but no one stopped her. Mama was standing outside of Grandmother's room, her hands twisting around and around a piece of cloth. As Naya got closer, she recognized one of Grandmother's scarves.

"Mama! I brought some things for Grandmother. Look!" Naya pushed the tote at her.

"Oh." Mama's face was doing something funny. "Oh, my love."

A chill raced down her spine. "So when does she get to come home? We'll have to help with her treatment plan, right? We should get a ramp for the back steps." Naya could hear herself talking faster and faster, as if she could stave off whatever Mama was going to say. "Doesn't physical therapy usually set up exercises? We'll have to learn those too."

"Naya," was all Mama said. Then she pulled her into the room, to the side of Grandmother's bed. Mama stood behind her, hands patting her shoulders like she used to do when Naya was young and unsure of being in a new place.

Naya couldn't stop staring at the bed. If it was possible, Grandmother looked like she had shrunk even further into herself. Her hair seemed whiter, more fragile. Her skin was papery thin and lit from within, but not with her usual fire—with something else, something that looked like it might be burning her into ash. She was barely a shell of the woman she normally was. *Like an old woman*, Naya thought.

"Grandmother had another stroke last night. The medicine didn't work to clear the clot this time."

Naya's heart made a funny little stutter. She whispered, "What does that mean?"

"She's not doing well, honey. Worse than yesterday."

"But she'll be all right? Won't she?"

"She's . . . not awake right now," Mama murmured. "We don't know if she'll wake up."

Like a coma? thought Naya. "Of course she'll wake up," she said instead. Her grandmother could survive anything. She'd be up and about soon. She knew it.

But she felt so cold inside.

⟞⟝

Hours stretched out. They dragged chairs near the bed. Mama kept having to get up, to talk to doctors, to make phone calls. Naya curled deeper and deeper into her chair, doing research on her phone when she wasn't studying Grandmother's still face, waiting for a sign she was awake. She remembered eating food that Cecilia pushed into her hands, but she couldn't remember what she ate or what it tasted like.

Doctors came and went, always speaking in hushed, firm tones. They checked Grandmother's pulse or chart. Nurses swapped the IV bags. But from what Naya had read of treatment plans, no one was really doing anything. She might have snapped at one of the doctors, might have gotten reprimanded by Mama, but the doctor just smiled grimly.

Sometimes Grandmother mumbled or moved her head in her sleep. Naya's neck hurt from freezing rigid in her chair, from jumping up to go to the bed, from being disappointed.

Next time, she thought. *Next time she'll wake up.*

She almost missed it when Grandmother made a sound again. But something stirred her, disquiet buried under hope; something was different. She must be waking up!

"Mama!" Her arm stretched toward Grandmother's on the bed.

Grandmother took a choking breath, almost a gurgle, and then sighed a long stream of air that seemed like it would never end.

Naya felt a jolt down to her bones. The lines shifted violently and writhed like whips. "No," Naya whispered.

Mama started weeping softly, her head bowed next to the bed. One hand still clutched Grandmother's over the worn quilt.

"Did she just . . . did she just . . . ?" Naya's heart flattened and folded inside her like paper closing. "No!"

"Come here, baby." Mama reached for her.

"Where's the nurse, the doctor? We need a crash cart!"

Naya ran into the hall, but a nurse was already stepping in. She followed him back into the room. "Do something!" she yelled at the man.

"Baby, my love, calm down . . ." Mama held her by the shoulders, keeping her out of the way as the man checked on Grandmother. He looked at the machines and took her pulse. Finally, he sighed and then nodded to Mama as he left the room.

Naya stared at his receding back. "No, the lines are still moving. She'll be fine!" *Don't look, don't look, don't look.* "This is a mistake! Where did the nurse go? We need a crash cart!" The movement of the lines increased, and she felt like she was being pummeled by strong winds. She wanted to lash out, to push back.

Mama's voice was raw. "Oh, my love, I forgot . . . my father died before you were born . . . and there's no one else close by . . ." She stumbled over her words, her face tired, so tired. "The lines do that when one of ours passes. Because we're the watchers, see. We're tied to the lines stronger than most people."

Tiggy's words came back to Naya—*You should have seen this was coming*—and she recoiled. "No! This is Grandmother. This is not happening!"

The lines settled around her, back to their usual steady trajectories. It felt like they sank into her, deeper than before, brighter than before, like they needed to fill up Grandmother's presence. Naya was suddenly furiously angry.

"You don't get to hold me!" she raged as the lines rooted in her. "You can't do this! I don't owe you! You owe Grandmother! You owe Grandmother!"

Mama gaped at her, her eyes shocked and hurt. Then she must have realized Naya was yelling at the lines, because the emotion smoothed out, even as her face twisted into grief. "It doesn't work like that, baby. I wish it did. I wish it did."

"No!" Naya bolted out of the room.

CHAPTER TWENTY-THREE

She couldn't remember getting on the bus. She thought she might have taken the long way home, but it was just a blur. She knew her phone had pinged with Mama's texts. Naya finally answered, *Going home to rest*, so the sound would stop. Then she was walking, walking, walking, until suddenly she found herself staring at the lot. The little kids running in circles in the center. Dust kicking up around their feet. The older kids leaning against the cement tube. The tires casting jagged, afternoon shadows. She shuffled toward her usual seat. Her tree, her favorite tree, looked flat, like a paper cutout.

"Naya?"

She wanted to sit down, but her tire seat looked wrong. Bits of rubber were flaking off, scattered all over the lot in a million pieces. The rubber would get all over her clothes. Had it always been like that? She swung aimlessly back toward the center.

"Are you okay?"

"She's gone." It came out numb, flat—flat as the tree. "Grandmother. She . . . died." No, that couldn't have really happened. It was a mistake.

"Oh my God!"

"What?"

"What did she say?"

Naya heard the whispers spread out around her. She shuffled away from the murmuring voices, away from the middle of the lot. She stared at a patch of ground where the dirt faded into scrabbly grass. Why did she walk here?

"Naya? What can we do? Should I call your mom?"

The question didn't make any sense. She could still hear the whispers. She knew the other kids were trying to help, but whispers never helped anything. Words never helped. Words just made things happen that you never wanted.

The voices fell tensely quiet. It took her a long moment before she looked up.

"Hello. Naya? I'm afraid you'll have to come with me. I have some questions for you." A man in a no-nonsense gray suit and wrinkled tie stood near her. He slouched slightly, his hands in his pockets, but his face was serious.

"What?" she asked. He spoke like he was a cop, but she knew him already. He was the man around the edges. "What are you doing here?"

The kids who had come close perked up their ears. Then they fell back, giving him room. He sounded authoritative, and the police were still investigating the shooting. They waited to see if he was going to ask about that day, craning their necks for other cop cars to drift down the street.

"Hey," Short Shorts spoke up. "Hey, this isn't a good time . . ."

The man ignored her, his gaze locked on Naya. "I'm here about recent . . . events. Naya, I'm sorry to pull you away from your friends, but there are questions only you can answer. Your cooperation is appreciated." He smiled, automatic and shallow.

She blinked at him. The words didn't make sense, and it took her a moment to work through them. "Who are you?" she muttered to herself. She didn't think he was a policeman after all, but he sounded like someone . . . similar. Maybe a detective or a grief counselor or someone from court. Lawyers had come around school, pulling kids out to ask them questions. Maybe this was why she had seen him around the edges; he was here about the shooting. She had just stopped paying attention after Grandmother got ill.

Grandmother.

Her throat burned. She pushed all the thoughts out of her head. If she didn't think about it, everything would be all right. She looked at the ground again. Someone spoke, but it sounded very far away.

It didn't matter. She didn't want to answer any questions. She didn't want to do anything.

"Naya?"

Her head turned slowly until his face came into view.

He pulled one hand from his pocket and held it out, brisk and slightly bored, as if his request was routine. But in his eyes, he seemed suddenly . . . pleased? She flushed with irritation, and it broke through the numbness. Why did he show up now?

"No," she whispered. "No, I don't think so."

If anything, his eyes gleamed more. She scowled at him.

"I don't think you understand," he said, his brown eyes large. "This is very important." His face made a funny twitch, like he wanted to look stern and was trying not to laugh. Or maybe he was trying to smile and it wasn't coming out right, so he changed his mind.

The hair rose on the back of her neck. She shook herself. Who the heck was this guy? She automatically blurred her eyesight, to check the lines. The lines trembled and shifted, like they had after the shooter. And after Grandmother . . . their hooks still in her, shining bright. She took a shuddering breath and flashed back to the hospital, to Grandmother lying on the bed.

No, no.

"I can't," she tried instead. "Not right now."

The man stepped closer, intruding on her thoughts, her space.

She frowned again.

"I didn't make myself clear," he said. "This is not a request. Now come along. Time is of the essence." He guffawed under his breath before quickly smothering it.

A thread of alarm curled through her. She fell back a step.

"What's going on?" Tiggy was there, abruptly, squinting at the man.

Naya was suddenly relieved the lot was full of kids, that the man hadn't found her daydreaming under the oak tree by herself. She didn't know what he wanted. He *could* be from the police station, odd though he was. But she wasn't sure. He was too intense, and she couldn't deal with it right now. "He says he has questions," she announced loudly. "He wants me to go with him, but I don't want to!"

"Hey, don't you need her mom? To talk to her? Everyone else had their parents with them." Tiggy puffed out his chest.

The man barely glanced at him. "I hardly think you would know." He waved a dismissive hand. "I have matters to discuss with her, and this is none of your business."

"Where are you from again?" Naya asked, looking at Tiggy for backup.

"Yeah, let's see a badge or ID!" Tiggy made a move like he was going to push between them.

The man turned and focused on Tiggy. "I'd think about what you're doing, young man. You're interfering in important matters." The man straightened to his full height. He was broader than she'd realized.

Tiggy stiffened, looking suddenly unsure. He shifted his eyes, from her to the man, back and forth.

The man fixed his gaze on Tiggy. "Didn't your brother just get in trouble recently?"

Tiggy goggled at him, and so did Naya. How did he know about that?

A grin flashed briefly across the man's face before he suppressed it. "What would your parents think?" he continued. "Do they know how you talk to your elders?"

Tiggy's chest deflated, his bravado melting away before her eyes.

"Tiggy?" she whispered.

"I don't think you want to get in trouble now, do you? Maybe you should head on home."

Tiggy blanched and wavered a step. "I can't get in trouble. You know I can't get in trouble." He wouldn't meet her eyes.

The words pierced her, a cut so clean and sharp she couldn't feel it for a moment. She stopped breathing. *He's . . . leaving me?* she thought, confused. Shock snaked around her heart and squeezed.

Tiggy backed away. "I'm sorry."

"Tiggy!" Her eyes went wide. She gasped a great ragged breath. Betrayal and hurt bled out of her, coated her in mind-numbing awfulness, and she couldn't think. Behind the man's back, Short Shorts was gaping at Tiggy as he hurried out of the lot.

"See? He understands." The man spread his hands. "This is important, and there's no need to get in trouble. Now come along."

"She doesn't want to talk to you!" Short Shorts sounded furious behind her. Naya wasn't sure if she was mad at the man or at Tiggy. For the first time, Naya noticed the other kids drifting in close, almost surrounding the man.

She knew she should talk to him. The shooting was important. There were even rumors it was a terrorist act. But with Grandmother . . .

Naya gasped and shook her head sharply, as if that would help, as if she could shake the hospital out of her mind. The feel of the writhing lines was still fresh. Maybe they were still happening. She couldn't tell. She couldn't tell anything except that she felt exhausted and overwhelmed, and her unease made everything look even more like paper cutouts. She just wanted to go back to being blank, to not think about anything, but she was alarmed now. Something didn't feel right, and her alarm was growing.

The man took another big step closer to her. His hand darted out and she jumped back, icy fear washing over her.

Short Shorts launched herself onto the man's back. "Run, Naya!"

She ran furiously, flying through the alley to her house. But no one was home! Mama wasn't there. Grandmother was . . . was gone. Her stomach cramped, and she almost stopped running. She whipped around the last corner and grabbed, frantic, for her key. Her hands fumbled and shook, and she couldn't get it in the lock. Right as she finally fit it into the slot, she heard a soft scrape behind her.

"Naya."

She whirled around, prepared to scream for the neighbors.

The man looked rumpled and dusty, evidence of Short Shorts jumping on him, and whatever else the other kids had done. But he still had that pleased air, like he'd won some sort of invisible prize. "I'm sorry. I think we got off on the wrong foot."

She shrunk against the door, and he held his hands up in surrender.

He pulled his tie off and shoved it in his jacket pocket. "I'm your father. Your mother called me when your grandmother fell ill. I came as soon as I could."

Naya froze. "Why . . . why didn't you say so back at the playground?"

"I didn't want to say anything in front of strangers." He shrugged. "Too many questions, and it's none of their business. This is a family matter. We needed to talk in private."

"Well, why did you say you were with the police?" Her voice had gone squeaky.

"I never said I was with the police. I said I had questions for you. About your mother and your grandmother. How is she doing? Have you heard any news? I haven't been able to reach your mom."

She replayed the conversation at the lot in her head. He was right. He'd never said he was a cop or what he had questions about. They all just assumed it was about the shooting. A wild hope blossomed inside her.

She had assumed. Maybe she'd had it all wrong.

Could he really be her father? She studied his face for a resemblance, to see if his eyes matched hers, or if he smiled in the same way. His washed-out tan skin didn't match hers, not at all. But that didn't necessarily mean anything. Genetics could be funny that way. His eyes and hair were brown like hers, so that was something.

He made that weird under-the-breath chuckle again.

She frowned at him. She didn't know what was so funny.

"It's so good to see you!" he said in a rush. "I haven't seen you since you were a baby! I've been wanting to visit you for so long. I'm just sad it's under such terrible circumstances."

Maybe he *was* glad to see her. Maybe that's why he looked so pleased. Naya couldn't quite wrap her head around the idea of her father just showing up like this, even if she had wondered about him.

"Could we sit down and talk?" he asked. "I can explain everything. I'm sure you have a lot of questions, and I do too. Then we'll go to the hospital. Your grandmother is at Mercy General, isn't she? How is she doing? I haven't talked to your mother since late last night."

Naya's breath went out with a whoosh. Her shoulders were trembling. She hadn't realized how tight she had been holding them.

He peered at her face. "Oh. Oh, no. I'm very sorry for your loss."

"You don't . . ." She swallowed. "You don't look surprised."

"Your grandmother had a stroke. Those are difficult at her age." He seemed unruffled, even though he was making a sympathetic face.

Queasiness hit Naya. She was curious about him. And she shouldn't be, should she? Grandmother had just . . . Then suddenly a new family member, *her father*, shows up? She suddenly felt like she was . . . replacing Grandmother. Even talking to him felt like a betrayal. But she wanted to *know*.

"You don't look well. Why don't we get you some water?" He shooed her toward the door, and she turned automatically and walked in. "We'll finally get the chance to know each other!"

She stiffened slightly, hope warring with caution. Even if he were her father, she didn't know him. But how would he know about Grandmother's stroke if he hadn't talked to Mama? She gave him a sidelong look. He seemed . . . a little odd but not threatening. She didn't want him upstairs in their private space, though—in Grandmother's space. She led the way to the downstairs kitchen, the one Mama had turned into her painting studio. In between the easels and stacked paintings were a few chairs around a small table. A mini fridge and an electric kettle were set up next to the cabinet that held painting supplies. Mama kept a few cups for tea there as well.

He sat down at the paint-splattered table and beamed at her, a high-octane beam that seemed too bright for the occasion.

She stared at him, confused. He didn't fit the artsy surroundings, but he didn't look awkward. She couldn't decide how to feel.

"Drink some water—you'll feel better," he said. "I could use some as well."

She got two cups out of the cabinet and filled them at the sink. She set one in front of him and took a small sip from hers. He took a drink and then grimaced.

"Do you have lemon, by any chance? I love lemon in my water."

She froze. Mama loved lemon in her water too. "Um, yeah." Naya set her cup down and checked the fridge. "Oh, I'll get one from the garden. I'll be right back."

Halfway to the garden, she realized she'd left a stranger alone in the house! But it would be rude to go back empty-handed. She raced to the tree and grabbed a lemon at random, tugging at it twice before it came loose. Then she raced back in. There, she couldn't have been gone more than a couple minutes.

The lemon was a little green, but she cut it and offered him a slice. Her stomach felt like something was rooting around in it. She stared into the bottom of her cup. Maybe she should have some lemon too. That was the sort of thing Grandmother would give her—with honey, or ginger ale.

He rapped his knuckles sharply on the table. When she jumped, he hurried to say, "I've wanted this for so long. To see you. You have no idea." He smiled.

"If you wanted to see me, why haven't you come before?" she asked. "Where have you been?"

"Well." He scrunched his lips together as he picked over his words. "I know your mother is very careful about her privacy. I was . . . a musician. It garnered too much notice. We didn't always get along, and I travel a lot. I'm . . . I'm ashamed to say I lost track of where your mother lived. She's moved before, you know."

Naya didn't know, but that sounded like Mama. She had hazy memories of someplace different when she was very small, but most of her life had been here in this house. "Um . . . what do you play?"

"Pardon me?" He looked surprised.

"You said you were a musician?"

"Oh, that!" He smiled. "Tickle the keys, strum a few bars. A little of this, a little of that. It pays the bills."

He was studying her intently. All the million questions she had suddenly unraveled, and she didn't know what to say. She took a big gulp of water to cover the silence. Then another. He swallowed another giggle.

He was so strange! Distrust bit at her. Maybe there was a reason Mama had never told her about him. "What's your name? I mean"—she caught herself—"what . . . what do I call you?"

"Mr. Lindy." At her startled expression, he continued, "Let's keep it formal for now. I always find formality encourages respect . . . until trust is earned. And I'll call you Miss Naya. How about that?"

Mr. Lindy, huh? Very carefully, she let her eyes blur. Just a little. She tried to find his line, even though it was blocked to her right now because it was crossing hers. But if she could go back along the lines, maybe she could find it, maybe even go back far enough to see if he knew her mother. Maybe Mama talked to him on the phone sometimes; there would be a blank spot if they did. She felt a pang of hurt at the thought. Did Mama keep that a secret too? Maybe he had been in and out of the lines all along, and she just didn't notice until a few months ago, when she saw him on the edges. Maybe there were other blank spots where they had crossed paths, unknowing moments that would account for him.

The lines flickered in and out of sight. She hit a wall. She could only go so far back without using her hands to trace the lines, and she didn't want him to see her. It took a lot of concentration to go backward.

Wait . . . if he wasn't with the police, if he had just gotten into town, how did he know about Tiggy's brother? Even if Mama had been talking to him, Naya didn't think Mama would mention that. Alarm pulsed through her.

She turned away slightly so she could follow a line. Suddenly, the room spun. As soon as she tried to focus on a line, another one seemed brighter and caught her attention. She struggled to find the right path, to find his face among the crowd of images. Why did she feel so sleepy all of a sudden? True, she didn't sleep well the night before, but her bed was soft, and her comforter was so pretty with all the colors . . .

Her thoughts stumbled before she got back on track. She hadn't even slept in her bed last night! She'd slept on the couch. She eyeballed the man sitting across from her and tried to find the lines again. One hand drifted up to a line before she remembered to drop it.

He laughed. And she laughed with him. Wait, why was she laughing?

The room spun again and went dark at the corners.

❦

Mr. Lindy could see what she was doing. It was much more obvious up close than it had been through his binoculars. She was trying to walk the lines without using her hands. Her eyes had lost their focus, but she was still tracking something he couldn't see. Most likely she was trying to validate his story. He smiled, delighted. The alignment of it, the perfect utter alignment!

She was too young to walk the lines *and* pay attention to the room around her, however. He'd seen older people of their kind do it successfully. He suspected they could flit quickly between the

WALK THE WEB LIGHTLY

lines and the present, like watching two fast-moving objects. She hadn't learned that yet. But she had plenty of time to grow into her skills. He would make sure of it.

Of course, she was having difficulty now. She was so small that the drug was working faster than anticipated. How convenient that she had the lemon tree! Her trip outside had given him ample opportunity to slip it into her water and was a much less messy option than he thought he would have to resort to—almost like it was meant to be. This time the laugh slipped out of him, and she giggled along with him.

She looked more surprised than frightened. Then she slumped in her chair.

He sprang forward to catch her before she fell.

There. He lowered her to the floor and fished her phone and keys out of her pocket. Mr. Lindy walked casually from room to room, feeling fabrics, running his fingers along the paintings. Just in case, he found two other landline phones in the house. He unhooked them from their wires before burying both landlines and Naya's phone in the depths of a crowded supply cabinet. Then he washed the cups and put them away. No sense in alerting anyone else that she'd had a visitor.

He hadn't seen the other children sneaking up on him—sloppy on his part. He had underestimated the bond there.

She should be out for at least a few hours, time enough to pick up a car and a duffel bag. She'd fit in one like a bug in a rug.

He laughed loudly in the quiet outrage of the house.

CHAPTER TWENTY-FOUR

She woke up on a couch, not recognizing where she was. But, for the space of a few breaths, she couldn't remember anything, not where she should be or where she had been last. For a second, she couldn't even remember her name.

"Naya," she whispered. With the whisper, events rushed back, one at a time. First the hospital, then Mama looking so worried, then Grandmother . . .

Half a sob choked her throat, but she was still confused. She tried to sort through what had happened after that. She had a vague recollection of a dream she didn't like. No, she was at the lot. And the man was there—the man around the edges.

She lurched upright on the squishy leather couch, dizziness making her stomach turn. A large semi-studio flat was in front of her, decorated in modern industrial, all cold, shiny metal and muted brick. It was so far from the bright-colored chaos of her home she couldn't register the space for a moment. An open-floor-plan kitchen was off to her left, and a steel door was across from where she lay on the living room couch. The smell of old fries lingered in the air. A big desk to one side held a sophisticated-looking laptop, and a pair of binoculars sat next to tall windows. Night sky showed through the windows, but the last Naya remembered, it was only afternoon.

She blinked at the setup. Where the hell was she?

The room seemed too expensive for their part of town. They weren't in a bad neighborhood, but it wasn't fancy, in between downtown and the suburbs as they were. Even most of their boutique's clients lived on the pricier north side of town and drove over for their clothes. Was she even in her neighborhood?

Panic crashed over her through the confusion. She reached for her phone, but her pockets were empty. Why was she here? How did she get here?

The doorknob jiggled, and Naya could only gape at it.

The man from the lot walked in. He stepped inside briskly and locked the door the regular way. Then he used a key to lock a big padlock across the bolt. Naya felt her eyes go wide. He waved vaguely in the direction of the couch, like he was saying hello to an invited guest and he would bring out drinks any second.

"What?" Naya gasped. "What's going on?"

"Don't you remember?" The man smiled. "We talked at your house, and then you agreed to come here."

"I don't remember that." The memory of lemon and water trickled into her mind, and fuzzy words drifted up. He said he was her father, that he had talked to Mama about Grandmother's stroke. She thought she had asked him something. Everything after the lemon tree was hazy.

But Mama wouldn't have wanted her to go with anyone—not at all. Especially with Grandmother . . .

"No, I wouldn't have agreed to that. I didn't agree to that," she said, suddenly sure.

He clapped his hands together and smiled widely. "Well, you're here now! Best make the best of things!"

Naya stared at the padlock and fought down nausea.

He walked to the couch, and Naya scooted to the far side. He perched on the other edge, beaming at her.

"You," he announced, "may call me Mr. Lindy."

She stared at him, a horrible dread building inside her. Tears swam in her eyes, blurring her sight, but the lines didn't appear like they normally did. She tried to bring them into focus, but the lines remained just out of reach, her head aching. "You did something to me?"

"Just a little something to help you relax. Don't worry, it'll be out of your system soon."

But she didn't feel relaxed. "You're not my father, are you?"

He smiled, that pleased look on his face again. "No. No, but I could have been. If things had gone differently." He reached out and smoothed her hair like a father would.

A sick feeling crawled over Naya's skin, and she thought she might vomit. "What do you want?"

"I want you to walk the lines, of course!"

"What?" How did he know about that? Her eyes flew to the binoculars by the window.

"Yes, I have been watching you! Clever girl!" he crowed. "We're going to get along well, I just know it. You see, I had one of you once, but she slipped through my fingers. I pursued her, romanced her. It worked for a while, but . . ." He made an exploding gesture with his hands. "Ultimately, it ended. So I had to change tactics."

He's bluffing, she thought distantly. The confusion lingered, but it was dissipating, rolling away like the fog in a bad horror movie. She shivered and rubbed her hands along her arms. He couldn't really know what she could do.

"I can tell you don't believe me. Very well!" He clapped his hands again. "Let me elucidate. Your people can see the timelines and trace them, backward and forward, through all the cause and effects of people's choices. Most people tend to think you're psychic, but what you can do is much more concrete than the average flimflam fortune teller. Your people, although rare, have been around a very long time, and you stay hidden for the most part."

He watched her face as he talked, and she shivered again. He seemed to enjoy the knowledge she knew was growing in her eyes.

"I know *you*"—he pointed a finger at her—"like to sit under the tree in that empty scrapyard and look at the lines. You pretend like you're daydreaming, but I know better."

Naya's throat felt tight and hot.

"And you're right, you know." He leaned forward conspiratorially. "You *should* be looking. You have a tremendous talent. It shouldn't be wasted."

He beamed like his compliment would make her feel better. She gulped in a great ragged breath.

"Okay, okay." Her mind raced desperately. He already knew what she could do, so there was no point in trying to hide it. He was like all the high school kids who kept bugging her. He probably wanted to know something he thought only she could help with. If she told him what he wanted to know, then it would be over. "You want me to walk the lines. Fine, I'll do it. And then you take me home."

He cocked his head to the side. "I'm sorry, you misunderstand. Your home is with me now."

She'd thought she was cold before; now it felt like ice in her veins, ice creeping toward her heart. "No," she whispered.

"I'm giving you a better life. One where you can watch the lines as much as you want! Grow your skills. Let you tap into your true potential. You're going to be amazed at what you can do. At what we're going to do." The conviction in his eyes scared her. "You're much better off with me."

Her temper flared. "You can't kidnap me!" she shouted. "What's wrong with you?!" Fear pulsed through her. She shouldn't have said that. She shouldn't make him mad.

But Mr. Lindy only chuckled. "It's not kidnapping when I'm giving you a better life."

"My mother will come get me!"

"That frightened thing? She won't come after you. Oh, maybe she'll try. She'll go to the police, raise a fuss locally. They'll expect us to leave town." He explained it to her slowly, relishing the story. "They'll throw up some roadblocks, check the buses and train station. It will make the news maybe. Briefly. But we won't leave town." He spread his hands wide, his smile huge. "And when they don't find us, everyone will move on, assume you're just another runaway. Missing teens don't really hold the public's attention like they used to, unless the girls are rich and white and pretty. Girls from your circumstances are a different matter. Then what is your mother going to do? Track us down? Come after us? She's much too timid. Besides, she won't be able to find us. I know your kind can't see your own lines. Or a close family member's."

She hated that he knew that. He sounded so sure of himself, so right. It drove her crazy. "But they've *seen* you!" she crowed, pouncing on that forgotten detail. "All the kids and people walking down the street. They saw us together, and you'll be recognized!" Naya's hands flew to her face, too late to snatch the words back. What if he snuck her out of town, after all?

"Oh, I'm not worried about that. For now, we'll take a staycation, but I see no reason why we can't get to work soon." As if it had just occurred to him, he said, "You probably don't feel at your peak right now, but I have something that will solve that!" He popped up off the couch and into the kitchen.

He reappeared with a Coke, and salt-and-vinegar chips. "These are your favorite, aren't they?" He presented them like a prize.

Then she really was sick, right all over his repurposed barnwood floor.

He tutted through his teeth. He walked into the kitchen nook, tossed the Coke and chips on the counter, and came back with a bottle of cleaner and a roll of paper towels. "Clean it up. There's the garbage."

He returned to the kitchen and nudged a trash can toward her with his foot. Then he leaned on the island counter and stared her down.

The reek of vomit hung in the air. Shame inexplicably swept through her. Numb, she sprayed the floor with cleaner and wiped the mess up.

He pulled a phone out of his pocket and checked it. Without looking up, he said, "I'm off on an errand, but I'll be back soon. Help yourself to anything in the fridge."

He moved toward the door. As soon as it cracked open, she bolted to push past him, or tried to. He blocked her neatly with a leg like iron, grabbed her wrist, and twisted her back and behind him as easily as if she were a kitten.

Naya sprawled on the floor and yelped, a sharp pain in her wrist.

He smiled genially and gave a little wave goodbye.

Then he was gone, the door clicking behind him, and Naya was left with a yawning emptiness in her gut. She stayed perfectly still for several minutes, waiting for him to come back, waiting for this to *not* be the reality that seemed to be happening.

He acted like it was no big deal for her to be there. Like . . . like he kidnapped kids all the time. Like he was *entitled* to her. Like he could pick up anyone, just because.

Why did I clean up the vomit? she berated herself. *Why did I do that? Why did I let him in the house?*

She sat on the floor and stared out the window. All the glass and steel provided a pretty view, but it let in a chill. Clouds had gathered, blotting out the stars, and fat raindrops first spattered, then grew into a steady stream. The sound the rain made was like footsteps skittering along the windows. For a minute, a brief minute, she felt like she was outside of the cage and the raindrops were like so many rats trying to escape the glass of their sky-filled prison. She felt fierce, hopeless pity for the rain.

Then Naya rushed back to herself. She needed to do something! She jumped up and frantically pulled on the door. The door was solid. The deadbolt didn't even rattle. "Help!" she yelled. "Help me! I've been kidnapped!"

A neighbor had to pass the door sometime! She crouched down and shouted through the bottom crack, the side, anywhere she thought there might be a gap, even if she couldn't see one. The door couldn't be so thick no one would hear her, could it? She put her ear up to the keyhole, holding her breath as she waited. She couldn't hear a thing.

She grabbed at the padlock of the second lock. He couldn't lock that from the outside! If she hid it, at least that was one less lock. Then when she found her moment, she could escape! But the shank was closed, and she couldn't pull it off the metal latch.

A quick search revealed there wasn't another phone—or a balcony, or a fire escape. She didn't recognize the part of the city she was in, from the view. The windows opened, but that didn't help her; she was much too far up to jump or climb anywhere. She wasn't sure anyone would even hear her yell. She didn't recognize the streets from the window, but she wasn't used to looking at them from above. She didn't see the empty lot either, despite the binoculars sitting there. Naya went to the computer, but it was password protected. So was the tablet she found in a desk drawer. A TV hung on the wall, and she checked it for Internet access. All she found were local channels.

She put up her hands, then stopped and stared at the door, scared he would come in and catch her. *But he already knows,* she thought. *He knows what I can do. It doesn't matter.* She could search right in front of him, and he wouldn't know what she was looking at. She scoured the lines for a moment she could get away, a weakness she could exploit, an allergy to peanuts, anything! But she couldn't see anything useful in the short times he was by himself. She could tell from his future lines that he was planning on sticking close to her most of the time, blocking her view by proximity. She'd have to trace his line farther backward, but that took time, and right now, she just wanted to get out of there!

She searched the lines for Mama instead. Even though she couldn't see her line, she had to try. She called up Mama's face like a talisman. At first there was nothing, just that stubborn blankness that occurred whenever the lines involved family. But then . . . maybe the universe knew how much she needed it, because a flash hit her, quick and painful. Naya focused all her concentration on that fleeting line. There was Mama, at the hospital, talking to a doctor, an administrator, crying quietly in a chair, talking on her phone. Every elusive image came with a new shot of pain and vanished. Then Naya saw her walking into the house, calling her name. The clock on the wall showed it was past midnight before Mama was home. Naya's head hurt fiercely when she pulled out of the lines.

The sky had grown even darker. She snuck a peek at the tablet for the time. She had been in the lines a lot longer than she thought.

Her wrist ached. What was she going to do?

The lock turned. A well-oiled *snick* was her only warning. She jumped off the couch as if she were about to be caught at something.

"Guess what I brought?" Mr. Lindy swept through the door with a large shopping bag. He kicked the door closed behind him, dropped the bag, and busied himself with the locks.

"Go on, go on! Look!" He stared at her over his shoulder.

She crept toward the bag, curled her fingers around the top edge of paper, and pulled just enough to see. Inside the bag were a pair of jeans and a designer sweatshirt, the height of trending fashion. The clothes sat on top of a shoebox she was sure held fancy kicks. Some of the kids at school would have been mad jealous. She knew they were expensive, but more importantly, they didn't look like the artisan clothes she usually wore. She fingered the embroidered hem of the blouse Grandmother had designed just for her, the skirt Mama had sewn. If someone spotted them, she wouldn't look like herself in the trendy clothes. Not at all.

Mr. Lindy turned from the door and looked at her expectantly. "There's a few necessities on the bottom. I never had clothes like these when I was a boy." He smiled to himself. "I can just imagine what the other children would say if I had them back then." He guffawed, loud and sudden. "Of course, what would they say now?"

Naya stared at him.

"Your friends would be envious, I'm sure," he continued. "There's nothing like name brands."

She didn't need name brands. Her clothes were special. A deep grief started to well up, and she squashed it instinctively. She couldn't start crying. She couldn't fall apart. She had to think.

"What would your mom think about you kidnapping a kid?" She shouldn't provoke him, she knew that, but it slipped out, mean and hard between them.

Mr. Lindy didn't even blink. "Oh, I don't have parents," he said easily. "But I imagine they would be quite proud. I've already gone so much further than the other kids in foster care. There is difficulty in starting from such poor circumstances. We have further to climb, you and I. But we're going to overcome that!

After we get started, we'll go shopping for you properly. A real spree, don't you worry."

Naya felt like she was going to lose it. Her chances were better if they stayed in town. She should play along until she saw a moment to escape, but his tone infuriated her. She shouted, "You keep saying 'we' like I'm part of this plan. I'm *not* part of your plan! We're *not* a team!"

"You will be. Once you see. The life I'm going to give you!" He leaned over to look her in the eye.

She cringed, fear tightening her throat.

He didn't seem to notice. "We're extraordinary individuals, you and I. You were never going to reach your potential where you were. Our gifts shouldn't be squandered."

Squandered—that was Grandmother's word. That was Grandmother's word coming out of his mouth. Naya thought she would be sick again.

"You can only climb so far when you start from circumstances like ours. We're extraordinary individuals, and we're going to do extraordinary things." He repeated it like a mantra. "Then nothing will hold us back. Not anymore." His eyes looked faraway and shiny. Without realizing it, she had backed away from him, all the way to the window.

Where there was nowhere else to go.

◆◆

Dinner was more greasy food, burgers delivered from a kid on a bike. When the doorbell rang, Mr. Lindy turned up the TV, slapped a hand over her mouth, and pinned her behind the door as he reached out for the bag of food. She squirmed and kicked as her surprise wore off, but he held her immobile, and she was too late. He smiled the whole time.

Hunger overtook her. It had been hours since she last ate, and then she was sick on top of that. She choked down her food, feeling vaguely guilty that she was hungry at all.

After dinner, Mr. Lindy turned the TV to a loud action flick, settled at the desk, and busied himself with his laptop.

Naya perched on a barstool at the kitchen island across the room. She was grateful he was ignoring her, but she didn't know what to do. She didn't want to turn her back on him. When he seemed absorbed in his computer, she sidled into the kitchen, quietly opened drawers and cupboards looking for . . . what? A knife? There was next to nothing in the kitchen at all—a couple of forks and spoons, two settings of dishes, as if the place wasn't a true apartment at all. The coffee maker on the counter looked like the one in the motel room from that trip to the ocean so long ago. Next to it were single-serving coffee and tea packets.

She wiped away tears. She had taken tea to Grandmother, her robe and her magazines. She didn't even know where they were now. She didn't know where Mama was. She suddenly, inexplicably, wanted a warm cup in her hands. She threw a glance at Mr. Lindy, then crept around the kitchen, heating water in the microwave for tea.

She settled back on the stool, the warm steam caressing her face. If she closed her eyes, it was almost like she wasn't in this apartment at all.

"Good!" he called without looking up. "You're making yourself at home! I knew you would."

Her whole body went rigid. She didn't know how long she sat there, watching him do nothing but type away on his laptop. It was long enough for the movie to end and another one to begin. Tears kept coming, and she kept wiping them away but silently, silently. Exhaustion dragged her thoughts toward a deep well.

When he stood abruptly, she couldn't help but jump.

"Well, I'm off to bed," he announced. "Your bedroom is at

the end of the hall. Make your bed, and get some sleep. We have a big day tomorrow!" he said cheerfully.

He clicked off the TV and disappeared into a bedroom, shutting the door behind him.

She stared after him, numb. Rustling and the sound of running water came from the room. She hadn't noticed another bathroom in there, but she'd been in such a panic. She would need to search more carefully the next chance she got. Maybe tomorrow.

When all sound in the room had stopped, Naya slunk stiffly to the front door to try it one more time. She tugged on the lock before giving up and tiptoeing to her "bedroom." In the room was a narrow bed with sheets and blankets folded on top. Everything was baby pink. He said he wanted her to make the bed. *Like a servant*, she thought bitterly. Was that what she was supposed to be now?

What did he want from her?

CHAPTER TWENTY-FIVE

"Morning!"

Naya woke up shivering, her heart pounding. The blanket was clenched in her sweaty hands. She hadn't meant to sleep. Anything could happen while she was sleeping. Last night, she couldn't decide which was worse: having the door closed, or open. So she cracked it and then stared at the sliver of lighter shadow.

Mr. Lindy loomed in the doorway. He curled his lip at the state of the bed—one sheet, half unfolded, tucked under her, and a single blanket in a crumpled wad. In her sleep, she had kicked the rest of the linens to the floor.

"I was going to make you pancakes, but messy children don't get breakfast. I expect that corrected by tonight. I like a clean household." He turned with a sniff and left.

She jolted upright, feeling like she hadn't slept at all, and stumbled into the bathroom. Naya reached for a lock, but the knob didn't have one. It looked shiny and new and didn't match the door. She drank from the faucet and splashed water across her face, then crouched anxiously on the toilet. She couldn't stay in the bathroom all day—not if she wanted to go home.

When she stepped into the big front room, Mr. Lindy was back at his laptop with a cup of coffee and crumpled napkins beside him. Despite the talk of pancakes, there was only a box of donuts on the counter.

Naya was hungrier than she expected. She pulled out a sticky chocolate-glazed donut, scarfed it down, then reached for a second.

"There's milk in the fridge. I know you're a growing girl!" He sounded proud of himself.

She shot him a dirty look before opening the refrigerator. A carton of chocolate milk stared at her, next to leftover takeout. The donuts were sugary already; chocolate on chocolate was too much. She made another cup of tea instead.

Mr. Lindy swooped in abruptly to refill his coffee, making her jump. He lobbed his dirty napkins at the trash can before going back to his desk.

Naya scowled. He said he liked a clean household, but she noticed he threw his garbage *toward* the can, not *in* the can. The trash lay in greasy heaps on the floor. His counters weren't the cleanest either, with crumbs and small spills dotting their surface, like he was used to people picking up after him, or he stayed in hotels with room service. He had said he traveled a lot. She got the feeling that was true, even if he wasn't a musician. Maybe he never stayed any place long enough to make a mess.

Her blood chilled. Maybe when things got too dirty, he just left.

She couldn't let that happen. They had to stay in town, like he said. After she finished eating, Naya gritted her teeth and put the garbage in the can, then wiped the counters down with wet paper towels. They needed to stay as long as possible, so that Mama and the police could find her.

"We're going out!" Mr. Lindy announced.

Naya's heart leapt into her throat. *Out where?* she thought. *Away from the city, her home?* But outside also meant a chance to catch someone's attention. It meant a chance to get away.

She'd play along. She'd play along, and then she would scream her head off as soon as she saw someone, anyone. Then she'd run. She pictured herself kicking him in the shin and running, practiced it in her head. Trying not to seem too eager, she turned toward the door.

"Not in that."

"What?" Her head turned sharply. She was so focused on leaving, it took her a moment to catch on to what he meant.

He wrinkled his nose and waved a hand at her.

She was still wearing her skirt and blouse from the day before. The clothes were wrinkled and starting to smell, but she didn't want to take them off.

"Go change."

She felt her face go tight and squinty, just like when Grandmother went from irritated to angry. *Grandmother would never put up with this*, she thought. She looked down her nose at him.

Mr. Lindy regarded her steadily as she held her ground. After a moment, he said, "You had breakfast this morning. Would you like to eat the rest of today?"

She clenched her jaw stubbornly.

He chuckled under his breath. "Or tomorrow?"

But she didn't want to stay in this apartment any longer, did she? She'd never have a chance to escape if he kept her locked inside. She stomped back to her room, grabbed the new clothes, and pulled them on, ripping the tags off as she went. She didn't manage to pull all of them off completely, but she didn't care.

She folded her blouse and skirt carefully and lay them on the bed, brushing her fingers across the embroidery. The grief started to well up again . . . but if she started crying, really crying, she was afraid she wouldn't stop. She needed to focus. She needed to find a way out. So she imagined Grandmother wrinkling her nose at Mr. Lindy's rumpled clothes instead and stomped toward the front door.

"Wait." He held a baseball cap in his hands. He stepped close and pushed the hat down. Her curly hair was too big for the cap, but he managed to force it on. Then he tightened the strap on the back until it bit into her skull. "Much better!"

In the shiny stainless steel of the refrigerator, the warped reflection of some other girl stared back at Naya.

He slapped a hand on her shoulder, painfully tight. They walked out the door and into an elevator. In the brief walk down the hall, she could only see one other door, and it was in the opposite direction. Sound seemed ridiculously muffled, as if the walls were extra thick.

If she was hoping to run screaming into a crowd, she was mistaken. The elevator opened onto an empty side lobby with a door to the street. The street itself was bare and silent. It was between the morning-commute rush and lunchtime, but still, there should be some people out. Too late, she remembered how quiet the streets had been after the shooting.

Maybe she should just scream anyway? Someone might hear her. Naya took a deep, shaky breath.

Mr. Lindy's fingers dug into her flesh.

She gasped with pain. On instinct, she pulled away, turning to run.

Quick as a flash, his other hand came around and grabbed her arm.

"Now, now, none of that." He punctuated each statement with a hard shake and a laugh. "I have something to show you." *Shake.* "Something important, and you *will* behave." *Shake.* "Until you see what I have to show you." *Shake.*

He kept laughing, though, as if he were just horsing around with his kid. "Once you see, it'll make all the difference. I promise you." *Shake, shake, shake,* so she couldn't catch her breath, her body jerking around so any sounds she made were cut off.

They didn't go far. Mr. Lindy steered her quickly down the block and around a corner. He was still talking and shaking her when they arrived. He had completely derailed her from screaming. He stopped in front of an old bar, with one plain door and no windows. A simple sign hung over the entrance. She couldn't move her neck, but she rolled her eyes from side to side, looking for street signs before he ushered her inside.

They stood off to the side of the bar doors. His hands loosened on her neck.

"What are we doing here?" she asked.

"We're going to run an experiment. You're going to help me."

She tried to shrug out of his grip. He pushed her against the wall so she was shadowed and partly blocked from view, his body trapping her. He loosened his hand on her shoulder but hovered close enough that the threat was clear. Her eyes searched for someone who could help. The weary patrons were scant and scattered around the bar, men who looked desperate and apathetic. The only energy was a card game between three men at a scuffed table.

"That man." He pointed to a short, twitchy card player. "Tell me his three most likely futures. Don't lie to me now. I'll know if you're lying."

She pushed him, but he was rock-solid. "Why should I help you with anything?"

"Because you are the perfect candidate for what we're going to do. And because I'll hurt your mother." He smiled genially, as if he hurt people all the time. As if it didn't matter at all.

It was suddenly hard to breathe. Naya struggled to get enough air as his hand tightened again on her shoulder.

"But if you work with me," he continued, "well, only good things will happen. So go on."

Mama. A panic bubbled deep inside her. There had to be a

way out of this! But her mind went completely blank, and her hands shot up as if she had no control.

"He loses the hand and walks away upset." The words tumbled out of her, fast and squeaky.

"Take a breath now," Mr. Lindy murmured.

But it was hard to breathe when she was drowning. "He loses the hand and starts an argument with the other player. They get in a fight." She hesitated, because that fight would turn out bad. Then she took that breath after all. Maybe she could get away in the confusion, run straight home to Mama, make sure she was okay.

"And the third outcome?" His eyes were huge in the dim room, intense and eager.

"He cheats, and he wins. He moves the cards around when he shuffles them. But that line is fainter than the others. He probably won't do it."

Mr. Lindy smiled and leaned his whole body against her so she couldn't move. "Now watch," he said. He narrowed his eyes at the squirrely man.

Naya wasn't sure what was happening. Mr. Lindy just stood there, but it felt like waves were coming off him. The waves made her stomach tighten and curdle. The twitchy man stilled for a moment. Then the lines shifted just a tiny bit, just a fraction. The brightness of the lines shifting from one to the other. The faint line growing stronger.

The man at the table took the cards. He shuffled them fast and loose. That, Naya knew, was when he moved the cards around! A shiver ran over her skin. She watched the game, waiting for the other lines to brighten, waiting for Mr. Lindy to be wrong. The players made bets and showed their cards. The other two men groaned, and the twitchy guy raked in the pot. She stared wide-eyed at Mr. Lindy.

"Do you see?" he crowed. "Do you see what we can do? We're going to have such fun together!" He waved to the bartender and ordered a red wine.

The bartender craned his neck and spotted Naya in the shadows. "She can't be in here."

"We're on our way out. Just needed to wet our whistles. Can I get a water too?" Mr. Lindy flashed a fifty-dollar bill.

The bartender grumbled but poured red wine into a glass and handed over a bottle of water. "That'll be twelve bucks, plus my tip," the man said, raising his eyebrows meaningfully and nodding toward Naya.

Naya opened her mouth to shout she was kidnapped, but she felt those waves coming off Mr. Lindy again. Something in her froze, trying to see what he was doing, as he answered, "Of course! Just take it out of what I gave you. In fact, keep the change."

The bartender looked blank for a moment. Then he nodded and turned away. Mr. Lindy steered Naya out the door, his wine glass in hand.

"But you didn't pay him," she said.

He grinned, delighted, like they were sharing a secret. "Now do you understand? Between your gift and mine, we're going to have everything. Everything! Everything you ever wanted is ours for the taking!"

But she just wanted to go home.

CHAPTER TWENTY-SIX

Half a block from the apartment, he took someone else's meal off a bicycle delivery guy. Still gripping Naya's arm, Mr. Lindy had stepped right into the bicycle's path. The young man had braked, a stormy expression on his face, then blinked vaguely and handed over the food. Naya managed a startled half scream before Mr. Lindy twisted her arm, and she dropped to a whimper.

"Oh, don't mind her," he said, offhand and genial. The man shook his head and bicycled away.

A few people had filtered onto the street while they were in the bar.

"Help!" she yelled as they passed a woman. "Please! I need help! He kidnapped me!" She tugged frantically against Mr. Lindy's arm.

But Mr. Lindy only nodded to the lady, and she kept walking.

Naya was horrified. Now that she knew what to look for, she could feel the waves coming off Mr. Lindy. He was using them all the time! Even if she started screaming bloody murder, she wasn't sure if anyone would do anything. How many people could he control? How far did the waves go? Did his power wear off after a while?

"Hey! Help me!" she screamed one last time, before he chuckled and pushed her through the same door they had left.

In the apartment, Naya ran to the bathroom and shut the door. She crouched on the toilet, her breath coming faster and faster until she thought she would throw up. He could control people! He could make them do things! How was she going to fight against that? Her head spun, and she leaned her forehead on the cool edge of the sink. She could hear Mr. Lindy puttering around in the next room. Could he control her from there?

She sat there a long time, until her breath slowed, and the edge of the sink grew warm against her head, and her back grew stiff from sitting in the odd position for so long. She kept waiting for him to knock on the door, to check on her. But he didn't knock.

A curl of anger crept in alongside the panic.

Who did he think he was? He pushed people around! He kidnapped her and then ignored her!

She stood and pulled up her sweatshirt to check her arms and neck. There were red marks but no actual bruises. He knew how to make it hurt just enough. He hadn't *hurt* hurt her, though. She bit her lip. He needed her for something. Maybe he needed her enough that he wouldn't hurt her.

But what could it be? She poked her head out the bathroom door and stared down the hall. She could just see his back and elbows. He was at the kitchen island eating the takeout, loudly.

She'd never escape if she stayed in the bathroom the whole time.

He nodded to her as she walked into the living room. The meal turned out to be quite the spread of Chinese food.

"Come eat! It's good!" He waved at the cartons littered across the counter.

Naya wanted to refuse the meal. The food in front of her blurred. She wanted to starve herself until she was useless to him. But her head spun, and her stomach roiled in protest. Her hands shook, and she wasn't sure if it was terror or because she'd only eaten donuts.

"Wait until we go into a bank or a jewelry store." He said it as if they were continuing a conversation and she hadn't been hiding in the toilet for the last half hour. He smiled congratulatorily, chopsticks in hand. "I mean, I could do that before. But this will really refine the process."

She wasn't even a "you" anymore; she was a "this." Naya scowled. She picked up a carton of chow mein and moved to the couch. She flipped on the TV, and her eyes shot sideways over to Mr. Lindy. She waited for the waves. She waited for him to say something or to take the remote, but he didn't do anything. She took a bite of noodles and scanned the channels for local news. Mama had to have called the cops by now.

Mr. Lindy wiped his mouth and tossed the napkins over his shoulder at the garbage can. He returned to his laptop, hunched over and peering enrapt at the screen. She tried, without being obvious about it, to see what he was doing on the computer.

Her stomach still roiled; the greasy food wasn't helping at all. But she didn't feel as faint as she had before. Naya couldn't decide if that was better or worse.

"The key," he said while he typed, "is balance. The balance of patience and prudence and risk. All extraordinary actions draw attention eventually. And you are extraordinary, as am I. Long-term investments will be our best course, then property. Building a legitimate portfolio will be crucial. Then we can pull back if we gather attention. Even disappear for lengths of time, if need be. I have a whole plan in place for us."

"Save the lecture. I'm *not* your partner." She tried to snarl it, but it came out a squeak.

He threw her a sidelong glance. "You will be. I'll be giving you opportunities that you would never have otherwise. But you're right, I'm getting ahead of myself. I waited until it was too late last time, spent too long on grooming and training. This time we'll start now, strike while the iron's hot."

He turned the computer toward her. On the screen were photos of three men, their names printed neatly next to each photo. "Each of these gentlemen are investment brokers. My research suggests that their morals might be flexible. I know you can find them in the lines if you have their face and name. I want you to look at their lines and tell me what you see."

"Can't you just do your trick?" Naya stuck out her jaw. "Like you did with that guy at the bar?"

"My results are best in person, and these are strictly phone contacts."

Naya's ears perked up. In person only? That was useful to know. Maybe she should keep him talking after all.

"Then . . . you could just . . . walk into a store and take anything?" she asked carefully. "Really? How does that work?"

"Well, it's rather like what you do! I can sift through people's . . . feelings, or motivations, and persuade them to act the way I want them to act. I make them lean one way or another." He leaned back and forth eagerly in demonstration. "The same way you can sort through the timelines for the best outcomes."

That's not what they did with the lines, but she wasn't going to correct him. "So you can feel what people are feeling?" she asked, astonished.

Mr. Lindy beamed. "No. However, I *am* very good at reading people, reading situations. I make it a habit to study people. Stores are easy because shopkeepers already want to move merchandise," he explained. "I'm happy to oblige them."

"But you have to talk to them to do it?" she asked.

"I didn't talk to the man playing cards, did I?"

Huh, that was true. "Do you have to be near them?" She found she was genuinely curious.

"Proximity helps. Having a connection is even better, but not necessary. Once, at the airport, I made a couple in the middle of a fight make up, and I wasn't even at the same gate as they were! I believe in young love," he bragged.

Naya had never been to an airport, so she had no idea how far apart the gates were, but she tried to look impressed. "But it wears off, right? Like . . . they wouldn't be permanently happy?"

"I encouraged what was already there," he said vaguely.

She waited for him to say more, but he just looked smug. She finally asked point-blank. "Can you make anybody do anything?"

He laughed. "I'm not going to give away all my secrets!" He seemed to be enjoying the conversation, as if he didn't get to talk about it very often.

That made her think of something else. "Are there other people like you?"

That sobered him. He sat back, chewing on his lip. "I'm sure there are. Somewhere." He clapped his hands. "But enough sharing stories! We have work to do!"

She looked at the computer, her mind turning over the new information. He had a distance limit; that was important. When she ran, she'd have to get far enough away that he couldn't use his power on her. He hadn't used those waves on her yet. At least, she didn't think he had. But the man at the bar didn't seem to know he was being manipulated. Neither did the delivery guy or the other people.

She needed more data. "Why even bother with this?" She feigned curiosity. "It sounds complicated. You can just walk into a bank and demand money! You said so yourself."

"Yes, I can. And I have. I have never lacked for cash. But

as I said . . . extraordinary actions draw attention. You walk into too many banks in a row and people start to notice the large sums of money missing. Then they start looking at video footage, calling people in for questioning . . . nothing I can't handle. But a pain, nonetheless. No, I'm ready to take it to the next level, a revenue stream that no one can question. What I'm planning will set us up for life! It's amazing what the upper classes can get away with once they've hit a certain financial bracket. Discretion services follow along like well-trained dogs. And then we can do whatever we want! Go into business, build a legacy."

She didn't understand half of what he was babbling. Maybe he had already used his power on her and she didn't remember. Maybe that's how he convinced her to give him water at the house. Or the lemon. She wasn't sure, though. She had been tired and confused and trying to be polite. She racked her memory but couldn't come up with any clues that seemed definite. "So . . . what you do . . . how did you learn it? If there was no one who taught you?"

Mr. Lindy smirked at her, amused. "Okay, now you're just stalling. Time to get to work! Trust me, you'll love this."

She slowly raised her hands as she thought it through. He said he'd had one of her kind once, but not anymore. If he could just make that person stay, why did he need Naya now?

Maybe . . . his powers didn't work on her kind at all.

Maybe she should test that theory.

"You can't make me." She watched him carefully. "You can't make me do anything." She watched to see if his eyes would go intense, if she felt those waves coming off of him.

"*Tsk-tsk-tsk.*" He waved a finger at her. "Remember your mother. I can go visit her at any time."

Naya's blood ran cold. She hadn't expected him to go back to that. He'd said it before, but she had half convinced herself it was an idle threat.

The look in his eyes didn't look idle.

"What does that mean?" she choked out.

"It means," he said, "that I have waited a very long time to be in this position." He rolled the words around like they were candy in his mouth. "I will not let anything jeopardize that. Least of all your mother. If she needs to disappear, well . . . accidents do happen."

"You wouldn't . . . You can't . . ."

"Oh, not by my hands! But if someone with violent tendencies happened to run across her path, someone who leaned toward anger, it could go badly for her."

Part of her thought, *It's not that easy. No one could just walk up and hurt my mother.* But the other part of her—the scared, exhausted part—kept thinking about how easily he had grabbed *her* and walked away. She hadn't even come up on the news yet. Maybe . . . maybe she wouldn't be on the news. Maybe no one was helping Mama look for her. Then it would be easy for him to hurt Mama.

But he was still talking. "You already know I'm very good at finding people. After all, I found the shooter, didn't I?"

"What?" she gasped.

Mr. Lindy looked pleased with himself. "That young man barely needed a nudge to go on his rampage. Finding another just like him would be a piece of cake."

It was him! It was him, all along. If he could use his power to push a man into shooting up a neighborhood, then . . . then he could hurt Mama, even if he couldn't use his power on her directly.

He narrowed his eyes at her. "I don't *want* anything to happen to her, you understand. But if circumstances force me . . . well, then it really won't be my fault, will it? *You* don't want anything to happen to her, do you, Naya?"

Her mouth trembled. She'd just lost Grandmother. She couldn't lose Mama too.

Mr. Lindy smiled as she worked it through in her mind. "Now"—he pointed at the first man on the list—"tell me what you see."

Her dread was a thick sludge weighing down her mind. She couldn't concentrate, couldn't focus on the lines. She tried to still her breath, to think of something besides Mama being hurt so she could do what he said. All that came to mind was how horrified Grandmother would be that she was using her gift this way, betraying all they'd taught her. As she put her hands up, Naya didn't bother to wipe away the tears.

The man was far away. It took a long time to call his line. The longer it took, the more sweat beaded along her neck and lip. She expected Mr. Lindy to get mad or threaten her again. He just stared at her, enrapt, his eyes shining.

She focused on the lines so she wouldn't have to see his creepy gaze. "I . . . I found him," she finally whispered. Her mouth was so dry.

"Good," he said. "I know you can see backward and forward. You're going to look backward, and you're going to look for these dates and these . . . let's call them 'keywords.' The first date is October nineteenth."

Naya's fingers flew along the line. "Okay. I'm there."

Mr. Lindy leaned forward, much too close. "Find all his phone conversations. Listen for these words, and tell me what he says on the phone." Then he said a series of words that made no sense to Naya.

Without being too obvious about it, she leaned away from him. "That's," she stammered, "going to take time." She coughed around her tight throat.

"I know, but it's important to get all the details right. I'll get you some water. Or maybe tea?" He patted her hand before moving toward the kitchen.

She couldn't decide which was worse: his threats, or suddenly switching back to normal-guy mode, as if they were friends, partners. She didn't want any of this! Even if she *had* messed up and let him in the house. Her eyes went blurry with new tears. She wiped them away and meticulously searched the lines. It took her a long while, maybe an hour or more, to find all the phone calls and repeat back what was said. It was easy to lose track of time in the lines. When she looked away from the lines, there was a cup of tea next to her. She grabbed the cup and gulped it down. The tea had gone bitter and cold. "What does that mean?" she asked. "Those aren't even real words."

"They're stock symbols," said Mr. Lindy. "In particular, they're stock symbols for transactions that the SEC would not approve of. I need to find the trader who is most likely to make the trades anyway."

"I don't know what any of that means."

Mr. Lindy's eyes lit up eagerly. "Have you heard the term 'insider trading'? It means when someone has inside information about a company that could affect its stock. For example, say a car company has to issue a recall—that will make the price of their stock drop. Someone who knew about the recall ahead of time could sell their stock before the price went down." He droned on about stock pricing.

He was enjoying this, Naya realized, taking on the role of educator. She knew about other people trying to control business deals or win the lottery using one of their kind's gift, because Grandmother had told her. But it never worked. Their gift didn't work that way, not for concepts or numbers, things without decisions attached. Sure, you could look ahead and try to see someone's winning lottery ticket, but it was like looking for a needle in a haystack. Even if you managed it, numbers had a funny way of changing at the last second.

He probably thought she could predict the future. What would happen when he realized it wouldn't work?

She should stall. The more time she gave Mama and the police, the better. She didn't know all that much about stocks anyway.

"I don't understand." She spoke slowly. "Why is it bad if someone understands what's happening with the company? Isn't that how business works?"

"Yes, but they're supposed to keep that information confidential. Since the stock market is supposed to be based on chance, it's unfair for one person to make money and not others. To have an advantage. If a stockbroker suspects insider trading, by law he should refuse to make the trade."

"So why does that matter . . . to us?" Her stomach turned over as she said it.

Mr. Lindy smiled encouragingly. "A little birdie has told me some very important information about a company for tomorrow's stock trades. So today you and I are doing research on my brokers to see who is the right fit!" He clapped his hands together before she could ask another question. "Now! The next one!"

Mr. Lindy made her find the timeline of the next trader, then the next. Each time, he fed her stock symbols to listen for in the phone conversations. Halfway through the names, he stopped her for a dinner of cheese pizza.

She dropped her arms, her hands shaky. The beginnings of a headache tapped its fingers at the edge of her eyes. Outside the window, the sky glowed sunset orange.

The whole day had gone by while she was in the lines!

But they weren't done. He made her stay up to finish the

list, while he hunched over the computer doing his own brand of research.

When she finally finished the last phone conversation and pulled out of the lines, her whole body trembled. She expected she would be tired; she had never spent so long in the lines before. What she didn't expect was to feel so dizzy and lost and insubstantial, as if she were bobbing along like a balloon in the air. When she blinked slowly, the afterimage of the lines danced behind her lids.

Mr. Lindy hadn't bothered to turn on the lights. He sat bathed in the glow of his laptop, the room strange with shadows.

"Excellent job, Naya!" The look he shot her was proud and pleased.

Like she cared. She groaned and put her face in her hands. Her head ached fiercely.

"It'll get easier. Trust me." He pushed another cup of tea toward her, all smiles.

She'd never trust him. Never. But she took the cup of tea as she pulled her thoughts together.

"Why are those conversations important?" she asked after a long drink.

"Those are times when a trade was made from inside information." His energy was high, almost gleeful, even though it was the middle of the night.

"How do you know that?"

"Oh, I've been doing research for a long time, collecting brokers for a very long time. I've met lots of little birds over the years. Some of them practically begged to tell me their secrets." He laughed.

She snorted tiredly. She had no doubt he could get people to talk with that power of his. His plan suddenly clicked. He wasn't looking for winning numbers or to predict the future; he was looking for brokers who wouldn't report suspicious deals. Deals he would make after he'd gotten insider information.

A pulse of adrenaline shot through her. Holy crap—his plan could actually work. If it did, he'd never let her go!

"But . . . what if it was just a coincidence that someone's stock did well?" She sounded insincere even to her own ears. "I mean, the lines are wrong all the time. You can't repeat things all that often."

He looked at her sideways, his lips twitching in a smirk as her voice trailed away. "Trying to lead me down the wrong path? Nice try, but I've studied your kind for a very long time. I know more than the average rube. The future isn't set. Not completely. Numbers change, but people are very predictable. That's how we're able to do what we do. Now"—he turned back to his laptop—"the fun begins. Just wait! Soon we'll see it!"

❧

She wanted to know if his plan would really pan out, but she was so tired. She got up to go to the bathroom and then sleep. But before she could collapse on her bed, Mr. Lindy was there, dragging her back, excitedly pointing out his accounts on the laptop, the stocks he would be buying. She perched rigidly on the couch and jerked alert every time he jumped up or swooped toward her. She knew she needed to come up with a plan, but when she tried to hold on to ideas, they wriggled away into cold numbness. Finally, she fell into a fitful sleep on the couch.

CHAPTER TWENTY-SEVEN

The morning sun was high when Naya awoke. Her jaw and back ached with stiffness.

Mr. Lindy was pacing back and forth between the window and his desk. He whirled toward her, and she squeaked in alarm. His clothes were rumpled, and he didn't look like he had slept at all, but his fevered eyes were triumphant.

"We made a hundred thousand dollars this morning!" he crowed. "All from our work last night. You and I, a hundred thousand dollars! A small amount, a small amount to be sure. We have to be careful, of course. But this is only the beginning." He stared out the window, then spun back toward her again. "And twenty thousand of that is yours!" His eyes dropped to the floor, and she wasn't sure if he was talking to her or himself. "I think twenty percent is a fair amount. True, your skills are invaluable, but I will be doing the majority of the background work. Securing the necessities and so on. I'll have to set up an account for you. For your own investments. Offshore, of course. After I've gotten you the proper ID."

He was too jumpy.

She leaned away, then moved to the kitchen to put some distance between them. She was famished anyway. Leftover donuts sat on the counter, stale and crusty. She drank a large glass of chocolate milk instead. It settled her stomach more than she expected, but her hands still shook slightly from the night before.

"We need cereal," she muttered to herself. "And some fruit."

"Yes, yes, of course! Anything you want!" He sounded magnanimous.

Naya jumped. How did he always manage to hear her?

She was disappointed his plan had worked, but she was also relieved he was happy. His moods made her nervous. She didn't know what he would do if it didn't work. But if it hadn't worked, would he have let her go? It would be harder to escape now; she knew that.

His face swung up again, piercing her with his stare. "Twenty thousand dollars! What do you think of that? That's a good chunk of pocket change. And this is only the beginning! Much more than your seamstress family could ever make, isn't it?" He smiled, wide and manic.

Naya realized with a shock that she had never worried about money. The thing about running an exclusive boutique is that exclusive work demanded higher prices—much higher some-times. Mama and Grandmother were high-end artisans. She'd never thought about that before. She'd always chafed at the pri-vacy restrictions, the rules, the unending hemming. But Mama and Grandmother did well for themselves; they had a reputation. Honestly, if they weren't so private, they could have set up their own designer label. Even Naya's own scarves and small weavings cost quite a bit. She already had her own account, money she was saving for med school, and she had another college fund on top of that. He really didn't know anything about their business. He didn't know Mama and Grandmother at all.

He thought they were poor. He just assumed. Why? Because she looked a certain way? Because she lived in a city instead of a gated community? He'd picked her, not just because of her gift but because he thought no one would bother to look for her.

The realization was crushing in a different way than the terror of being taken in the first place. The little hopeful part of her almost broke under the weight of wondering . . . what if he was right? What if no one looked for her?

No. She couldn't think that way. Mama knew people all over town, knew people in other businesses, other neighborhoods. She was *popular*, even as reserved as she was. She had enough contacts that she could get help. She'd go to the police. Naya bit her lip. She'd be quiet about it, though. Mama would probably try to keep it out of the news.

But he could still hurt Mama. She probably wouldn't have anyone at the house except Cecilia, if Mama wasn't still at the hospital. No, Naya had been gone two whole nights. Mama would know by now.

Mr. Lindy was still babbling. "I knew I was right. I knew it. I'm giving you a better life. You'll see. And once you've tasted what we're going to do, what we'll have . . . you won't think of your old life at all." He swung around. "You did great last night!" he called over his shoulder as he hurried down the hall. "Good job! Make a list and I'll pick up groceries."

She could still hear him talking to himself in his bedroom, presumably getting dressed. An idea suddenly lit inside Naya like a fire. She looked around the kitchen for a pad of paper and settled instead for a paper napkin. After the usual list of milk, bread, and fruit, she wrote down all the ingredients to make Grandmother's secret fudge recipe. Most of the ingredients were basic, but Grandmother always put in dried cherries and Marcona almonds, and that meant Mr. Lindy would have to go to the organic market. It was the only place in the area that carried them as far as Naya knew. Grandmother always had to ask the manager, Mrs. Rodriguez, for them too. It was a long shot, but maybe she would notice Mr. Lindy and tell Mama.

She added a few more items at the end to disguise her clue. Plus she could really use a toothbrush.

Mr. Lindy reappeared in fresher clothes, although still rumpled. Grandmother would sniff her nose at his messy state, and the thought gave Naya a vicious satisfaction. She smirked at him as he snatched the list she held out.

"International waters," he mumbled to himself. "International waters will be our happy place."

He left then, still talking as he locked the door behind him. The room fell into silence. She drew in a deep, relieved breath to be alone and padded to the bathroom. Grime was starting to coat her skin in an unpleasant way, and the greasy food didn't help. She poked through the shopping bag and found underwear and another shirt. She washed her face and neck, wiped under her arms with a damp towel, but she felt dirty as she pulled on the clothes he had bought her.

Panic seized Naya by the throat. She couldn't wait for the slim chance that Mrs. Rodriguez *might* notice the dried cherries and almonds and put two and two together. What if she didn't even know Naya was missing? She had to get out of there!

Her hands shot up, and she searched the lines for the streets near the apartment. It was all the same images as before, nothing that would help her. Mr. Lindy was too careful, and everything else was too broad, too big. If she knew what the neighbor in the apartment down the hall looked like, or where Mr. Lindy would be going next, she could zoom in on someone else's movements to find a way to get help. But she couldn't find the right line. Her head swam suddenly, the lines dancing in and out of her vision. She collapsed, boneless, to sit on the floor of the hall, her forehead on her knees.

Wait—there was something she hadn't tried. She'd been looking for a hole where he wasn't paying attention, or a point where she could run and find a police officer. She'd been looking at the future. She got up unsteadily and walked to the desk where the laptop lay, shiny with fingerprints.

She should try the past—his past, just like she did for the brokers. Specifically, it should be before he met her but after he had set up this apartment. Her hands ran backward down the line: images of him spying out a window, a different window than this one. He must have had more than one place. Then scenes of him lurking near her house unfolded in front of her eyes, and she suppressed a shudder. He'd been watching her longer than she thought, almost right after she noticed him as "the man on the edges."

Then she saw him walk into this apartment, talking to a manager about privacy. And . . . there he was, bent over his keyboard. She zoomed in on the image. He was typing, typing . . . She had it! She had his password.

She slid his laptop toward her, opened the lid, and pushed the enter key until the screen brightened and the password box appeared. She held her breath as she typed the password. It worked! She was in.

He had a browser window already open with multiple tabs: stock information, Google searches on people, property listings in foreign countries, even one page with boats for sale. Her blood chilled. If he took her out of the country, how would she ever get back? Especially if she was trapped on a boat?!

She opened a new tab and then paused, her hands shaking over the keyboard. Most of the apps she used were on her phone. Could she get to Snapchat on a computer? Mama wasn't on the same apps, but she put her paintings on Instagram. Naya didn't know how often she checked it, though. She could post to one of her friends. They were on all the time, but most of them had seen her leave from the lot already. She jerked her head in a sharp shake. Her friends would take too long. Even if she told them she'd been kidnapped, she still didn't know what street she was on. What could they do? She should go to the police first. The police could do things like trace Internet connections. Right?

Her hands hesitated, though. She needed help, but she had to warn Mama. Before she could think about it, she typed "Instagram" into the search bar, logged in, and went to her mother's page. She hadn't posted anything all week. Naya clicked the message icon. *Mama, I'm close but don't know where? The man at the edges took me. Be careful. I love you. Naya.* She hit "Send" and changed the tab back to Google.

She googled the city police department. A site came up immediately in the search list, and underneath the website was a link that said, "Report Crimes Online." A rush of adrenaline pulsed through Naya as she clicked the link.

At the very top of the page, in red letters, it said, "If this is an emergency or a crime is in progress, please call 911." Below that was a long form of questions with "Yes" and "No" boxes to click. Despite the message at the top, the first question was, "Is this an emergency?"

Yes, she clicked.

"Are you reporting a lost or stolen firearm?"

No, she clicked.

"Did the incident occur on the highway?"

No.

"Come on, come on," Naya muttered, scanning through the questions. She wanted to skip some of them, but she was afraid she'd mess up the form and the police wouldn't look at it.

Finally, there was, "Do you believe you are the victim of a crime because of your race, religion, sexual orientation, handicap, ethnicity, or national origin?"

"*Yes!*"

"Are you the victim of the crime you are reporting?"

Tears welled up in relief. She blinked them away.

In the "Comments" box, she wrote, *A man kidnapped me. I'm in a high-rise apartment. I think I'm near Claremont . . .*

She was so intent on the screen, she forgot to check the lines. A rattle at the door brought her head up with a sharp snap. The lock was already turning.

She clicked the "Submit" button at the bottom of the form. She didn't have time to shut down the laptop. She shut the lid and scrambled to the window, staring out like she had before. She prayed the screen would time out. Maybe she could shut it down later.

Don't check the laptop, she prayed. *Don't check.*

He swung the door open. He walked in with a grocery bag and a leather portfolio in one hand and smiled cheerily at her.

She hadn't finished the form. She didn't even get a chance to type in her name.

He turned his back to place the bag on the counter.

She took two steps farther from the desk.

"I haven't gotten all of the groceries yet, but guess what? I have your passport!" He reached into the portfolio and tossed it to her.

She caught it on reflex in sweaty hands, flipping open the small book. Her stomach curdled in dread. The passport looked legitimate; her name was listed as "Naya Lindy." There was even a picture of her, smiling into the camera, even though she had no idea when he'd taken the photo. Could he really make her leave the country?

"Once things quiet down, we'll be traveling. It's better to set up offshore accounts when you're actually offshore." He laughed at his own joke. "And don't you worry, I'll have your account set up by then. You'll need spending money, after all. You're absolutely right—you should pick your own food, have the essentials, shop for clothes. Whatever you need. Never say I don't take care of my investments."

He walked past his desk and paused. He studied his desk, tapped two fingers on the wood, and gave her a flat, measured stare.

She hoped her face was as blank as she thought it was. Her heartbeat pounded in her ears.

Then he flipped open the laptop.

He was quiet a long moment while he clicked through the screens. His face went through a series of twitches before settling on a funny half smile. "Why, aren't you clever?" he said conversationally. "You must have looked backward down my line."

He didn't seem particularly angry.

It was terrifying. She bolted away from him before she realized she had nowhere to run. "How disappointing. My fault, really," he mused. "You just don't understand yet. Come here."

Before she could decide between ducking behind the kitchen counter or hiding in the bathroom, both terribly useless options, he caught her hand in a quick dart. He yanked her toward the desk but kept her at arm's length. He tapped at the laptop's keyboard while it was out of her line of vision.

"There. I'm changing my password. Now it's part of your line too, so you won't be able to see it." He smiled something at her that wasn't a smile. "See? I'm clever too."

He snapped the laptop shut. He stared up at the ceiling, deep in thought. He hadn't let go of her hand yet. She tugged against it, but not too hard, just to see if he would let go. He didn't. "You are a very naughty child. Do you know, I'm almost hurt?"

She stopped tugging.

"I thought you were starting to understand," he explained, in a slow, patient voice, as if she were stupid. "We are going to do extraordinary things. No more wanting things you can't have, no more struggling to make ends meet, no more looking in from the outside. Everyone wants you when you're financially set. You will be rewarded beyond your wildest dreams. But only children who behave get rewards."

He moved the desk chair to the center of the room. He pulled her with him while he positioned it just so. "You are not behaving now, and we must make a correction. Sit."

She shrunk against his grip. "What? Why?"

He yanked her, hard enough for pain to jolt through her arm, and pushed her into the chair. Then he walked to the bathroom. She clutched her shoulder, too frightened to move. When he came back, he was holding an electric hair trimmer.

"What are you doing?" Her voice sounded high and panicked. "What is that for?"

"I don't want to hurt your mother, but I will. I don't want to hurt . . ." He paused and looked at her significantly.

Me, she thought, her shoulder throbbing. *He'll hurt me.* But she knew that, didn't she? He hadn't yet, not really, but if he was pushed? He talked about hurting people without batting an eye.

Would he hurt her before the police got there? Were the police even coming? The police might start searching for her, if her form had gotten through, if Naya was reported missing. They wouldn't know to protect Mama. Mr. Lindy could go to the house at any time.

Her thoughts crashed around like trapped birds. She sat frozen while Mr. Lindy turned the trimmer on. His hand came down like a weight on her head.

"Do we understand each other?" He said it solemnly, like he was making her promise something. But underneath . . . underneath there was a touch of glee.

She loved her hair. She loved the way her hair felt against her cheeks when she whipped her head back and forth. Or the way Mama would wrap her fingers around the curls, coaxing them into shape.

He held her skull while he ran the trimmer, turning her head sharply this way and that. Her hair fell in soft chunks to the floor.

"This was for the best, in any case." He sounded jovial. "I always feel a fresh start needs a fresh look. I feel lighter already. Don't you?" He released the vise of his hand.

She bolted off the chair and raced to the bathroom. In the mirror, her hair was much, much shorter, butchered into uneven lengths and sticking out from her head. She slammed the door shut and kicked it, kicked the place where the lock should have been. She burst into ugly tears.

Through the door, she heard him say, "You might want to trim that up a little."

The snark in his voice stopped her tears and blew her shock away. Fury took their place. Her body shook with the force of it. She stormed into the living area. She gaped at the floor, at the piles of hair thrown aside—so much of it, so much of *her* on the floor. Mr. Lindy made that stupid low chuckle of his, and her anger became a fire inside her. Her glare traveled from the hair on the floor, up his body. She didn't want to see the look on his face, that ridiculous smug confidence. She seethed as her eyes hovered below his chin, and that's how she saw it . . . a stray, mouse-brown hair on his collar. She flew at him. Snatched it. She snatched it before she thought about what she was doing. Then she swooped for a section of her own hair on the ground. Now it was Mr. Lindy's turn to gape at her, flabbergasted.

She crouched on the floor and wrapped the hairs around and around.

"If you harm me, so too shall you be harmed!" she screamed

at him, clutching the hairs together, infusing them with her rage. She thrust forward her hand like a curse.

The two hairs wound together tight and turned a violent shade of red.

"We're bound now," she spat. "Our fates are twined together, just like you said! We're going to do amazing things." Her voice dripped with sarcasm. "Only . . . if I get hurt, you'll hurt now too, so you better treat me nice."

She didn't know if it would work, if she could really make a curse, if she was doing anything but faking it. She didn't know anything but the rage and the fear and an instinct, and she wanted to scare him. She wanted him so scared.

By the look on his face, she could tell he didn't know if it would work either.

Maybe he didn't know as much about her people as she thought.

"You don't touch me again." She realized she was panting. She probably looked like a crazy person on the floor. Furious. Unpredictable.

Good.

Mr. Lindy wasn't quite as confident as before. There was not a trace of a smile on his shocked face.

"Perhaps we both overreacted," he said after a long moment. He stepped toward the kitchen counter. He pulled out a sandwich from the grocery bag and retreated to his bedroom. "Just wait. You'll see, it's all for the best."

When the door clicked shut, she couldn't hold back the tears.

➤◆

He never came out of his room. She waited a long time before she ate one of the sandwiches, washed down with a flat soda. Her stomach churned and roiled. She forced herself to chew and swallow. She was used to regular meals, healthier food, not fast food all the time. At least there was a loaf of bread in the bag, along with peanut butter, a box of cereal, and a toothbrush. No items from her secret-message recipe, though, so he must not have gone to the organic market. *The police will come*, she told herself. *I submitted the form.* She hoped what she filled out was enough.

Naya crept around the room. She didn't know what to do with herself. It was worse than when he was gone. He wasn't in the room, but she didn't feel safe. She couldn't look at the computer again, and she didn't want to turn on the TV. Every time she made a sound, she spun around in case he came out of the room. But the door didn't budge. The bedroom was silent.

How long could he stay in there?

Finally, she got a dustpan that was under the sink and swept the hair up as quietly as she could. Then she put the rest of the food in the fridge. She threw away the last of the fast-food bags without letting them crinkle, and she wiped the counters down. Then she tiptoed around the room, dusting, straightening as she went, until everything was exactly the way it looked before he came in.

By the end, she was so tired, she swayed on her feet. She had no idea what time it was anymore, but the windows had grown dark again. She picked up the chair from the center of the room and carried it quietly, her arms shaking with effort, to the bedroom, where she wedged it under the doorknob. She huddled under the blanket in the middle of the bed.

He hadn't bought her any pajamas.

CHAPTER TWENTY-EIGHT

A loud clatter startled her awake.

Mr. Lindy, looking bizarrely cheerful, had thrown the door wide open. The chair hadn't stopped him at all.

Naya groaned. Her head pounded with a dull ache, and there was a terrible taste in her mouth.

"Wakey, wakey!" He clapped his hands together. "It's time for work! I've got a hot tip that I think we can turn around in a few days. A much higher payout this time. I normally like the slow path, but I think you need an example of what we can really do, so this one time, let's push the envelope. We need to do some research though, so up and at 'em!"

He trotted briskly across the room and yanked the curtains open behind her. The sky was the shade of dark gray that comes right before the sun rises, the dim trickling in through the window.

Naya moaned again. It wasn't even properly morning yet. "I don't feel good. I think I'm sick." She tried to burrow back into her pillow.

Mr. Lindy ripped the blanket off the bed. "Oh, you'll be fine with a good breakfast in you! Now get up." That last part was said in a hard tone.

She stumbled into the bathroom, feeling hot and staticky at her edges, like a TV signal that wouldn't come in right. Her toothbrush got rid of the taste on her tongue, but the smell still lingered at the back of her throat. She was starting to stink too, but she didn't want to take a shower, not without a lock on the door.

"Hurry up now, we have some research to do before the morning bell," he called from the front room. "Chop-chop!"

Every muscle hurt as she shuffled to the kitchen. She had dreamed she was walking the lines all night. Maybe she had been. She grabbed the cereal and had no choice but to pour chocolate milk over it, because Mr. Lindy hadn't bought the regular kind that was on her list. She perched on a kitchen stool, and the first bite both settled her stomach and made her realize how much she didn't feel like eating. She stared at the bits of cereal floating in brown soup. Out of the corner of her eyes she saw the lines flickering and random images. Blocking them took a lot of effort. All she wanted to do was sleep.

"I really don't feel good," she tried to tell him again. "I think I have a fever."

"You'll be fine. But that's a thought! I might have to convince this gentleman not to go into work. Calling in sick would do just fine. I'll give him a call."

She stared at him. "I thought you couldn't do that over the phone."

"I never said that," he replied archly. "I *said* my talents work best in person."

"Did you make Tiggy leave me?" she whispered.

He smiled. There was a meanness behind it, control. He was still mad about the hair curse. He *could* answer the question, but he wasn't going to.

"I've found most people will always save themselves before they put themselves at risk for others. Just like your friend. It's hardwired into human nature, left over from our primordial beginnings, to survive at all costs. That's why none of your friends will be coming after you. They might cry and make a fuss, but who's going to listen to a bunch of children? There's so many of you . . . poor, grungy kids on a pitiful, grungy lot. You all just blend in with the dirt. Probably no one else has even noticed you're gone yet. And in the end, if the authorities don't notice, what are those kids going to do? Get themselves hurt? No. It goes against people's instinct."

He said it with finality, and doubt bit sharp at her heart. Maybe Tiggy really did just leave her. He was afraid of getting in trouble, after all.

But Short Shorts had put herself at risk. She had jumped on his back! Naya held on to the image fiercely. She wondered if Mr. Lindy had used his power on the other kids after she ran out of the lot. She hoped not, but after what she'd seen, it was likely he did.

"Back to work! Look up this man." He showed her a photo and name on his laptop.

"You know what?" She squinted at him while part of her brain screamed at her to shut up. "Make me. With your power. I dare you."

Mr. Lindy narrowed his eyes back. For a moment she felt those waves coming off of him, almost automatically, as if he couldn't help but use them. She felt the waves and braced herself. But she felt . . . nothing. No compulsions, or her mind being changed, or anything. His face twisted, and the waves cut off abruptly.

He can't use his power on me, she thought triumphantly.

"Oh, but haven't we gone through this?" he said, forcing cheer into his voice. "There is your mother to think about. And your friends! Wouldn't it be so sad if something tragic happened to them, one by one?"

Naya sucked in a breath and swayed in her seat.

"Now." He nodded. "Tell me what he did last Wednesday."

"What time?"

"Oh. All day." He smiled spitefully.

Naya put up her hands. They trembled in the air in front of her. Her eyes blurred from wooziness. The lines sprang up around her, but it took a long moment before she could concentrate.

The man was another one of those Wall Street guys Mr. Lindy liked so much. At least that made it easier to find him.

Mr. Lindy's phone rang, abrupt and shrill. Naya almost leapt out of her skin.

"Hello?" he answered. "Yes. Yes, of course."

He hadn't taken any calls before. She didn't think he had friends. Naya's fingers itched for the phone. Would the person on the other end of that line help her if she asked?

"And you've got him on the hook for what? I see." He paced back and forth in front of the windows. "Yes, I could lean on him; my standard fee applies . . ." Mr. Lindy gave her a sidelong, considering look. "However, I'm offering a new service that you might be interested in. Research of an extremely lucrative nature and potentially a much bigger hook for you. Let me do some digging. I think you'll be pleasantly surprised. You want a better deal going in, don't you?"

Naya's shoulders fell. It sounded like the person on the phone was someone like Mr. Lindy, someone who wanted to cheat to make money—probably no help at all. Naya poked at her chocolate soup while the person on the other end of the phone talked. She took a tiny bite of cereal. A line flickered in front of her. She put up her hand, almost vaguely, and followed the line. She watched a man work in a mini-mart while she listened to Mr. Lindy talk on the phone.

"My fee? This type of work is for partnerships only. If I get the information to increase your demand, I get a thirty percent cut." He held the phone away from his ear while the other voice yelled. "Hear me out! If I don't find anything, I'll work my usual service, take my fee, and you'll get your payout. However, if my research provides a more lucrative angle, maybe double or even triple what you're asking now, then I get my cut. Either way, you get paid."

He paused in front of the windows, fixing his gaze on Naya. She dragged her sight away from the line and back into the room.

"How? I happen to have access to a very exclusive . . . line of information." He chuckled at his own joke. "Now, I have to ask you—have I ever let you down?" He smiled. "That's right. Tell you what: give me twenty-four hours." He pulled a napkin toward him and jotted down notes. "Really? How interesting. I'll be in touch." He ended the call and swung to face her. "We're going to switch gears." Mr. Lindy hunched over his laptop, typing rapidly. "You're going to find these two men and this woman." He turned the screen toward her so she could see the photos. "You're going to see where their lines converge in the past. All the points they converge . . . and what happens around each time."

"I don't know how to do that." She thought about how long it had taken her to find Brandon when she traced backward from the fire at the parking lot. She couldn't imagine how long it would take to trace three people. She swayed in her seat. It made her tired even thinking about it. "I'm probably not old enough to do that yet."

"It's quite easy." His eyes were intent on her. "You find the first person, and then put your people's equivalent of a pin on that line. Then you find the next person and the next, and put pins on their lines too. Then you take the high view to find where the lines touch."

"A pin?" What was he talking about?

"Yes. You take a tiny bit of your energy and place it like a drop of color on the line."

"I've never . . . I've never done that before. How do you know that?"

"Remember, I had one of you before. She told me about it. I know you can do it. It's part of your instincts. You just need to try."

Naya thought about Mama and Grandmother and the other lady in the room, all walking the lines at the same time. Was that how they looked at the big pictures? With "pins"? She bit her lip. She hadn't learned that yet. It bothered her that he might know something about the lines that she didn't. It always seemed like Mama and Grandmother could see farther than she could, but she always thought that it was just practice. A fierce pang of regret pulsed through her. She shouldn't have brushed off training, especially with Grandmother.

Mr. Lindy was still staring her down. "Will you try, Naya?" He cocked his head at her. "Or do I need to go visit your mother?" He had that mean look in his eyes again.

Her stomach twisted as her jaw clenched. "You don't have to keep saying that! I got it."

"Just making sure we understand each other."

She put her hands up, the worry for Mama making them shake worse than before. She held the first man's face and name in her mind and skimmed through the lines that came to her until she found him. He was gray-haired and balding and sat in an office chair as if it were a throne. His line stretched behind him and branched out before him, and all she could think about was sticking pins into bugs for scientific study.

"Listen to your instincts, Naya," Mr. Lindy whispered.

A shudder shook her whole body.

Color, she thought. *Drop of color.* She turned the threads into colors with her energy. She had learned how to do that when she was small, even though she wouldn't need it until she was much older. Could the pin be like that? But instead of using thread, she'd put it on the lines. Would that even work?

"How long do the pins last?" she asked, flicking her eyes to him.

Mr. Lindy's face soured. "I don't know."

She went back to staring at the line. If she didn't try, he would do something horrible to Mama. The fear bit her, strong and poisonous. Her fingers tensed involuntarily. Then, before she could think about it, she pushed that energy toward the man's line, just like she was holding one of her spools of thread.

A tiny spot of vile green yellow glowed on the line.

She did it! A thrill curled through her. Then it twisted around the knot in her stomach and soured the sense of accomplishment.

She watched the green spot a moment, taking her hands off the line to be sure, but the color didn't fade or disappear. She jerked her head, too quickly, to see the woman's picture next, and the whole world tilted and went black.

Slowly, the room brightened. Had she fainted? She saw the lines first; then the room came back into focus. But the dizziness didn't go away.

From far away, a voice spoke.

"Okay, okay. Fine! Clearly, you're not faking. I'll get some Tylenol. Go sit over there so you don't fall again." Hands guided her to the couch. "Keep working. I'll be back." Mr. Lindy scooped his keys up, and the door locked behind him before she knew it.

She lay flat on her back and stared at the ceiling until it stopped spinning. For a long moment, she didn't move. Her head still hurt, and it was hard to think, and she was so tired. It took too much effort to block the lines, so she let them dance in and out of her vision. For a long moment more, she thought about not doing any work for him, not doing anything ever—just lying there forever, until he gave up.

But he wouldn't give up, would he? He'd just hurt Mama. Then he'd hurt her friends.

He would be back soon. She wondered about the pins. How long would they last? Could she see pins made by other people?

The idea made her carefully raise her hands again.

If she put a pin on a line near her, would Mama see it?

First, she tried to find Mama's line again, just in case . . . but it didn't work, and a new pain lanced through her headache. Naya looked at the lines closest to her, instead, of people she didn't know. She scanned through them quickly, just like she used to surf the lines. A number of the lines belonged to people in the building around her.

Her heart pounding, she reached for the nearest line, and thought about how glad she'd be to see Mama. A little push, and the pin glowed a rosy pink.

She wiped the sweat off her hands, then quickly added three more pins, all on people's lines near the apartment. She zoomed out to check, high above the apartment lines, then zoomed out again, high enough so she could see that part of the city. Her pins glowed like love on the lines. If Mama saw them too, she'd know the apartment building Naya was in, as long as they stayed in the city.

The doorknob rattled. Naya froze where she lay on the couch. She sat up slowly and kept her hands up as if she'd been working the whole time. Mr. Lindy swept through the door, a paper bag under one arm.

"Here you go!" He pushed a bottle of DayQuil at her. "I got orange juice as well. How are we doing?"

She knew he meant walking the lines, not her health.

"Fine," she ground out between her teeth. She stopped and made an elaborate show of studying the DayQuil label before walking gingerly toward the kitchen for water to chase the medicine down. She wasn't as dizzy as before, but he didn't need to know that. Her head still pounded with headache, and her legs were shaky, and she was still kidnapped. If he had to wait awhile or get her special medicine, he damn well could.

Mr. Lindy twitched impatiently. The medicinal syrup was sticky in her mouth. The wooziness came back, sharp and swooping. Suddenly, she couldn't wait to get back to the couch. She slid down, boneless, resting her head against the back of the cool cushions. Images flickered in and out of the corners of her eyes, the way they had when she was small and hadn't learned control yet. She wondered if this was how their people went mad.

Mr. Lindy cleared his throat. Naya didn't bother stifling the roll of her eyes. She lifted her hands and went back to work.

>—◆

"Where are you, Naya?" Mr. Lindy whispered near her ear, sometime later. "Where are you in the lines?"

"I found him. I found her. I just need to find the second man," she lied.

She needed more time.

"And the pins?" he prompted.

She wanted to smile, but she scowled instead. "They worked."

She had added more pink spots. She tried to make a beacon of them, tried to aim all the pins like an arrow pointing around her, even if she couldn't see her own line. Now that she knew how to make pins, she could keep adding more. And now that she was zooming farther, she had a better idea of where she was. That was what she was doing when he spoke like a gnat in her ear—tracing the streets through people's lines around the building. Naya smiled grimly to herself.

After she had put pins on the three people he wanted her to track, she had to zoom way, way out to find the spots of green again. She could see her pink spots too, but those green spots were in another part of the country altogether. At that height, the lines converged into a vast network of flickering white, like fine woven lace or a living tapestry, the possibilities appearing and vanishing as quick as thought—like the most complicated spiderweb in the world, with her at the center. It was a heady feeling, but it made her wary, as if she were carrying something precious and breakable that didn't belong to her.

There was something else too, something she'd never zoomed out far enough to see. There were different lines, huge in comparison to the regular lines. Their light was different, more beautiful but harder to see. It was as if she wasn't meant to see those other lines at all. She zoomed in and out between tracing the neighborhood streets and studying the giant lines. Were those something that could help her? She moved her hand through one, tried to feel it, but it was so huge that it was like touching air—all around her, and she had never truly noticed.

It was fascinating. There was more in the lines than she had imagined.

"How much longer, Naya?"

She scowled again. Even if the giant lines couldn't help, she'd much rather spend time studying them than dealing with him. She couldn't tell how long she had been walking the lines anymore. Maybe she could just stay in the lines until he fell asleep.

He prodded her shoulder.

She reluctantly focused on her task and found her spots of green—the three people. Two were often close together, but the third only crossed their lines a few times.

"What am I looking for?" she asked.

"My associate thinks the man and the woman are taking bribes. Maybe dealing in unscrupulous business dealings with the other man. Look for anything that looks like money changing hands—cash, checks, envelopes of money—especially if it's not in the usual business settings, like if they meet at a coffee shop or at a park. Listen to the conversations, and tell me what they're talking about."

Naya's face pinched. Walking the lines meant her people saw all sorts of private business, even when they didn't mean to. She had been trained to observe without judgment, but it was hard not to judge sometimes. But they also didn't purposely spy on obvious private moments either. It was . . . rude.

"The woman is his assistant," Mr. Lindy continued. "She may be his girlfriend, or she might just be part of the bribes. I want you to look for anything that seems scandalous—good blackmail material."

An itchy, grimy feeling crawled along Naya's skin. It was bad enough listening in on people's phone calls, like the brokers. This was something else altogether. This is what he would have her do all the time if she didn't escape. She knew it.

Her hands flew along the lines. "I found something," she said. "The man and woman are talking about creating an account. Then she contacted the second man and told him it was all set up. That was months ago. Is that right?"

"Good! Tell me the details! What type of business are they talking about?"

"I don't hear anything about business. It's about the other woman. They're talking about how they all need to meet together." She scanned the lines carefully, but she didn't see more meetings.

"The other woman?"

"Yeah. She's really young. And pregnant. Wait, I have to go forward." Naya's hands strummed the air. "They're helping her move somewhere, but she keeps crying. I don't think she wants to move, but they're making her. The second man is putting her bags in the car and driving her away."

Mr. Lindy went very still, more still than she had ever seen him. Usually, he paced, or twitched, or typed in an irritating way.

"How young? Your best guess."

"Um . . ." Naya bit her lip. "Older than me. High school or college, maybe?" Her hands skimmed down the young woman's line. "It looks like . . . she just started college."

"And after the baby? Do any of them visit her?"

"Let me see." Her hand strummed the air. "The first man does. The one you thought was taking bribes. He's really excited to see the baby. He's kissing her, so she must be the girlfriend, not the other lady!" She sat back, her shock pulling her focus from the line. "Ew! He looks old enough to be her father!"

A low chuckle rumbled through Mr. Lindy. The laugh sounded like it started in his belly and was clawing its way out, getting louder and higher as it climbed. He finally threw his head back, a high, almost hysterical-sounding peal of laughter bouncing off the loft's walls.

Before she realized she was moving, Naya had scooched away from him on the couch. It was alarming how excited he looked. When the laughter trailed off, he clapped his hands and jumped around in a jig. He looked at her as if he expected her to join in.

All she could do was stare.

"He's a politician! He's also married!" Mr. Lindy crowed.

"Um?"

"This is perfect! Perfect!" Mr. Lindy's voice quivered and cracked. "What's her name? Oh! Can you see where they moved her to? The city or address?"

She didn't have to blur her eyes before the lines snapped back into focus. They seemed to be coming to her faster, almost out of control. But anything was better than watching his maniacal glee. Her headache, kept at bay by the DayQuil, surged back, throbbing and fierce. "142 Front Street, apartment B, Pinecrest, Pennsylvania."

"You clever, clever girl! I knew this would pay off! I told you we were going to do amazing things!"

Naya sank deeper into the couch, staring at the ceiling. The more excited he got, the more she felt her own energy draining away.

"I only found her because of the connection arc," she said tiredly. "There was a strong one between her and the man. Otherwise I wouldn't have seen it, looking for the other three. They all met a bunch of times, but they only all met with her once."

"Connection arc?" Out of the corner of her vision, he went still again.

She darted a furtive glance at him.

Mr. Lindy's eyes were voracious. "Tell me about the connection . . . arc."

A shiver cascaded down her spine. *He doesn't know about the arcs*, she realized too late. "Well, that was a fluke. You can't see anything from those . . ." She tried to backtrack. "They're temporary. They don't tell you anything . . ." Which was true, mostly, but she didn't elaborate. She didn't want him to learn anything more about the lines. "They're useless, really."

Of course, he knew she was lying. His mouth pinched, but his eyes gleamed even more, as if the sour look was just for show. "We'll talk about this later. Right now, I have business to attend to. Why don't you get some rest?"

She narrowed her eyes at him, but he only turned away, punching a number into his phone. He talked smoothly to the other person, but he was fidgeting again, excitement running through his jerky movements. He mentioned the politician's name, then spoke in circles and innuendo. The person on the other end of the line also seemed excited. After he ended the first call, he immediately dialed another number. It was boring and seemed like it would go on for a while, and she was so, so tired that she finally got up and walked quietly to her room.

CHAPTER TWENTY-NINE

She fell asleep without really planning to, stretched out on the bed. She dreamed of pink dots, and waterfalls of giant lines, drowning her with light. When she woke with a jolt, she wasn't sure if she was still in the lines. A blanket was clutched around her, trailing off the bed's edge, but images brightened and faded, in and out of her vision, obscuring the walls. She blinked until she half recognized a bedroom. Not her bedroom at home. It was the apartment Mr. Lindy was keeping her in, full of lines all around her. An urge to walk those lines pulled at her like an ache, and she raised one hand. She liked being in the lines. She could look at anything she wanted there. She didn't have to see Mr. Lindy's face. She could make dots. Had she done that yet? Wait, where was she?

She felt . . . lost.

A surge of panic went through Naya. Was this the "lost in the lines" Mama had warned her about? Was this how it happened?

Adrenaline made her sit bolt upright. She needed to pull it together. She couldn't escape if she went mad or got lost in the lines. Gritting her teeth, she willed the images away, forcibly pushing and blocking the lines until she could only see the ugly half-made bed in front of her. She could feel the lines, though, just at the edges, pulling at her, ready to be called back in a flash.

She made herself stand, her feet cold on the wood floor, and take several deep breaths until the lines fell farther away and the here and now felt closer. Late afternoon light poured in through the window, so she hadn't napped long. She felt better than she had earlier; the pain in her head had faded to a dull ache. But her hands trembled ever so slightly.

"Stop it," she whispered at them. They didn't listen.

She stumbled toward the kitchen, hoping there was something to eat besides orange juice and stale donuts. She'd feel better if she could just eat something real. She had to stay sharp, look for another opening to run, and watch for Mama when she saw the pins. If she let the lines distract her, if she got lost in the lines again, she might miss her chance.

Mr. Lindy stood in front of a jumble of items piled haphazardly on the floor: discarded clothes, scattered papers, a pair of binoculars, something that looked like a mini satellite dish that she thought might be for listening in on people. Where had he been keeping all of that?

He whirled toward her. "Naya! Naya, my dear girl!" The light in his eyes was disturbing.

She kept walking until the kitchen bar was between them and fumbled for a cup. The cereal box sat on the counter, and she crammed a handful in her mouth, before reaching for the tea. As sugary as it was, the cereal steadied some of the trembly feeling in her hands and in her head.

"What's that?" she asked cautiously, nodding at the items on the floor.

"Oh, just sorting through the discard pile. We'll be leaving earlier than expected, and I always like to start fresh in a new place."

A chill washed through Naya. They couldn't leave town! Not when she'd just figured out where she was!

"What?" she yelped. "I thought we were lying low?"

"Things change. You!" He pointed. "You should know that most of all! I need to meet up with an associate. With the info you've given me, we have an opportunity not to be missed." He gave a great belly laugh and then abruptly cut it off.

He scrutinized her. She could practically see the wheels turning in his head. A shiver crawled over her skin. Why was he staring at her? Was he thinking about whatever opportunity he had going on? A flash of bitterness wrestled with her fear. He wouldn't even have that "info" if it wasn't for her! Maybe she could come up with a reason for staying in town a little longer. She racked her brain for an excuse.

"But that isn't important." He waved a hand at the pile like shooing away a fly. He stepped toward her, too quickly.

She was cornered between the kitchen counters. She didn't want him to get close. She didn't want him to touch her.

He crouched, almost enough to bring them eye to eye but still high enough to loom over her. "I want to learn more," he said quietly.

Another shiver coursed over her. "What do you mean?"

"I know you have other talents. Other . . . skills. Remember? I had one of your kind once. She let me see the lines. She whispered and took my hand, and I saw them. You're going to do that for me too. Not just the lines. I want to see the arcs. I want to see . . . everything."

She stepped back, away from the manic look in his eyes, her back hitting the stove. "I . . . I don't know how to do that."

"Oh, I think you do. I think you know more than you're telling me. You did the trick with the hair." His face twitched. "That's . . . fairly advanced."

He was pretending he knew what she did with her curse, but she could tell he was lying, because she'd been bluffing. She didn't know if she'd done something with the curse or not. But it didn't matter. She'd seen a pit bull once with a piece of meat it wouldn't give up. Mr. Lindy looked an awful lot like that dog.

She tried anyway. "I'm too tired. I'm not used to spending this much time in the lines," she stammered. "I think it's making me sick. I might faint again."

He dropped a hand on her shoulder, and she squirmed. "I know that this is a period of adjustment for you. I also know that in time, you'll see this is for the best. However, I decided . . . after our little tiff last night . . . to add some insurance." He smiled, brief and savage. "There is a gentleman under my employ keeping tabs on your mother. He's sending me texts on her whereabouts right now."

He flashed his phone at her. The screen showed a text thread with a photo. It was blurry, but Naya instantly recognized her mother stepping through the front door of their house, before Mr. Lindy squirreled the phone away in his pocket. Without thinking, Naya lunged to grab the phone.

The hand on her shoulder squeezed, pinning her in place, not quite hurting, but a promise that it could.

"Heeeeee"—Mr. Lindy drew the word out—"unfortunately, is a brutal, violent man. I've given him very explicit instructions if he hears from me. Do you understand? So . . . no more stalling. No more fighting. You're going to be a good girl now, aren't you?"

He might be lying, she thought to herself. It could be an old photo, from when he was spying on them. He kind of had that look when he was lying. But the thought fell like a cold weight to her stomach and froze her all the way through. All except her hands—those went from trembling to shaking.

"Yes," she whispered, her tears spilling over.

"Good!" He released her shoulder, straightened up, and paced back to his pile. He prodded the clothes with a toe. "Good, good, good."

Naya clutched at the counter, her breathing ragged, staring at the tiles through a veil of tears.

But Mr. Lindy couldn't leave well enough alone. "I'm glad we understand one another." His snarky tone was back, smug and slow. "Yes, we wouldn't want a terrible accident to happen, would we?" He threw her a look and griped, "Especially if it was all *your* fault. Since I'm doing you the favor of a better life."

Fury engulfed her so quickly, she sucked in air. The rage pushed aside the dizziness, the tears, and the fear. How dare he? How dare this . . . this petulant child kidnap her? Threaten her mother? And now he was *whining* about it?! She recognized distantly that the anger had been building the whole time. This twitchy, hyperactive toddler who couldn't clean up after himself, or know a healthy meal if it hit him in the face—he thought he could just take her away? After her grandmother had just died! Like he had a *right* to hurt people?! Grandmother would never have put up with this . . . this bullshit!

And Naya wasn't going to either.

Whatever showed on her face made his eyes go quite wide. Then he flipped, fast as a dime. "But you did a very good job this morning!" he hurried to say. "I'm proud of you! So proud! And you'll only get better! Now be a good girl until we leave town."

Like she would care about his praise. "Do I get to be a bad girl after we leave?" she bit out, sharp and bitter.

He flipped again, his face going smooth and hard as he ignored her statement. The weird gleam was back in his eyes, stronger than ever.

"Drink your tea, eat, or whatever you have to do, and then you're showing me the lines."

She smoothed her own face out, wiping the tear tracks away. She nursed her tea between her hands and ate cereal slowly, slowly, straight out of the box, while she thought things over. She thought about the new things she'd learned about the lines. Finally, she looked at him, straight and regal.

"We can't do it here," she said. "We have to be around people and more active lines. You want to see everything, right? It's the only way you'll see the arcs. And . . . everything else."

—◆—

They left the building. When her feet touched the ground outside, she staggered, like she had jumped off the high tires at the lot and had finally, finally landed. Suddenly, her hands stopped trembling, and the floaty, lost feeling disappeared. She stared at the cement and pavement, so solid under her feet. As steady as her resolve. She had been far from the ground longer than she ever had before, walking the lines for far, far longer than she normally did. She had always thought Grandmother's talk about grounding was metaphorical, but maybe it was something physical they really needed and she had just never noticed.

Mr. Lindy clutched her shoulder and wandered down the street crowded with people leaving work. He looked from one person to the next, hungrily, as if he could already see their lines.

There was a patch of dirt with a thin tree next to the sidewalk. On instinct, she veered, turning him with her. She planted her feet on the soil and went still. It felt like her feet were roots stretching into the earth forever and ever. Like she was a sister to the thin tree next to her, a tree who would live long past her lifetime, watching these lives go by. She breathed the scent of dirt, touched the silver bark, and the last fogginess cleared from her mind.

"Come on, come on." Mr. Lindy jittered her shoulder excitedly.

"Down there," she pointed. "At the crossroads. That will be the best spot." She added, just to mess with him, "But you know that."

"Of course, of course," he lied. He gripped her tight but let her lead him to a spot a few blocks down, where retail stores were built into the bottom floor of office buildings and apartments.

People milled about, leaving work, or shopping, or going to dinner, the neighborhood crowds coming back after the shooting. She watched Mr. Lindy sidelong, but he didn't stop her. She halted next to the crowded seats of an outside café and a busy intersection. A calmness swept over her. "We have to keep touching. Don't let go. You'll have to give me your eyes," she said. "Say, 'My sight is yours.'"

"My sight is yours," he whispered. Triumphant. Smug.

She gritted her teeth. "And yours is mine."

He blinked.

"Now unfocus your eyes," she said.

He blinked again, and she knew he saw what she did. Light, thin lines shot between people on the street, between buildings and cars, between trees and plants and birds, and back to people again. Long, steady lines streamed out behind people, and short branches formed in front of them, flashing, quick as thought. But there was more. Some lines almost seemed twined together, couples or families who had spent a life with each other. Some lines were steady and thick, with few branches forming in front of them. Other lines branched so much, they looked like fractal patterns. And still there was more. Arcs appeared and faded, appeared and faded. Light bursts crackled around them. A girl spoke to a small boy, and her words were sparks flying outward. The sparks were picked up by a woman, and she smiled at an old man. A couple in love walking hand in hand had their own glow. A man shouted angrily out the window of his car, and the light arced between him and another vehicle. There were a million different connections, and possibilities, and . . .

This was how she had learned—giving her sight to Mama and Grandmother. She could always see the rush of images, since she was small. When she was a toddler, she had stumbled into things, trying to chase the lights. But this was how they had shown her how to walk the lines, how to separate her sight, to make sense of what she saw: the difference between the temporary arcs and each person's line, the energy that gathered around and between people with its own light, the lines of animals and the hum of trees and how even places could have their own energy. The vibrations of *life*. It struck her what an honor it had been. She remembered the soft sound of Mama's voice, her grandmother holding her hand. Her breath came harsh in her chest, and her eyes burned, her calm unraveling. This training was sacred, and he was perverting it!

His fingers bit into her shoulder. "It's beautiful," he whispered, his voice shaking with greed. "Show me more."

Rage coursed through her again. He wanted more? She'd give him more. What he saw was only the first layer. She expanded her vision, let it slide sideways so the recent past floated up and interposed itself on the present lines. That used to take a lot of her concentration, but it was easier now. She wasn't sure if it was because she was so angry, or because she'd been walking the lines so much, or because of how the lines had sunk deeper into her after Grandmother passed.

Next to her, Mr. Lindy staggered. She knew the extra images were confusing him.

"Look," she said. She pointed to where a young man wavered in front of a shop. For a brief moment, there were two of him, one walking into the shop and the other turning away. Then his past showed like a ghostly image, walking up the street, coming to this shop four times before, standing on the sidewalk. Then she zoomed out, just a little, still keeping Mr. Lindy focused on the young man. A small glow formed around the young man's head, a sun, with all his connections' arcs radiating out like rays. She went another layer deeper and pulled up the young man's past, farther back on the line, and superimposed it over the here and now—the man at work, in his apartment, at the grocery store. There were so many lines now of the past and future, they formed a dense, tangled web.

And just there, hard to see, was the edge of one of the huge lines. She could pick them out now, because it made the other smaller lines shine just a little bit more. She edged toward it while Mr. Lindy stared at the ghostly images.

He clutched her shoulder, greedy and drowning, his steps unsteady, his breath a ragged cry of triumph. "Show me more! Show me how we'll use them! Show me . . ."

"Okay." She reached up and put her hand over his where it clasped her shoulder, gripping it firmly.

She screwed her eyes shut as tightly as she could and fell gently to the side, careful not to jerk out of his hand, pulling him with her.

And she fell into the giant strand of light.

Even through her closed lids, she could see the brightness. It was everywhere, everywhere. There was so much light, she felt translucent. Bright pops of color burst behind her lids, and she hoped it wasn't her brain exploding. Everything slowed down. She knew she was still falling, but she couldn't feel it anymore. It was like she was frozen in time. Or maybe in between. In between time.

And underneath the light was something more, something she couldn't sense when she was walking the lines. The lines always felt so big, the way they stretched forward and back, all of human existence and their endless possibilities. But underneath that was something vast, something complicated and precise, like energy, like movement. Was this part of the huge lines maybe? Or something even larger? And there were others there, in that light, that brilliance—beings outside the lines. She sensed it for just a split second before her mind couldn't hold it any longer. *That's how it works*, she thought to herself. *That's the universe working.*

The lines she walked were just a fraction of it, a tiny, tiny part.

"You're not supposed to be here," a voice spoke in her ear.

"It's not time yet," said another in the brightness.

"I know," she whispered, or thought she did. She begged forgiveness in her mind.

From very far away, she could hear Mr. Lindy screaming in agony. The light was so brilliant, it was starting to creep in around the edges of her screwed-shut eyelids. There was no pain, but she knew it was burning her anyway. It would blind her too, if she stayed there much longer.

She fell through the strand of light. She knew she was through when the light shut off, shocking and blinding in a different way, like her home was suddenly yanked away from her. And as she came out the other side, only then did her shoulder break free from his grasp. She bumped the ground with an "Oof."

She felt night-blind and deaf for a moment.

Mr. Lindy was still screaming, lying on the ground, clutching at his eyes. Blood ran down his face under his fingers.

People were staring at them in the street. She scrambled away from him on her hands and knees.

"Help me!" she screamed. "Help!"

Most of the crowd only stood there, their mouths agape. One man ran toward Mr. Lindy, pulling out his phone to call 911. A woman held her phone up like she was recording, spinning back and forth to see what had hurt Mr. Lindy, as if there was a car she had just missed.

They think I mean help for him, thought Naya, flabbergasted. *I should run.*

But he was already stumbling up, reaching for her before she could stand. Snarling through bloody eyes, moving his head back and forth, not completely blind. He managed to focus on her, his head tilted at a funny angle, and he lunged.

"No!" she shrieked, and scuttled backward. "He's a kidnapper! I think he hurt my grandmother!" She burst into ugly sobs.

People rushed forward, finally, and stood between them. But they were only trying to help him, not protect her. Someone steadied him on his feet. Someone else offered a tissue, as if that could help the mess of his eyes.

As the crowd closed in, Mr. Lindy quickly changed his tune. "I was maced!" he shouted. "Mugged! My daughter! My daughter, where is she?"

"She's here!" A hand settled on her shoulder.

Naya shook the hand off. "He's not my father! He kidnapped me!" Her voice sounded high and funny.

"Did you hit your head?" A woman peered at her. "You shouldn't move."

"*No!*"

"Is she in shock?"

"I don't know him!" Naya pointed. "Look at him! We don't look a thing alike!"

And they did look at him—a clean-cut white man in nice clothes and expensive shoes, with a fakey-fake look of concern on his face, like she was really his daughter and he was so worried. It didn't matter that they looked nothing alike.

"Yes, yes," he said, wiping at the blood on his face. "I think she hit her head when she fell! Naya, are you okay? Naya?"

People faded back again, making space for him to reach her.

"No! Listen to me!" She tried to turn and stand, ready to run. Ready to kick and bite him if she had to, to get away. The woman who had asked about her head had trapped her from behind, bent over so she couldn't rise. They were all pinning her in. A cage of legs and concerned faces, and no one was actually doing anything to help her.

His hand reached out like he was going to stroke her face.

The fake concern was still there, but his eyes gleamed triumph. Triumph, and that look he got when he was influencing people, making them go his way, and she felt the waves coming off him. Naya's heart froze in her chest.

Someone shouted.

Then Mr. Lindy staggered. He looked alarmed, but he kept moving toward Naya. He lurched again and went down, the waves abruptly cutting off. The crowd gasped.

Mama stood behind him, breathing hard, one of the heavy rods they used to hang their weavings in her hand. The light coming out of her eyes was the most beautiful thing Naya had ever seen.

"Get away from my daughter!" Her hair stood out around her face like a lion's mane. "Predator! You vile . . ."

Mr. Lindy pushed himself to his hands and knees.

Mama cracked the rod across his back.

He collapsed, twisted to the side to gape at her.

"Stay down," she snarled.

"Mama!" Naya scrambled past him and launched herself at her mother. Mama caught her tight, shifting her arm so she could still hit Mr. Lindy if she had to and hold on to Naya at the same time.

"What are you all doing?" Mama turned on the crowd. "He took my daughter! Call the police. Now!"

The woman who had pinned in Naya pulled out her phone, her hands shaking. She mumbled, "Sorry, sorry, oh my God, sorry."

Mr. Lindy's face contorted, desperate and greedy and angry. He stared his influencing look, and Naya clutched Mama's arm in warning.

"You really think that works on me? On any of us?" Mama leaned over and hissed at him. She used the rod to pin his shoulder down. "You think you know? You don't know anything."

"The police are on their way!" a woman's voice called out.

Mr. Lindy suddenly looked at the crowd. A number of phones were aimed in his direction, taking pictures. He wrenched his shoulder out from under the rod. Mama staggered. He scrambled to rise, and he put on his victim face on his way up.

"This woman is a violent stalker!" He pointed. "She lost custody. My daughter! Mine!"

The crowd wavered. Some of the people backed up a few paces, like they were witnessing a domestic dispute and didn't want to get involved.

"No!" Naya screamed. "You took me from my house. You drugged me. I don't know him!"

A shocked rumble moved through the bystanders. More phones popped up, taking pictures. A siren grew in the distance. Mama dropped the rod behind her feet, out of Mr. Lindy's reach but still close enough for her to grab. Her arms closed fiercely around Naya.

"You are going to be held accountable!" Her voice sounded like doom.

Someone called Mama's name. She turned her head. Cecilia was running to them. Naya felt Mr. Lindy turn his concentration on the crowd, his power leaking out like poison as he stepped toward the onlookers.

"Don't let him go! Don't let him leave!" she cried.

But the crowd drifted apart, almost aimlessly, like the people didn't know what they were doing. No one left, but they didn't bunch so tightly together either, and they opened a path for him. Mama swooped for the rod, but he was already running, faster than Naya thought he could move. The crowd closed behind him as he fled.

CHAPTER THIRTY

Mama had found her through the pins.

"That was really smart, my love," she said. "You brought us to the right area."

Mama and Cecilia and a bunch of adults from the neighborhood had volunteered to canvas the city to look for her. When Mama saw the pins, she suggested the area to the group. And because it was Mama, they went, just like they piled up sandbags at their doors before the storm.

Naya's throat went tight and funny when she heard that her abduction had never made the news, not until *after* she was found and made that big scene on the street.

So he was right about that, she thought. *No one was going to make a fuss over one missing teenager.*

The house didn't sound right. Mama was clattering in the kitchen as usual. The washer was running like it normally did. Naya could hear the neighbor next door closing up shop. Traffic had picked up outside as people went home from work. It was the symphony of evening sounds she was used to hearing.

It took her a long minute to figure out what note was missing. The shuffle of papers, the click of a pen, Grandmother muttering under her breath . . . were just . . . gone.

The tears came so heavy and sudden, Naya couldn't move

her homework out of the way. Then she didn't bother. Her whole body shook with racking sobs as she watched her math homework blur and run.

She was so, so happy to come home. But it felt like every time she turned a corner, there was a new devastation to stumble over.

➤◆

She didn't go back to school. She got all her books and homework and did independent study, and emailed teachers if she had questions. For the first time ever, Naya's grades slipped, except in science. On the nights she couldn't sleep, she'd pick a subject to study and write a report on it. She learned about fractal patterns, and X chromosome inactivation in calico cats, and how Antarctic fish had antifreeze proteins that allowed them to live in subzero temperatures. By the end of the semester, Mr. Ned said she had 160 percent and didn't have to take the final.

Nightmares plagued her, nightmares where she and Mr. Lindy and Grandmother were doing an odd waltz around and around a room she didn't recognize. She couldn't shake the feeling that someone was watching her, the way she used to walk the lines to watch other people's lives.

➤◆

Grandmother would be dressed in her soul wrap for the Viewing, their people's version of a wake. Mama pulled it out of Grandmother's closet, yards and yards of fabric. Naya draped the material on the bed as Mama handed it to her, running her fingers over the glowing silk. She remembered the special times when Grandmother would wear the dress, wrapping the material into elaborate folds. Naya had asked her once why her soul wrap was so big. Grandmother replied grandly that she had too much personality for just a "skimpy cover-up."

The memory made her smile, and she told Mama the story.

"My daddy used to talk about how shy your grandmother was when he first met her," Mama said softly, as she smoothed her hand over the wrap. "Shy and serious. He said she studied all the time, and worked two jobs to buy art supplies."

"That doesn't sound like Grandmother at all!" exclaimed Naya. "Well, she always worked hard. But shy?"

"She changed. My father knew how to make her laugh. Daddy said . . . certain things you had to make a habit, and he kept her laughing until it was one of hers. He would take her out dancing or to the carnival. After I came along, we'd go to the beach, or barbecue after church. He could make anything into a party. She said once she didn't know how to live until she met him."

Naya had never heard this much about her grandfather before. It was like Mama was under a spell. She didn't want to break it, but she couldn't help but ask, "What happened to him?"

"He used to tell fortunes sometimes, down in front of a club. More of a lark than anything, laughing with his buddies. Or when he really wanted to make some money your grandmother didn't know about, so he could buy birthday or holiday gifts. He didn't do fortunes very often, and he played it up like he was a clown, but there were enough times he was right over the years that people . . . certain people . . . started to believe."

Naya's stomach tightened. "Like people believe that we're psychic?" she whispered.

Mama shook her head at her. "Oh, my love, there's no use in . . ." She stopped and sighed heavily. "People are going to think what they're going to think. We're not flashy. We don't hang out a shingle doing fortunes, but that didn't matter, did it?" She was quiet a long moment. "Sometimes you get caught in the path of others, despite your best efforts. Back then, there was one man who was rich, but new rich, you know? He had made his fortune,

fast and unexpected on some one-off investment, and he was flying high. My father told him he would lose everything before he
died. Then he said the man would know his death by a ribbon
tied around a horse.

"That man had my father killed. A mob of men dragged
him out of the house one night, right in front of us, calling him a
thief. They beat him down until he couldn't get up anymore. The
mob killed him, but we knew that man was behind it. He riled
everyone up."

Naya was horrified. Mama had been eight when he died, and
she'd seen the whole thing?

"We picked up and moved right after, afraid they would
come back. Mother didn't even have time to bury him."

Something clicked in Naya's mind during the awful story,
something she didn't have a name for but felt like threads weaving into place, making a picture she didn't know she had been
looking at. Little things—routines Grandmother had, or words
Mama did or did not say, all the precautions—they made a lot
more sense now.

"Did he . . . did he make a soul wrap?" she finally asked. "Can
I see his art?"

Mama looked at her with a sad, almost lonesome expression.
"He never made a soul wrap. My daddy, he didn't take art as seriously as most of our kind. He was a very active person, and art
can take a lot of sitting and stillness. He was good with wood and
building, but mostly he did leather work. Fine belts and bags, and
he could always get work making or mending horse tack.

"I know your grandmother was passionate about art, downright bossy about it at times, but I think it was because of my
father. Maybe she thought that if he had had something, something to concentrate on, a passion, then he wouldn't have gotten
caught up in trouble." Mama bent over Grandmother's soul wrap

on the bed, smoothing out any wrinkles. "He was right about making laughter a habit," said Mama. "Despite everything, Grandmother never went back to being shy and quiet after he was gone. If anything, she got bolder after she was done grieving, as if she had to live both their lives for him. But she didn't want to talk about him very much. Too much pain. Too much anger."

Naya's head spun. "Are we going to move now? Like after Grandfather was killed?"

Mama stood upright, her back straight in her favorite sweater. It was Mama, the same as always, but somehow she seemed taller to Naya's eyes.

"No, baby, I don't think so. Not this time."

"What if . . . what if Mr. Lindy comes back?"

Mama was quiet for a long moment. "Naya, my love, I made a mistake, and I'm so sorry. Grandmother and I, we kept too much private. We separated ourselves from our people. Lots of our people do—our gifts are more noticeable when we gather in groups. But we did it too much, I think. And I kept our circle of friends in this city small. I was so worried about keeping our secrets safe, of keeping you safe, I made us . . . invisible. Everyone knows what happened to you and who we are now. His face has been plastered all over the Internet. Even though they haven't found him yet, that visibility is protection. And now that I know who he is, I'll be able to track him through the lines. He'll be recognized if he comes near us or others of our kind.

"There's something else," she continued in a hushed, heavy voice. "I didn't always live with Grandmother. Mother and I used to fight, and I wanted to see the world, not be tied to a shop all day. Before you were born, I met a man while I was traveling. I fell for him hard, and he said he loved me. I think he did, in the beginning. But he figured out what I could do, and he wanted to use it. He said my gift could set us up for life. I went along with it at first, small ways to make money or find opportunities." Mama stopped, swallowing hard. "It was even fun, I'm ashamed to say. I enjoyed the money, the freedom it brought, of making my own way. But he took things too far. He started breaking laws, taking dangerous risks, asking me to be in the lines all the time. He cut me off from friends and family. I kept making excuses for him. When I finally tried to leave, he locked me in a room. No one else knew. It took me three months before I found a way out. I ran straight home, and your grandmother packed everything up without blinking an eye, and we moved again."

A shiver took Naya and didn't want to let go. Mama turned and wrapped her arms around her until the shaking slowly subsided. It had happened to Mama too! Oddly, the burden felt better and also worse, knowing she wasn't the only one.

"Sometimes when you have so much knowledge at your fingertips, you lose sight of which information is the most important. Everything begins to blend." Mama spoke into her hair. "We talked about the wrong things. We should have told you *our* stories, mine and Grandmother's, not just the ones about our people's history. We avoided the pain, instead of embracing the wisdom that pain brings."

Something in her tone made Naya pull back and look at her. "But that wasn't your fault! None of it was your fault!" Her voice was too loud. She almost shouted.

"I know that now. But I blamed myself for a long time. All the stupid mistakes I made. I did love him, so I thought I needed to shoulder the responsibility. But then your grandmother said, 'It didn't matter how much love you poured on him. If his mind was set on evil, then evil he would do.'"

Naya steeled her heart from breaking. "Was that man . . . Was that my father?"

"No," Mama breathed. "Oh no. Your father is a good man.

I met him later, when I needed to, when I needed someone who would heal my heart. You don't always have to watch the lines to find good. The universe will bring it to you when the time is right."

"Why don't you ever talk about him?"

"I still love him very much," said Mama. "It hurts when I talk about him, and we couldn't . . . His gift is very strong. He can see the lines farther than anyone I've ever met. I don't think he can block it out the way we can. It's too hard for him out here."

"Out here?" Naya asked, bewildered. It was great to finally learn about her family history, but it hurt that Mama and Grandmother had kept so much from her.

"In the regular world," Mama explained. "There are places, older places, hidden places, some of them, that are not as busy or as fast as being here in a city, with noise and media and too many people all the time. Images and lines that you can't stop seeing. Your father couldn't do it. But I needed to be here, so I could make the things I needed to make."

Naya knew she meant her clothes and her paintings. It was hard for their people to stay away from what inspired their art. She imagined not being able to watch surgery videos or have access to a library.

She imagined seeing the lines all the time. She remembered the light and the voices, the pull of the lines, how hard it got to block them out—how easy it would be to get lost, obsessed with trying to see everything.

Mama continued, "And I stayed here so that I could give you the life *you* deserve, my love."

Naya swallowed. She imagined having to choose between Mama and Grandmother, two people she loved, the way Mama had chosen . . . all for Naya's sake. Mama was so much stronger than she had realized.

"But no, we aren't going to move again. I've let fear rule our choices for too long," Mama said firmly and gently. "Our gifts let us see so much . . . but it's not really living if we're not *in* our lives. Do you understand?"

"Yes," whispered Naya. "I know exactly what you mean."

CHAPTER THIRTY-ONE

Grandmother looked beautiful, but not like herself, not really. The casket looked wrong and much too somber. Her soul wrap, though—that looked like her. It laid in shining folds around her, glowing in the light. Naya drank in the rich colors and textures, the flamboyant flair. For the first time, she noticed a spot that reminded her of Grandmother frowning over paperwork, contented and comfortable. Another pattern was bright with Grandmother's laugh. Still another section felt like the intensity of her passion for art. There was even a section that reminded her of the younger self that Mama had described, studious and shy.

Naya was glad Grandmother wouldn't be buried in the dress. It was tradition to pass soul wraps on to the family after a person's Viewing, but Naya still felt selfish about it. She wanted to pore over the wrap, to learn everything she didn't know about Grandmother. She wanted to be able to see her gorgeous soul wrap every day, as if Grandmother were still there. A soul wrap was meant to be shown, to share the stories within it, but for now Naya wanted to keep it close.

They had the Viewing at the house. A little makeshift platform was set up in the backyard, right next to the door facing Grandmother's garden. They put rows of chairs on the patches of grass and worn paths around the vegetables and flowers. It was a little crowded, but Grandmother would have wanted it that way. They put up pictures and displayed her art all over the house, and had food and more chairs in every room.

A preacher came from their local church who would say a few words and give a blessing. And there was someone else too—an "Elder," Mama called her. She would lead the Walk of Life.

The house was soon crowded with people. Most were friends and neighbors and clients, but there were a number of guests Naya didn't recognize at all.

"So many! Where did they all come from?" asked Naya.

"I know we don't see visitors very often, but we do keep in touch," said Mama. "Not only with family but with other members of our community. It's a network of sorts, but it can take a while to get a hold of each other."

Because people moved or hid, Naya thought. *Or disappeared.*

"We walk the lines for each other when we can," Mama continued. "I had already put out a call for help finding you. But there aren't that many of us, and sometimes it's hard to find someone with enough distance to see the lines you need. Sometimes we get blocked from other walkers, not just our family."

"I didn't know that," Naya said.

"I need to start teaching you more, my love, about our people's practices today. You've always been my baby girl, and I didn't want to let go of that. I didn't realize how quickly time was passing." Mama gave her a hug and moved off to greet people coming in.

Naya wandered the house while people murmured at her or patted her back. Cecilia brought her food that she couldn't remember eating. Tears stopped and started intermittently, until she stopped paying attention to them.

Her friends were standing all bunched together in a corner.

Short Shorts and Tiggy, the twins and Arnie, and all the rest from the lot. Plus a few of the older kids and parents had come to pay their respects. Touched, Naya's throat went tight and hot when she saw them.

Tiggy was staring at his feet, but he was there nonetheless. She hadn't seen him since he left her at the lot. Naya wasn't sure how much of Tiggy's actions were him and how much were influenced by Mr. Lindy. She chewed her lip. It turned out, the things you don't know are as important as the things you do. She wasn't sure if she could ever trust him quite the same as before.

But she missed her friend.

Short Shorts came up and silently put an arm around her shoulders. Naya leaned gratefully against her as the other kids gathered around them. Short Shorts really was a good friend— the best kind, really. The kind you don't know about until everything turns awful and they're right there for you. She hadn't known about those type of friends before. She wouldn't forget.

Across the room, a tall man, thin and spidery, bent down to take Mama's hand. She nodded at whatever he murmured to her. An older woman, not quite as tall, came to stand beside him. The woman enfolded Mama in a hug.

"Naya, come here," Mama called. She looked tired but pleased. "This is your aunt Bekah, from your father's side. And this is her son, your cousin."

"I have a cousin?" she asked, wondering.

He was younger than she thought, now that she was up close, maybe college aged. She had to crane her neck to meet his midnight eyes.

"Hi, I'm Charlemagne," he said. "But everyone calls me Chaz. I'm sorry for your loss."

"I've always wanted a cousin." She didn't know it was true until that moment.

When the preacher gave his blessing, she sat with her new cousin on one side, and Mama and Cecilia on the other. Short Shorts sat right behind her. Grandmother's garden was in full bloom, glowing with color. The blossoms nodded and swayed like they agreed with all the nice things people were saying about Grandmother.

Then the Elder called for the Walk of Life to begin. Naya had never been to one before, but the Elder led everyone to the front half of the house, and everyone crowded in. Most of the guests just stood quietly, respectfully, looking at Grandmother's art on display. But the guests who were family, those who could walk the lines, put their hands out—with their palms up, as if they were in church. Naya cocked her head quizzically. Mama moved over to Naya's side and held her hands up, nodding at her to do the same. Naya held up her hands and let out a small gasp. The lines glowed in front of her, without blurring her eyes, without concentration. Was she supposed to touch one? Walk the lines in front of all these people? She glanced around, but everyone kept their hands frozen before them.

The Elder's voice rang out. "We are here to honor the life walk of Althea Bernadette Clementine . . ."

She began a recitation of Grandmother's life, all her art, her achievements—the big and small details, the stories Naya knew and some she had never heard. The Elder took her time and moved slowly through the room, pointing at art or keepsakes. The tone of her voice chimed through Naya like a bell. The Elder stopped at a hanging on a wall, recalling where Grandmother lived when she made that piece, pointing out the symbolism. Naya was amazed at how much the Elder knew. Mama must have gone over it all with her, but Naya didn't remember them spending that much time together.

The chime vibrated through her again, and the lines gleamed

bright and beautiful. A shiver took her. Bits and pieces of the stories unfolded slowly before her eyes, in time to the Elder's voice.

Puzzled, Naya watched the images a moment, before it clicked . . .

She was seeing Grandmother's line! The line that had always been blocked to her, the life that had been part of her own. Tears burst out of her without a sound, dripping off her cheeks.

In shock, her gaze traveled around the room. Only their kind could see this, she was sure.

The Elder led the way into another part of the house, more images unrolling with her as they followed. Naya was suddenly sure that Mama hadn't told the Elder about Grandmother. This was the Elder's talent at work, seeing the life of someone who had passed.

The Elder pointed out a mural of birds dancing through the air that Grandmother had painted when Naya was small. It was a different style than Grandmother normally painted, and Naya wondered, as she had many times before, what had prompted the mural. As quickly as she thought it, the lines seemed to hum, like a voice calling to her, and Naya saw an image of Mama playing with her when she was a toddler. They were lying on a patch of grass, with Grandmother's picnic basket off to the side. Mama tossed her toward the sky, and Naya laughed and squealed, flapping her tiny arms.

That was what had inspired the painting—her and Mama playing. The tears came faster, fresher. As if she would never stop crying and just float away on the river of them. But Naya was smiling too, so broadly that her cheeks hurt.

The images weren't the Elder's doing after all, but a gift from the lines.

CHAPTER THIRTY-TWO

A line had already formed outside the boutique. Cecilia and Short Shorts lugged bolts of cloth and other supplies out of the shop and up the stairs while Naya straightened racks of clothes. Mama was still setting up the sample pieces for preorder, but the doors would be open any minute.

Summer sales were always a bit crazy, but to Naya, this time, they felt like relief. Summer had been hard. She'd spent most of her time in a haze, where nothing felt quite right. After a nightmare, she stumbled downstairs half asleep, expecting to see Grandmother in the weaving room or at the sewing machine or at the kitchen table. Then she would remember, and the douse of grief and guilt over forgetting for even a moment made it hard to breathe.

They had to work extra hard to prepare for Fall Open Studios before school started again, and the summer sales were the first step. It felt good to be tired, to think of something else. Mama sat next to her at the kitchen table most nights, teaching her the paperwork. Naya took over many of Grandmother's weavings. Mama decided to sell some of her paintings. They'd lost time and finances, and somehow, without Grandmother, *for* Grandmother, it was important they do well.

She finished hanging up the last of the bikini wraps and summer dresses and checked the room for anything out of place.

Without Grandmother's decorating panache, they decided to hang upside-down parasols along the ceiling as a quick, easy way to add bright summer color. The shop didn't look *quite* as pretty as it did at the Spring Tea, but it still looked nice.

Cecilia and Short Shorts clattered down the stairs.

"I think that just about does it," said Mama, as Cecilia and Short Shorts found their stations. "Why don't you do the honors, my love?" She rubbed Naya's shoulders.

She stood tall, her chin up, as regally as Grandmother, and opened the doors.

She greeted customers: "Come on in." "Hi, Ms. Norris, it's good to see you." "Welcome."

After they closed for the day, she fell into bed and didn't dream at all.

◆━◆

Naya dug through a stack of mending jobs. Both she and Mama were terribly behind, but the clients were being extra patient. Still, Naya knew she should get on those hems before Grandmother said . . .

She blinked rapidly. She never thought she would miss Grandmother's lectures so much.

Naya moved a pile of pants off a sewing machine, and sitting there was a pair of Grandmother's readers. The frames were yellow and orange, and Grandmother had added some crystals along the temple. Naya put them on, scrunching her nose to keep them from slipping, and walked to the hall mirror. The world was sharp and angled and fuzzy all at once. She tilted her head until she found an angle that didn't hurt her eyes and peered at herself in the glass. In the blurry reflection, she almost looked like Grandmother.

She took off the glasses and folded them carefully. Naya walked to her room and tucked them into the pocket of a yellow sweater hanging in her closet. She never wore that sweater much, but it was Grandmother's favorite color for her. The weather would turn soon. The sweater would be perfect for fall.

◆━

Naya had to sign up late for her high school classes because she'd missed the last part of school. She'd already been accepted into the honors science class as a freshman, but there was also an anatomy class she could take as an elective. She stared at the form, chewing her lip. The high school had more of the art options Grandmother had always talked about. There were the usual drawing and painting classes, as well as graphic design courses, screen printing, photography, ceramics, and even metal sculpture classes.

She grinned to herself. Cecilia would be so excited if she took something with metal.

Her smile faded. She signed up for Life Drawing I, with graphic design as an alternative. In between class and shop work, she studied the art around the house as if she were seeing it for the first time.

◆━

Naya was in the weaving room, finishing the last weaving Grandmother had started, the one where Naya's little spider sat in the corner, next to Grandmother's. She wasn't sure if the final pattern was as complicated as Grandmother's would have been, but she was pleased with the way it turned out anyway. She had asked Mama if they could keep this one, instead of selling it. Mama had already put the rod up to hang it in her room.

Naya sat back after the last row was woven and stared at the rows of spools on the walls. The room was deeply quiet. It should be peaceful. *She* should be peaceful. She loved this room, her times here with Grandmother. But she knew deep down this still wasn't for her. She would probably always weave; she enjoyed it. But taking the drawing class had shown her that science would always pull her more than art.

She felt a sudden, fierce rush of sorrow for what she was not. For not carrying on the legacy that Grandmother had started.

Her throat tight, she stood up and trailed her hand along the threads.

"I'm sorry," she whispered. "I love you."

It didn't feel like enough. She wondered if it ever would.

A violet-purple spool, almost glowing in the light, caught her eye. She didn't remember it being there. It was in the section of white and cream threads, the ones waiting to be dyed if they needed a custom color. She picked up the violet spool, and it pulsed with her grief over Grandmother.

Somehow she'd been infusing threads without realizing, without even touching them. How did that happen?

When she turned her eyes back to the wall, she saw that there were more.

◆━

The afternoon was quiet, waiting. No clients were scheduled, and the usual traffic outside had died down. Even the sky felt hushed, the color of it that shade between blue and gray, when the summer heat finally admits defeat to autumn. She thought it was time.

Naya walked to the kitchen and laid her weaving gently on the table. "Mama?"

Mama turned from chopping vegetables.

The silk threads glowed and shifted in the light. Naya had woven in spirals and waves, lines that blossomed into color, shapes that hinted at something bigger, fractals and energy and ordered chaos dancing together. To Naya, the patterns felt like night skies and outer space and the way life could be birthed by single atoms. All the things that could be started if they just had a single spark.

Like love. Like art.

"It's beautiful," Mama breathed. "Is this your soul wrap, then?"

"This isn't my soul wrap," Naya said in a rush, startling herself. "I know it looks like one, but it isn't. It's just . . ."

Mama stayed silent, listening.

Naya groped for the right words. "It's just me . . . me right now." She gently touched a spot of deep purple; grief and love thrummed quietly through the threads. She had woven in all the threads she had found: Threads about Mr. Lindy and Grandmother. Threads about being home, and her friends. Threads about the strange, disconnected haze she'd been walking through until she started weaving again. Threads that hinted at the vastness underneath the light. The quick, quick glimpse of patterns, of cogs, of purpose moving beyond anything she could know. It was all so much bigger than she thought.

She looked up at Mama. "You were right. I wasn't ready."

Mama stroked Naya's hair and then moved to a closet in the hall. She took a box down from the highest shelf and opened the box on the table. Inside was Mama's soul wrap, a long cloak made in simple lines and panels. The wrap was very different from Naya's patterns or Grandmother's, but it was still beautiful. At the bottom, where the hem should be, long, loose threads were bunched together and tied neatly into bows—like the soul wrap wasn't quite finished, like it was designed that way, like Mama could pick up and add on any time she wanted.

"I'm not done either. I don't know when I will be," said Mama. "I'm okay with that." She laughed. "Your grandmother didn't approve. She said, 'Art is meant to be completed!'"

Naya wrapped her arm around Mama, and they leaned against each other.

"But I always thought, life is messy and so is art." Mama kissed the top of her head. "Luckily for us, they both grow. Right?"

"Right." She smiled.

"I spoke to your teacher from last year . . . There's another medical science camp coming up, a short one over winter break. Do you still want to go?"

Naya thought about it for a long moment. The haze still came and went, but it was fading enough that she knew it wouldn't be there forever. From very far away, she thought she heard a voice hum from the lines. The voice sounded happy, like Grandmother at her sassiest. Her chest loosened, and she breathed in air.

"Yes."

ACKNOWLEDGMENTS

feel like I just finished writing one set of acknowledgments, and here I am writing another. A lot happened, for my family, at the tail end of this book. My husband had a health crisis and I was left floundering, trying to keep everything afloat, let alone proceed with bookish, writerly things. The dedication for this book and the acknowledgments are pretty much the same. I knew I had great friends and family, but this amazing community rallied to help before I even had a chance to ask.

So, for everyone who kept showing up when they knew they were needed (even if I didn't know it yet), I am forever grateful. Thank you for showing up in my backyard when I was in a panic to move things out of the way. Thank you for dropping off food, and giving me breaks, and helping with the cars. For doing my dishes behind my back. Thank you for helping with the whole tree-trimming fiasco, and for taking care of the crap I couldn't. Here's to all of you: Christy and Rich Bulan, Jeanne and Fred Rupprecht, J.T. Everett, Jeanne and Kristen Diaz-Kleiboer, Darcy and Harold Ogle, Thuy-Anh Do, Sonja Jeter, Kira White, Carlos Ariojas, Joe and Krista Samatua, Anthony Olyaee, Paul and Marita Villareal, Cindy and Dan Tarangioli, Kitty and Dave Pascual, Robert and Charlene Kuehnis, Matthew Kuehnis, Monica Pulizzi and Albert Vargas, Tracy Briseno, Bob and Bette Baines, Darren and

Michele Seaton, Christy and Mike Brandenberry, April and Leo Pursley, Justina Weibender, David DaCunha, and last but by far not the least: Junko Tanaka, Carmen Cheung, and Angel Man.

Thank you, Brooke Warner, for taking another submission. Especially considering, in my overwhelmed state of mind, I sent about the vaguest, most incomplete query letter ever! Your consideration and deep commitment to writing and women's voices is such an inspiration. Thank you to Shannon Green for shepherding this book through to print. You've been an absolute joy to work with, and I really appreciate your patience and positivity. Thank you to Rylee Warner, Grace Fell, and Crystal Patriarche for everything you do and for always answering my questions, even when I've already asked them several times before. (Sorry about that.) And Maggie Ruf . . . my website is amazing and it's so fun working with you! ❤

Thank you to all the ladies at the Her Spirit conference for providing a safe place to be vulnerable. You are all so inspiring! Thank you, Sean Stewart, for being incredibly kind when I reached out and for your wonderful words. To my fellow Spark-Press and SheWrites authors, who have been so friendly and willing to share resource tips on this publishing journey, I can't imagine having such a great community anywhere else.

And finally, a special thanks to Amelia Beamer. (Whom I should have mentioned in *The Byways*. I knew I was going to forget someone! Bad author!) Her early enthusiasm and thoughtful editing were invaluable. Your words and insight made this book and *The Byways* better, and I'm forever grateful.

Without all of you, I wouldn't be back at the place I needed to be. You are in my heart, always.

P.S. Brian and Chance, I love you.

ABOUT THE AUTHOR

Mary Pascual is a writer and artist who believes finding magic is only a matter of perspective. She loves stories about characters with heart and fantastical settings that are more than meets the eye. She grew up in California and enjoys reading, art, traveling, exploring outside, and building elaborate stage sets for Halloween. Writing has taken her on a number of unexpected adventures, including working in high tech, meeting psychics, interviewing rock bands, and even once attending a press conference for Bigfoot. She got hooked on reading adult science fiction and fantasy in the fifth grade—so in retrospect much of her reading material was completely inappropriate (which probably explains a few things). She lives with her husband, son, and assorted demanding cats in San Jose, California.

SELECTED TITLES FROM SPARKPRESS

SparkPress is an independent boutique publisher delivering high-quality, entertaining, and engaging content that enhances readers' lives, with a special focus on female-driven work.
www.gosparkpress.com

The Byways: A Novel, Mary Pascual. $17.95, 978-1-684631-90-2. Neurodivergent CeeCee hates how different she feels from everyone around her. But she doesn't know what being different truly means until she lands in the magical, terrifying world of the Byways, a place that does its best to save those who are different—but also exacts a steep price if you fail its tests.

The Goddess Twins: A Novel, Yodassa Williams. $16.95, 978-1-68463-032-5. Days before their eighteenth birthday, Arden and Aurora's mother goes missing and they discover they belong to a family of Caribbean deities. Can these goddess twins uncover their evil grandfather's plot in time to save their mother, themselves, and the free world?

The Thorn Queen: A Novel, Elise Holland. $16.95, 978-1-943006-79-3. Twelve-year-old Meylyne longs to impress her brilliant, sorceress mother—but when she accidentally breaks one of Glendoch's First Rules, she accomplishes the opposite of that. Forced to flee, the only way she may return home is with a cure for Glendoch's diseased prince.

Above the Star: The 8th Island Trilogy, Book 1, Alexis Chute. $16.95, 978-1-943006-56-4. *Above the Star* is an epic fantasy adventure experienced through the eyes of three unlikely heroes transported to a new world: senior citizen Archie; his daughter-in-law, Tessa; and his fourteen-year-old granddaughter, Ella. In this otherworldly realm, all interests are at war, all love is unrequited, and everyone is left to unravel the truth of who they really are.

Below the Moon: The 8th Island Trilogy, Book 2, Alexis Marie Chute. $16.95, 978-1-68463-004-2. Cancer has left Ella mute, but not powerless. When she finds herself in a parallel dimension, she must paint to communicate, fight alongside fearsome warrior-creatures, and—along with her mom, Tessa, and grandpa Archie—overcome the Wellsley family's past in order to ensure a future for everyone.

Inside the Sun: The 8th Island Trilogy, Book 3, A Novel, Alexis Marie Chute. $16.95, 978-1-68463-045-5. All worlds are dying, and it's up to one broken and dysfunctional family to save the day. Each overcoming personal secrets, illness, and trauma, the members of the Wellsley family discover their bravery in the face of all they must face: an enchanted maze, terrifying sea creatures, a fading sun, evil creatures, and a galaxy turned on its head.